THE MAN WHO CHANGED ROOMS

AND OTHER CRIMINAL TYPES

THE MAN WHO CHANGED ROOMS

AND OTHER CRIMINAL TYPES

JOHNSTON McCULLEY

WILDSIDE PRESS

THE MAN WHO CHANGED ROOMS
AND OTHER CRIMINAL TYPES

"The Man Who Changed Rooms" originally appeared in *Clues* magazine, February 2, 1929. "Initiating Noggins" and "Eternal Assets" originally appeared in *Detective Story Magazine* under the pseudonym "Harrington Strong." "Forbearance" originally appeared in *All Around Magazine,* January 1917. "Demons of Disaster" originally appeared in *The Masked Rider Western Magazine,* March 1946.

CONTENTS

THE MAN WHO CHANGED ROOMS

CHAPTER I

INSTRUCTIONS

Because he was not absolutely sure that the tall, hawk-nosed man was shadowing him and watching every move that he made, Creighton Marpe was compelled to stifle his feelings and resort to strategy rather than violence.

He had an inclination to turn abruptly and drive his fist squarely to the end of the hawk nose, and he was thoroughly capable of doing it. But he had to be sure. It would not do to make a mistake. It certainly would not look well for a man in Creighton Marpe's position to smash an innocent pedestrian on the nose.

Creighton Marpe was compelled to remember that he was in a most particular branch of government service, and that the enemies of the Government were his enemies. They were sly, crafty, even violent on occasion. It might serve their purposes to lead him into a nasty row.

So Creighton Marpe merely continued down the Avenue after the manner of a gentleman leisurely taking the air and enjoying the splendid afternoon, swinging his stick as though he did not have a care or suspicion in the world; and the expression on his face was as guileless as that of an innocent babe.

He stopped now and then and pretended to be peering in at shop windows and scrutinizing the latest wares, and once to touch flaming match to tip of cigarette. On these occasions he made certain that the man with the hawk nose was still in the vicinity. The latter certainly acted as though he was making it his business to keep Creighton Marpe in sight.

There must be some sort of big game coming off," Marpe

muttered, as he dodged the traffic in a cross street. "And the others evidently know more about it than I. Matter of fact, I do not know anything — yet."

He was on his way now to a rendezvous with his chief, who had arrived only that morning from Washington. The manner of rendezvous told Marpe that something was afoot; for he had been instructed by telephone to cancel previous arrangements and meet the Chief in a certain place near Washington Square, and to be very careful about it.

Creighton Marpe was rather an impressive-looking gentleman as he continued slowly through the crowd of afternoon shoppers that congested the walk on the fashionable Avenue. He was slightly more than thirty, tall, handsome, and fastidiously dressed. There was nothing of the fop about him, however. He had the appearance of an athlete, and bore an air of command.

Now he made his way through the crowd until he came to a big tobacco shop on a busy corner, moving slowly so that the man behind could keep in sight if he desired to do so. The tobacco shop itself presented a busy scene, with shoppers three deep in front of the counters, salesmen jumping about, men struggling to get to the cigar lighters and telephone booths.

Creighton Marpe sought a telephone booth and was fortunate to find one unoccupied. He entered it and closed the sound-proof glass door behind him. He went through all the motions of putting in a telephone call — dropping a coin into the slot, moving his lips as though in denunciation of an inefficient "central," then smiling like a man who finally has been given the correct number and is speaking to somebody with whom it pleases him to converse.

And all the time he was doing these things he was holding down the receiver-hook with his elbow. His acting was for the benefit of anybody who might be watching him. His subterfuge was for the purpose of learning whether the hawk-nosed man really was trailing him.

The hawk-nosed man entered the tobacco shop and made his way through the crowd. He glanced through the door of the telephone booth, and Creighton Marpe was quite sure that he saw the other's eyelids flutter betrayingly as their glances met. So! He was being followed, trailed, watched, shadowed like a criminal by the hawk-nosed man!

It was all in the game. Yet Creighton Marpe felt like rushing from the telephone booth and calling the other to account. But he decided that he probably would be confronted by an air of injured innocence if he did, and be termed a meddling fool. Also, by doing such a thing he would attract attention to himself at a time when he did not wish to do so; and he might even be walking straight into a trap prepared for him. The part of wisdom, all things considered, was to ignore the other man — and dodge him.

So Creighton Marpe stepped from the telephone booth with a whimsical smile upon his lips, aping the expression of a man who probably had just concluded a satisfactory conversation over the wire with a lady.

He thrust his way forward to the counter and purchased a package of cigarettes that he did not need. But it gave him an opportunity to look over those in the shop. The hawk-nosed man, he found, was standing in the rear, near the door that opened into the side street.

Creighton Marpe started toward the front door of the shop in a natural manner. As he reached it, he saw the hawk-nosed man dart out the rear door with the evident intention of circling the corner and taking to the trail again. But Creighton Marpe immediately turned and made his way back through the shop, and went out the rear door behind the other man. He started down the cross street and walked briskly.

"Hope that he runs in circles until he's dizzy!" Marpe muttered to himself.

When he reached the first corner, Creighton Marpe swung to the left again, used the parallel street for several blocks, and then returned to the Avenue. Here the walks were not so badly crowded. Marpe did not see the hawk-nosed man. He stepped along briskly now, thinking of keeping the appointment with his Chief, wondering what it was that had caused his superior to arrange a meeting in this section of the city.

He crossed the Square, turned into a side street, and passed the small apartment house which was to be the rendezvous. At the next corner he crossed the street and returned on the opposite side. So far as he could see, he was not under surveillance.

Now he went across the street again and into the building, where a girl sat behind a combined desk and switchboard.

"Ring Mr. Daggern, please," Creighton Marpe said, as he had been instructed. "Mr. Howland calling."

The girl surveyed him languidly and smiled. Creighton Marpe had a way of getting a welcoming smile from women. A moment later she assured him that he was to go right up, and that the room number was 316.

"Come in!" a man's voice commanded.

Creighton Marpe did not recognize the voice. It certainly was not that of his Chief. So he turned the knob of the door, threw the door open, and stepped swiftly to one side of it instead of into the room.

Nothing happened. Marpe then peered around the corner of the casement. The Chief was standing a few feet away, grinning.

"All right!" the Chief called. "Glad to see that you are so wary. Come right in, please."

Marpe closed the door and turned to face them again. The Chief beckoned and led the way into a little adjoining room. He introduced the other man as Captain Gaines, and the captain immediately went back into the front room and closed the connecting door.

"Sit down, Marpe," the Chief said, kindly, waving a hand toward a chair. "All this is rather mystifying to you, no doubt. Quite like intrigue, isn't it? Captain Gaines is working with the General Staff, and is with me as a sort of bodyguard."

"Bodyguard, sir?" Marpe asked, eyebrows raised in surprise.

"Exactly! We are playing with dynamite, or something that is stronger. The enemy is very active. I really do not know all about it myself. But we are rather secretive about this thing. That is why I asked you to come here to get your instructions."

"Then there is work for me to do?" Marpe asked.

"Exactly. You are to go at once, and as speedily as possible, to Kansas City, Missouri. There you will engage a room in the Hotel Baltimore. Captain Makker, an army officer stationed at Fort Leavenworth, will make himself known to you and deliver to you a certain paper."

"I understand, sir," Marpe said.

"You will register at the hotel under your own name, and Captain Makker will be watching and communicate with you immediately. As soon as you have that paper, Marpe, you will bring it with all haste back to New York City."

"Understood, sir," Marpe said, as his superior stopped and looked at him questioningly.

"Upon your return you will engage a room at the Hotel Magnificent here. A Major Sinlon will make himself known to you, and you will deliver the paper to him. That is all, except that you must make all speed possible."

"It does not sound difficult, sir."

"Ah! I have neglected to inform you that certain persons will do everything to get their hands on that document. My boy, I do not even know what that document is. But I know that the War Department had asked us to do this work, that their own officers are being watched, that they are — well, are really afraid — that the document will fall into the wrong hands. They especially requested that you be given this work to do. You have a wonderful record, Marpe."

"I am grateful, sir."

"I asked them why they didn't have this Captain Makker simply bring the papers on and deliver them to Major Sinlon. From the answer I received, I am led to the conclusion that there is something terrific back of this."

"But couldn't the stuff be memorized by a trustworthy officer, and couldn't he come here or go to Washington and make out the document there?"

"My own question, boy. I was told to mind my own business, in nice, polite words."

"Couldn't a couple of officers come with the paper, one remaining awake and alert all the time?"

"My own question again. Then it was rather intimated to

me that perhaps our service couldn't deliver the goods. I replied that our branch of the secret service could do anything from running errands to fighting a war. Matter of pride with us, now, Marpe."

"It doesn't sound like a difficult assignment," Marpe declared.

"Um! It doesn't at that. But it was hinted to me that the enemy, whoever they are, might go to any length to get that document, whatever it is. Confound it, they shouldn't make us work entirely in the dark!"

"My own initiative, sir?" Marpe asked.

"Just do the work, Marpe."

"Very well, Chief. I'll get a plane and —"

"Sorry! I know that you love to ride around the sky, Marpe, but the airplane stuff will not do this trip. Was told as much. It seems they fear the foe will be watching for an airplane. We have specific orders to use the good old railroads."

"Very well, sir; only it will be slower."

"Fast enough to suit them, I suppose."

"Can you tell me anything else, sir?" Marpe asked.

"Very little, I am afraid. They didn't tell me much more than I have told you. Just get to Kansas City, get that document from the Fort Leavenworth officer, come back with it, and deliver it to Major Sinlon at the Hotel Magnificent."

"I was shadowed as I came here today, sir."

"Um! No doubt! I presume they are shadowing every known man to see which gets the assignment."

"He was a tall, hawk-nosed man —"

"So? That gentleman's name is Lenserg. I have heard a few things concerning him, and he is what might be termed a bad customer. Lenserg, huh? Um! This may be more serious than I thought."

"Foreign government, sir?"

"Exactly! European government, the one we of the Service know as Number Six. I have to laugh sometimes, very quietly in the seclusion of my private study. With all these peace pacts and all this disarmament talk, a man would think that there was no sense in having a secret service and special couriers and all that. But we on the inside — well —"

"Yes, sir!" said Creighton Marpe. "I shall be watching for this Mr. Lenserg. I dodged him coming here."

"Good work," the Chief said. "All set now, Marpe?"

"I understand, sir. Any passwords?"

"Yes. I have to laugh again, very quietly, of course. The password will be given you by Captain Makker in Kansas City, and again by Major Sinlon in New York. It is Spanish."

"My favorite foreign language, sir."

"Uh-huh! Here it is — *¡Feliz Aventura!*"

"Happy Adventure," Marpe said.

"Exactly! Isn't that silly?" the Chief asked. "Let us hope that it will be a happy adventure for you, Marpe. I'd hate to lose you, my best man."

"You may be sure, sir, that I'll do my best to return," Marpe replied, laughing.

"That's the boy! Eyes and ears open, now! I do not need to tell you that you are in danger from the moment you leave this room. It appears that our friends from over the sea are very eager to get that document. Oh! Here is a photograph of Captain Makker."

He handed Marpe a photograph, and the latter looked at it for some little time, until it was impressed upon his memory to such an extent that he believed he would know the original instantly.

"Recent?"

"New photograph, front and side views, taken especially for this affair," the Chief responded. "And here is one of Major Sinlon, too."

Creighton Marpe inspected the second photograph well also.

"And the password is *Feliz Aventura*," Marpe said. "Very good, sir. I am to work alone?"

"Captain Gaines will join you in the outer room and stay with you until you take the train."

"But I thought that he was your bodyguard."

"He was, Marpe. But I do not need one now. I have given you my instructions. So you are the quarry now. Good luck, Marpe!"

The gray-haired Chief extended his hand, and Creighton

Marpe clasped it, then stepped back a pace and saluted snappily, and then turned to stalk with measured, military tread across the room toward the door.

"Oh, Marpe!"

"Sir?" Marpe turned.

"Along the way, you may encounter a little lady who bears the name of Alla Stimney. You have met her, I believe?"

Creighton Marpe's face flushed. "Yes, sir," he replied.

"All Stimney has no secrets from me, lad. She is the best woman we have in the Service. You are the best man. It is fitting that — er —"

"Yes, sir!" said Marpe.

"She has told me of your little romance. Congratulations, my boy. But do not forget, Marpe — the Service comes first!"

"Always, sir!"

"If there every comes a time when you must choose, and quickly, between the Service and your sweetheart, you will remember that —"

"That the Service comes first — yes, sir!" Marpe interrupted.

"And I sincerely hope that you never will have to make the choice, boy."

"Do I understand that Miss Stimney is on this assignment also, sir?"

"Tut, tut! You should know better than to ask me questions. You may run across her. That's all, Marpe!"

There was cold dismissal in his tone; the Chief was the Chief once more. Marpe opened the door and stepped out into the other room where Captain Gaines was waiting for him.

"When we leave the building, follow me at a short distance," Marpe requested. "Observe whether I am followed by anybody else. I'll give you the chance, now and then, to overtake me and whisper if there is anything to communicate. Then I'll repass you, and so on."

They went down together in the elevator, but did not speak. In the lobby below, Creighton Marpe stepped briskly through the door and down the short flight of steps to the street, and Captain Gaines followed him leisurely.

As he reached the street, Marpe gasped, and almost came to an abrupt stop. Just across the thoroughfare, leaning against the front of a building, twirling his mustache and smiling in a supercilious manner, was the tall, hawk-nosed man whose name the Chief had said was Lenserg.

CHAPTER II

THE SIGNAL

Creighton Marpe apparently gave him not the slightest attention. He turned up the street and walked to Washington Square, and across it. Captain Gaines followed a short distance behind, and the man Lenserg shadowed Marpe so faithfully that he did not observe Gaines.

Leaving the Square and starting up the Avenue, Marpe walked at a brisker gait. Lenserg kept the same distance from him. And suddenly Marpe stopped at the curb, extracted a cigarette and lighted it, and over his cupped hands observed that Lenserg continued to advance.

Marpe faced him squarely, surveyed him from head to feet and back again. Lenserg continued his advance, seemingly paying not the slightest attention to the man standing at the curb. He came opposite.

"Hello, Lenserg!" Creighton Marpe said.

Lenserg stopped abruptly, an expression of astonishment in his face.

"I beg your pardon?" he said. "Lenserg is my name. But I do not remember of meeting you, sir."

"Not socially. You scarcely would be in my set," Marpe told him. "But you know my name, I dare say. And, as you see, I know yours. Furthermore I know your game."

"Sir? I fail to understand you," Lenserg said.

"Rats! You followed me down the Avenue a short time ago, and I thought that I had dodged you in that tobacco shop. Shadowing me, are you? I dislike being shadowed, Lenserg."

"The streets are free, are they not?"

"Old stuff!" Marpe commented. "I had expected something better of you. Lenserg, I don't like your face. I feel quite sure that if I see much more of it I'll become enraged. And when I become enraged, I fly off the handle, if you can catch my meaning. You are a husky individual, but I feel quite sure, Lenserg, that I can lick you!"

"Aren't you rather belligerent?" Lenserg asked, smiling.

"At times," Creighton Marpe admitted. "I know the game you are playing. It is your privilege to play it. But I don't like to be followed. Lenserg, I am going to the Hotel Magnificent. I expect to have luncheon there with a friend. After that — who knows? Anything else that you would like to know?"

Lenserg's lip curled. "You are quite clever with your tongue," he said. "Are you as clever in other ways?"

"Possibly."

"And just suppose, Mr. Marpe —"

"So you do know my name!"

"Yes. Suppose that I mix it with you here on this corner? I can say that you attacked me for no reason whatsoever. And what would you say in court?"

"I wouldn't appear in court," Marpe told him. "I'd put up cash bail and forget it. If I really had to disclose my Service, I'd do so without detriment of it. And then what would you say? That you are working for a foreign government and trying to deter officials of the United States?"

"I'd stick to my story and pay a fine for fighting," Lenserg said. "But suppose, in that fight, you were injured so that you had to be taken to a hospital? That little trip of yours would be delayed, would it not?"

"Possibly — if I went to a hospital."

"That light stick which you are carrying, Mr. Marpe, would not avail you much against this heavier one in my hand. One blow against the head, and you certainly would be delayed. I may mention that I know how to fence with a cane."

"And can you also fence with a rapier?" Marpe asked.

"I can, if you'll pardon my seeming lack of modesty in saying so."

"You haven't a rapier with you, by any chance?"

"I have not."

"But I have!" said Creighton Marpe. As he spoke, he twisted the handle of the light cane and a blade flashed in the sun.

Lenserg retreated a step. "A sword-cane, eh?" he said.

"It is, and a beauty, too. Though I dare say that I'll not need it," Marpe told him, returning the blade.

Lenserg took a quick step forward. "I could smash you down before you could draw it!" he said, his face livid.

"Easy!" Marpe warned. "Three feet behind you, Mr. Lenserg, is a gentleman with his right hand in coat pocket, and I feel quite sure that he has a pistol in that hand."

"The old trick of trying to get me to look behind, eh, so you can catch me off guard?"

"Oh, I say! I am a man of truth," Marpe declared. "Captain Gaines, kindly step around in front and satisfy the gentleman. I thank you, Captain. There he is, Mr. Lenserg. Is it true that you have a weapon in your hand, Captain?"

Captain Gaines grinned and revealed it.

"You see, Mr. Lenserg?" Marpe asked. "We of the Service are generally doubly protected. Allow me to suggest that you catch a taxicab now and proceed wherever you wish to go. It is immaterial to us, so long as you rid us of your presence."

Lenserg bowed to him. "You win," he said, "for the present. But it is a long road to Kansas City and back." He turned from them and walked briskly up the Avenue.

"Confound it!" Gaines said. "Why wouldn't we beat him up, or have him arrested, or something like that?"

"This is not a time of war, Captain Gaines," Marpe pointed out. "All this sort of work is done under cover, and those connected with it have no official standing outwardly. We are representatives of our government. Would it look nice if a howl went up that we were abusing the nationals of a friendly power? But these are times, Gaines, when I feel like forgetting the Service and doing what most men would feel like doing. Let's catch a taxi, now."

They flagged a cruising taxicab and headed for the Hotel Magnificent.

"I am going to be rather open about this thing," Marpe said. "I'll engage a room at the Magnificent immediately, and have it held for my return. The enemy will find that out, naturally, and be prepared to greet me when I return. But I may not show up there."

"In that case, Major Sinlon will call up that room, somebody will tell him to come right up, and he'll walk into a mess."

"The major can take care of himself, surely. It is the paper that they want, the mysterious document. The major will not have it. What sort of man is Major Sinlon?"

"Middle aged. Capable," Gaines replied.

"Do you know Captain Makker, the man I am to meet in Kansas City?"

"Met him once. Don't know anything about him except that he has a good record."

"It seems to me at times that about half the trouble in the world comes from documents," Marpe offered. "Here I am, possibly running into danger and all that on account of some papers. And I do not even know what they are."

"Neither do I," Captain Gaines assured him. "But from the way they have been acting around the Department in Washington, that document is mighty important."

"And I wonder what Major Sinlon will do with it if I get it to him safely. If the enemy knows the game, they'll be prepared to go after Sinlon, won't they?"

"Don't you worry about that," Captain Gaines replied. "I'll be on the job again as soon as Sinlon gets that document — and possibly some others also. I have orders to wait here in New York for your return. I have a room at the Magnificent now."

"And are you fool enough to use it?"

"Not for sleeping purposes," Captain Gaines replied, chuckling a little. "I go there once a day, with my hand on an automatic when I open the door. But where I sleep is nobody's business."

"You've been around!" Marpe said, smiling.

"Yours is the job I'd like to have. There's some excitement and adventure in it."

"Loss of sleep, poky trains, poor hotels at times, peculiar hours and all that," Marpe assured him.

"But it is a great game!"

"No public acclaim like aviators get."

"But think of the service!"

"That's it, Gaines! We serve, and there is a lot of satisfaction in that, at least."

They reached the Hotel Magnificent and Marpe went directly to the office of the manager, to whom he was known personally. He booked a room, explaining that it was to be held ready for him. The manager knew Marpe's work, and promised secrecy.

"But that is not what I want this time," Marpe protested. "Just pretend to keep it quiet, but let it leak out. I want to register regularly, and I don't care who learns what room has been assigned to me."

"Then I'll have the house detectives keep their eyes on the room," the manager offered.

"No, you don't! Give my enemies a chance to work, if they wish to do anything. I have my own plans. 'The Man Who Changed Rooms' crooks called me in connection with a certain case I was working on. Well, I still live up to the name. I may change to another room as far as actually living in it goes, but I have my own reasons for being registered in this one."

"Anything that you say, Mr. Marpe."

Marpe and Captain Gaines went in to luncheon, then. They got a table in a corner, where they could sit side by side with their backs to a wall, and ordered lavishly. Their quick eyes took in the crowd of diners, but they saw nobody who looked at all suspicious, or who appeared to be giving them special attention.

Marpe started to say something, but stopped speaking abruptly, and Captain Gaines glanced up, on the alert. He beheld a radiant smile on Creighton Marpe's face, and he followed Marpe's gaze and saw a man and woman sitting down at a table not far away.

"What —" Gaines began.

"Friend of mine — Miss Alla Stimney," Marpe explained.

"Oh! I have heard whispers of that romance, Marpe. I congratulate you. She's a splendid-looking woman!"

"I do not know the man with her, but I'll have to step over

and say a word," Marpe said. "I may not get a chance to see her again until I return from Kansas City."

He started to get out of his chair. Miss Alla Stimney turned her head and saw him. The expression of her face did not change. No hint of recognition came into it. She raised her right hand and brushed it lightly across her ear three times, as though brushing back a stray lock of hair.

Creighton Marpe resumed his chair and sighed.

"What's the trouble?" Captain Gaines wanted to know. "Change your mind? I'd like to meet her."

"Confound it! She flashed me a signal. 'Do not recognize me,' that signal said."

"So you people go in for all that sort of thing, do you!" asked Gaines.

"Yes, we have out little eccentricities," Marpe admitted. "There are times when we need our little signals. We have —"

Once more he ceased speaking abruptly, and Captain Gaines glanced quickly at Alla Stimney. Now she was holding the lobe of her right ear between thumb and forefinger as she smiled at the man sitting across the table from her.

"Any meaning to that?" Gaines asked.

"Yes," Marpe replied. "She is telling me to follow her when she leaves the café."

CHAPTER III

BOUND WEST

They finished their luncheon, paid their check, tipped the waiter handsomely, lighted smokes, and pretended a conversation regarding business so that they could loiter without arousing suspicion. Alla Stimney did not look their way again. She was conducting an animated conversation with her escort.

Creighton Marpe and Captain Gaines inspected the man well from the near distance. He was of middle age, ample as to girth and florid of face. He had a sleek, prosperous appearance, and seemed to exude the thought that he was a sort of oily individual. Marpe's blood boiled at the manner in which he looked at Alla Stimney as he bent across the table.

"Never saw the scamp before in my life," Gaines said.

"Nor have I," said Marpe.

"Yes; and he acts like one who has just made his first killing in the market," Marpe added.

"Do you suppose, Marpe, that he is concerned in this affair upon which you are engaged?"

"I haven't the slightest idea," Marpe said. "Many strange things happen in the Service. Miss Stimney gave me that signal, and it cannot be ignored. There — he is paying his check. We'll get out and pick them up as they leave."

They left the café, descended the steps to the main lobby of the big hostelry, and there waited in the ever-changing crowd. A short time later, Alla Stimney and her escort d-scended the steps and passed within a short distance of them.

"I must send a telegram," Alla Stimney told the man beside her, in such a tone that Marpe could hear.

"There is a telegraph desk just across the lobby, dear lady," her escort replied.

Creighton Marpe ground his teeth in rage. "Dear lady" was one of his own pet modes of address when he talked to Alla Stimney. He felt like resenting the remark forcibly, especially when Alla glanced at him with her eyes twinkling, showing that she knew Marpe had heard. But the Service came first. So Marpe followed the pair at a short distance, Captain Gaines walking beside him and talking in a natural manner about nothing much at all.

Alla Stimney led her escort to the telegraph counter, and he stepped back politely and stood surveying the crowd while she picked up a pencil and reached for a message blank. But she seemed to be unable to decide just what to write. She looked at the wall as though thinking deeply, and tapped nervously with the pencil on the counter.

"Um!" Marpe grunted, suddenly. He moved a step nearer, and Captain Gaines went along with him. They, too, seemed to be merely watching the crowd — but Creighton Marpe was listening intently to the erratic tapping of the pencil in the hand of Alla Stimney.

It was the telegraph code that she was using, making the dots and dashes as she tapped the counter with the pencil. Marpe interpreted it readily:

"Take — good — look — at — him. He — is — one — of — them. Name — is — Herman — Carlmurg. That — is — all."

Then she turned and looked straight at him, her own face expressionless. Marpe would have started toward her, but once more she gave him the signal not to recognize her. And then she gave him yet another, which meant that he was to go his own way and attend to his own business.

She crumpled the telegraph blank and turned toward Herman Carlmurg again and touched him on the arm. Together they left the hotel. Marpe and Gaines, following, saw them get into a taxicab and drive away. Marpe hurried to the cab starter, exhibited his badge of authority and asked one question: "Where did they go?"

"Metropolitan Museum of Art," the starter replied.

"What do you think of that?' Marpe asked Gaines, as they went down the street. "Going to the Museum. She flashed me the message that the man was one of them, and that his name is Herman Carlmurg."

"I'll remember Herman," Captain Gaines declared.

"So shall I," Marpe assured him. "She is keeping an eye on him, I suppose. Well, Gaines, we'll walk down the street and get some railroad tickets now."

"Going to sneak it?" Gaines wanted to know.

"No, sir! My foes know that I am going to Kansas City, so why pretend otherwise? I'll not be in much danger until that document is in my possession," Marpe said.

"But they might keep you from getting to Kansas City."

"That would only delay matters a bit. If anything happened to me, another man would be sent."

"They may be able to handle another man easier. Confound it, Marpe, you are entirely too modest!"

"I may say," Marpe replied, "that I do not intend to sleep much. I'll be alert, naturally."

They walked down a cross street to a railroad ticket office, where Marpe sought certain information and then purchased tickets.

"It occurs to me that you are going to do considerable traveling," Gaines remarked. "Three tickets, a lower berth and a drawing-room, eh? Going to take along a party? What is this — a lodge excursion?"

"I am to be the entire party," Marpe replied. "I'm leaving this evening, and I'll be in Chicago tomorrow in time to catch a limited train to Kansas City, where I'll arrive the next morning. And I intend to get some sleep tonight. I may not be able to get much for some time thereafter."

"Going to sleep all over the Pullman car?" Gaines asked. "And why so many tickets?"

"You have to hold two to get a drawing room, as you perhaps know, and one for a lower berth."

"I know that. But —"

"And I like to patronize the railroads," Marpe added.

"Kind sir, your tone tells me that I am to attend to my own business," Captain Gaines said. "I'll try to do so."

"Stop long enough to light a cigarette! Glance toward the front of the office," Marpe whispered. "There is our friend, Mr. Lenserg."

"Why, so it is!" Gaines agreed, looking over the flaming match. "Rather persistent devil, isn't he? Still on the trail, and all that."

"And he'll probably continue to trail," Marpe said.

"Suppose that I pick a fight with him and you slip away during the fuss."

"Wouldn't do any good in the long run," Marpe explained. "I've got a better way than that. Come right along with me."

Creighton Marpe led the way to the front of the big office, where the man Lenserg was pretending to be looking at some railroad folders.

"Ah, Mr. Lenserg, we meet again!" Marpe said. "I told you once that your mere presence made me nervous, so you should remain away from me. However, you are only trying to do your work, and every man has his work to do. And I am going to save you some trouble."

"Indeed?" Lenserg said.

"Yes, sir! I'm going to give you all the information you

require, so you won't have to trouble of finding it out for yourself. I am going to leave the city by train at five o'clock today, my destination being Kansas City."

"Thanks," Lenserg said, sarcastically. "And from which station, may I ask?"

"Oh, you may ask! From the Grand Central Terminal, my dear sir. I have Lower Six in the car behind the club car. Probably we can have a rubber of bridge."

"It takes four persons to have a proper rubber of bridge," Lenserg insinuated.

"Yes. I take it that you may have a friend aboard," Marpe said, with meaning.

"And am I to assume that you may be able to scare up a friend also?" Lenserg asked, also with meaning.

"Stranger things have happened," Marpe admitted. "Always likely to meet a friend on a train. I may mention that when I am traveling I am very alert. There seems to be something about the clickety-clack of the car wheels that makes me snappy. I am awake and wary, if you catch my meaning. I am rather particular about my diet, smoke only my own cigars and cigarettes, and am a very light sleeper."

"Interesting facts," Lenserg observed.

"I do not carry a cane with me on such trips, hence rapier practice is denied me. But I dearly love an automatic pistol, and I always carry one."

"And are you a good shot?" Lenserg inquired.

"Man! You should see me mow 'em down!" said Creighton Marpe.

He laughed and turned away with a grinning Captain Gaines at his heels. Once more they hailed a taxicab, and started to journey uptown to the apartment house where Marpe had a bachelor suite.

Marpe packed a bag, and then they sat and talked and smoked until the proper hour arrived, when they started downtown again. At Grand Central Terminal, Marpe showed one ticket and the lower berth check to the gate man, bade farewell to Gaines, and hurried aboard the train.

He was conducted to his car and seat. He opened his bag and got out a traveling cap and some cigars. Then he sat back and viewed the arriving passengers in quite a normal manner, to all outward appearances. But he really was watching closely, trying to search out his unknown foes if there were any aboard.

He did not see Lenserg. He assumed that Lenserg would not be on the train since his identity was known to Marpe, but that there would be somebody else Marpe did not know by sight.

Just before the train started, Marpe got up and went into the club car ahead, where he made himself comfortable with cigar and newspaper. But he sat in a corner seat from which he could view the entire interior of the car.

CHAPTER IV

OUTWITTED

When dinner was called, Creighton Marpe went to the dining car and ate a substantial meal. The diner was crowded, and if he had foes there he was unable to identify them as such. They would be clever, he knew; not the sort to betray by furtive actions that they were other than innocent travelers.

He left the diner and started back through the train, searching for the Pullman conductor, and finally locating him sitting in one of the cars and going over his lists.

"Kindly follow me into the vestibule," Marpe said, speaking in low tones and stopping for an instant beside the seat as though trying to maintain his balance in the swaying train. "It is very important."

He went on without once glancing at the conductor, who arose presently and followed him. Marpe was standing back in a dark corner of the vestibule between the two cars.

"I am a government man on official duty, and may have enemies aboard the train," Marpe explained, swiftly. "I have Lower Six in the car behind the club car, and a drawing-room in the car behind that. Here are the tickets covering the drawing-room. Please have the porter make up both the upper and lower berths and hang the curtains. Explain to him only as much as is necessary."

"I understand, sir," the conductor said. "You don't want everybody to know where you'll sleep."

"Exactly!" Marpe replied. "I haven't quite decided. I'll be governed by circumstances."

"Anything I can do to help?" the conductor wanted to know.

"Thanks, no! This is the sort of game that we play without outside help," Marpe explained.

He started on through the train, secure in the knowledge that nobody had witnessed his short conversation with the Pullman conductor. He came, after a time, to a compartment car, and started walking briskly along the wide side-aisle.

A woman appeared at the other end of the aisle and approached him, a woman of perhaps thirty, fashionably attired, well-groomed, of the sort generally to be found on limited trains. She seemed to be on her way to the diner.

When only a few feet separated Marpe and the woman, the latter suddenly lurched to one side, grasped at the hand-rail, and started to fall. Marpe sprang forward and supported her.

"My ankle!" she gasped, her face twisting as though with pain. "I — I turned it."

"Ankles are treacherous things at times," Marpe said, smiling down at her.

"I'd have fallen, I believe, if it hadn't been for you."

"Nonsense! You caught the rail neatly. But I am glad that I was at hand and could be of service."

"I wonder if I could bother you a bit. I have a compartment in the next car. If you would be kind enough to assist me there, I'd appreciate it."

"Certainly," Marpe told her. "But perhaps you can continue in a moment. A twisted ankle hurts fiendishly for a time, and then is better."

"I feel half ill," she complained. "I can have some dinner sent in to me."

Creighton Marpe assisted her to the end of the car and opened the door and helped her out into the vestibule. His eyes made swift search of the dark recesses of that vestibule before he ventured into it, but found it empty. He opened the opposite door and aided her into the car and to the door of the compartment she designated.

"Thank you," she said. "Would you care to come in a moment?"

"I believe not," Marpe said, firmly.

"I am a bit lonesome, and you seem to be the sort of man that a woman would like to talk to."

"No doubt a conversation with you would be interesting," Marpe said. "If you care to go to the observation car —"

"The proprieties?" she questioned, laughing a bit. "We'll leave the door open. And I do not feel like walking through the train to the observation car. My ankle, you know."

"Ah, yes, your ankle," Marpe said. "Ankles are treacherous things, as I observed, and also convenient things at time. More romances have started from a sprained ankle — real or pretended —"

"So you are afraid of a romance? We can avoid that, can't we?" she asked.

"Certainly," he said. "Does the ankle hurt much now? I thought not."

"Do you mean to insinuate that I pretended to turn my ankle just to strike up an acquaintance with you?"

"Certainly! Didn't you?" Marpe said. "You see, madam, I caught sight of you peeking around the corner of the aisle as I entered that compartment car. And as soon as you saw me, you entered the aisle and started toward me — and sprained your ankle."

She laughed again. "Perhaps that is true. Am I so very wicked, using that means to strike up an acquaintance with an interesting man, when I am so lonesome?"

"That interesting man stuff would catch nine out of ten, but I happen to be the tenth," Marpe told her. "By the way, let me ask you something. Did you ever hear of Lenserg?"

He fired the question at her in such a manner that she was caught utterly off guard. A slight twist of her lips, the ghost of a frown, a tiny start betrayed her.

"I see that you have," Marpe continued. "Friend of your probably. Need we say more?"

"You think that you are very clever," she said.

"Dear me, no! That is not cleverness. It was all so obvious, if you'll pardon me for saying so. I really expected to meet foes more worthy."

With that, Creighton Marpe left her standing there and continued his journey through the train. He went to the club car and resumed his seat in a corner, and this time he perused a magazine. But he did not lose himself in the story he was reading to such an extent that he neglected to remain alert.

However, nobody made an effort to engage him in conversation, nobody seemed to be watching him. One by one, men left the club car and went to their berths. And finally Creighton Marpe closed the magazine, politely stifled a yawn, glanced at his wristwatch, and left his seat.

He went slowly the length of the car and into the car behind. The porter had made up the berths and the aisle was curtained. Marpe got into Lower Six and prepared for the night. Finally, he stretched out in the berth and turned off the light.

But he did not go to sleep. He had no intention of sleeping in that berth, where he might be caught off guard and prove to be an easy victim. He remained there quietly until about midnight, when he got into a light dressing-gown, put on slippers, and crawled between the curtains.

He started down the aisle of the swaying car, brushing against the curtains, squeezing to one side once to allow a trainman to pass. When he came to the end of the car he kept going, out into the vestibule and across it, into the car behind, and to the drawing-room that had been prepared for him.

Lights were burning in the drawing-room, and it took Marpe only an instant to make sure that no foe lurked there. So he locked the door and began a more methodical inspection of the room. There was nothing to indicate that an intruder had been in the place.

Everything seemed to be all right. But Marpe took the bed in the upper berth apart and remade it carefully. He had heard of such things as the prick of a hidden needle inducing a drugged sleep. Satisfied at last that his enemies, if they were on the train and active against him, had not tampered with anything in the drawing-room, Marpe got into the upper berth, made himself comfortable, pulled the curtains together, and turned off the light.

"*¡Feliz aventura!*" Marpe muttered. "Happy adventure, huh? Maybe it will be, and maybe not. You never can tell in a case like this."

He was asleep within a sort time. And evidently he had taken all his precautions for naught, for he was not molested during the night. It was about dawn when he awoke, inspected the luminous dial of his watch to get the time, and crawled cautiously out of the berth.

He slipped into his dressing-gown, clutched the automatic in the pocket, unlocked and opened the door. The Pullman conductor sprang out of a seat only a few feet away.

"I've been keeping an eye on your drawing-room, sir," the conductor said.

"Thanks! But was it necessary for you to go to all that trouble?" Marpe asked.

"Well, there were a couple of gents prowling through the train like they were looking for somebody who was missing. They are passengers and didn't create any disturbance, so I couldn't jump them about it. They saw that I had an eye on them, though, and stopped it."

"Um!" Marpe grunted. "Did you know the gentlemen?"

"Never saw them until this trip, and I've been on this run for quite a few years. They've got a compartment in the car where you reserved a lower."

"Thanks. I'll look 'em over," Marpe said.

He went across the vestibule and into the car forward, where he parted the curtains of Lower Six carefully. He found what he had rather expected to find — the contents of his bag scattered all over the berth.

Marpe chuckled as he returned the things to the bag, collected his clothes and dressed. He went to the washroom to finish dressing, packed the bag neatly afterward, locked it, put it beneath his berth, and went forward to the club car.

It was only an hour after dawn, but there were passengers in the club car. In one corner were four men who had spent the entire night playing bridge, probably for high stakes. And there were two others who sat side by side and smoked.

Creighton Marpe gave them a swift look and sat down opposite them. He pulled at a cigarette and watched the scenery rushing past. He watched the men across the aisle, too. Something seemed to tell him that they were foes; some unusual sense warned him to be alert. And he could be now, after a refreshing sleep. He glanced up quickly to find one of them men glaring at him, and then he felt sure. Marpe smiled in a knowing way and looked through the window again.

"My friend, you look as though had had a good night," one of the men said to Marpe.

"Never slept better, sir," Marpe replied. "But you and your friend look as though you haven't slept at all, if you'll pardon me for saying so."

"Only fitfully," the other replied.

"Possibly a troubling conscience," Marpe told him. "You might take a nap during the day. I'll not, of course."

There could be no mistaking his meaning. One of the men glared and the other almost snarled at him.

"It'll be a lonesome day," Marpe continued. "Not very much excitement on a trip like this. Though I did meet a charming lady."

"Some men have all the luck," one of them answered.

"She was inclined to get better acquainted with me, too. A charming lady, but I felt compelled to avoid her. You see, she knows Lenserg."

"Lenserg?" one questioned.

"Yes, Lenserg — the man under whose direction you two are working. She probably knows Herman Carlmurg, too."

"You appear," said the man across the aisle, "to be exceedingly wise."

"Oh, not exceedingly so!" Marpe protested. "Only moderately wise. By the way, while you were searching my bag, you uncorked my shaving powder. Dreadful mess!"

"Are you accusing us —"

"Tut, tut!" said Marpe. "What is a little face powder between friends? And you certainly annoyed the Pullman conductor, too. I imagine he thought you were bandits. Thanks, however, for not breaking into the drawing-room I was occupying and ruining my sleep. Now I believe that I shall go and have an early breakfast. See you later, gentlemen!"

CHAPTER V

OUTWITTED AGAIN

That evening when the train reached Chicago, Creighton Marpe took his time about leaving it, and allowed his foes to go ahead of him through the gates. He caught sight of the woman, alone, and of the two men he had met in the club car.

He had almost four hours between trains in Chicago and a change of stations to make. He did not know how many were arrayed against him, and if there was anybody at hand to aid him in a pinch he did not know that. For no member of the Service had approached to signal him that a comrade was in the neighborhood.

He continued to be alert. He went through the station crowd, carrying his bag, descended to the street level, and engaged a taxicab to drive him to the other station. There he checked his bag and went to the restaurant to spend considerable time over his dinner.

When he had finished eating, he still had an hour before the train would be open. He prowled through the waiting rooms, scrutinizing those in the crowd. This was the part of his work that Marpe disliked — the inactive part where he was compelled to be on guard constantly and he was denied a clash, either verbal or physical, with his foes.

Standing near the entrance to the station, he saw the woman again. She got out of a taxicab and went through the station, a porter carrying her bag. A short time later, the two men arrived. They passed into the station without seeing Marpe.

Marpe knew that the westbound limited was to run in two sections. He visited a Pullman officer, identified himself, and got space on both sections. And then he waited until the gates were thrown open.

He showed himself so that the others could see him. He fussed around the newsstand, purchasing magazines and fruit, and so gave them the chance to pass through the gate ahead of him. He went through a moment later.

Now he was watching them closely, through he pretended not to be, and he knew that they were watching him. Marpe went along the second section, found his car, showed his transportation, and gave his bag to the porter, who carried it inside.

Through a window he watched the others as they boarded the second section also. He caught a station porter who was just leaving the car, gave him his bag and a dollar, and told him to take the bag to a certain berth in the first section of the train on the next track.

Then Marpe walked through the train to the club car. He saw the two men in a compartment which had the door open, but acted as though he had not seen. The woman was not in evidence, and Marpe supposed that she was in one of the compartments.

He went to the club car, struck a match and ignited a cigar, and paced back and forth like a man eager for the train to start. His two enemies entered, glared at him, and sat down to smoke and watch him. Marpe gave them not the slightest attention.

He glanced through the windows now and then at the first section. And suddenly he darted through the door of the car, sprang to the platform, raced across it, and jumped upon that first section just as it started pulling out of the station. Standing on the steps, Creighton Marpe looked back and thumbed his nose at the two enraged men on the other train. "Compliments from The Man Who Changed Rooms," he shouted to them.

Now he was safe from annoyance for a time, he believed. He was on the first section of the train, and they were on the second. And those sections would not be together for some time. So Marpe claimed his berth, opened his bag, and made himself comfortable.

He had a talk with the train conductor later in the evening and ascertained that the two sections would be side by side at three o'clock in the morning at a division point in Iowa. Marpe made certain requests and went to bed. At half past two o'clock the porter woke him, and he dressed swiftly.

The train pulled into the division point for a change of locomotives and crews. Marpe watched carefully. The second section pulled in quietly beside the first. Standing in the deep shadows beside the baggage truck on the platform, Marpe watched his two foes leave the second section and dart across the platform and get upon the first just as it started to pull out. Marpe, grinning, got aboard the second section.

Now the enemy was rushing ahead of him on the first section, and he was safe on the second. And he had enjoyed several hours of sleep. He did not retire now, but went back to the observation car and made a friend of the lonesome brakeman.

He watched the dawn come, saw the banners of sunrise in the sky. The train was running on time, nearing Kansas City. Marpe went back into the car where he had a berth and performed his morning ablutions.

Then the station. Marpe dropped off as the train came to a stop, to find that the first section was on the next track. Marpe hurried across to it to get his bag. He came face to face with the two men and nodded pleasantly.

"It appears gentlemen, that we have been on different trains," said Creighton Marpe.

Neither of them had a reply for him. They turned their backs and stalked away from him as he got his bag, which convinced Marpe that somebody else was watching. And when he turned he saw him — Lenserg!

Lenserg here in Kansas City, and Marpe had left him behind in New York, and no trains could beat the ones upon which Marpe had traveled.

Marpe went straight up to him. "So I see your disagreeable face again, do I?" he said.

"As you see."

"Airplane, I suppose."

"Certainly. Been waiting here for quite some time for you."

"Nice of you to give me all these little attentions," Marpe told him. "By the way, I met two interesting gentlemen on the train, also a lady. But none of them was clever enough to be real interesting. Really, Lenserg, you should engage better people."

"I may, at that," Lenserg said.

"And now, Mr. Lenserg," Marpe told him, stepping a bit closer and the expression of his face changing and becoming stern, "let us forget these pleasantries and get right down to business. I understand you and your friends, and you had better understand me. I am on a certain mission, as you know. I have been playing with you, but I play no more. It is business now, Mr. Lenserg! Get in my way now, and I'll tramp on you!"

"The game isn't over," Lenserg said.

"I warned you, Lenserg!"

"Of course, if you call in the police, and the army and navy —"

"Don't need 'em, Mr. Lenserg! Good day!"

Marpe brushed past him and went into the station. He decided to eat breakfast there, and so entered the restaurant and sat at a table. He saw Lenserg glancing at him through one of the windows. He noticed, too, that the waiter who served him was of the same race as Lenserg. He watched the waiter narrowly as the food was brought.

"Took you a long time," Marpe commented.

"Very busy this morning, sir. Sorry!"

"I thought that maybe you'd stopped to talk to some-body," Marpe told him.

The waiter said nothing. Marpe attacked the breakfast. He put sugar and cream in his coffee, stirred it, inhaled the steamy aroma.

"Um!" Creighton Marpe muttered. "Thought so! Lenserg got to him, eh? Never would have noticed the taste, but you can always get it from the odor."

He pretended to drink the coffee, but he did not. At the corner of the table, there was a potted plant, and Marpe watered it with the coffee when he felt certain that there was nobody watching him. He called for his check, in time, gave the waiter an ordinary tip, got up, picked up his bag and put on his hat, and started from the room.

But something seemed to go wrong with Mr. Creighton Marpe at that juncture. He stopped, and weakly brushed one hand across his eyes. A far-away look came into those eyes, too, and Marpe's lower jaw sagged, and he seemed to be breathing with difficulty.

He passed through the doors and made his way to the street in front of the station. He leaned against the building there, dropped his bag to his feet, seemed to grow suddenly weak. His eyes rolled, he clutched his throat with his left hand.

Lenserg suddenly stepped up beside him.

"Marpe, you seem to be quite ill," Lenserg said. "You're in bad shape, man! Better get to your hotel. Let me help you to a cab."

It seemed that Creighton Marpe was trying to speak, to tell him something, and that he was unable to do so. Lenserg clutched him by the arm, picked up the bag, and urged him forward. Marpe went along with him like a helpless child, seemingly unable to think or act for himself.

Lenserg came to the curb and beckoned the chauffeur of the nearest taxi. The taxi darted forward and stopped, and Lenserg opened the door.

And then Creighton Marpe changed swiftly. He laughed lightly and his face cleared and his eyes twinkled.

"Thanks, Lenserg!" he said. "I'll take my bag now, please. It isn't every day that I have such an aristocratic porter. And, by the way, I didn't drink that coffee."

As Lenserg recoiled, his face purple with wrath, Marpe laughed again and got into the taxi. He slammed the door.

"Hotel Baltimore," he directed the chauffeur.

He laughed again as the taxi wheeled away.

CHAPTER VI

SEVERAL FOES

At the hotel, Creighton Marpe registered under his own name and addressed the clerk: "Got a room and bath for me?"

"Yes, Mr. Marpe. Reserved on telegraph from New York."

"When was the reservation wired?"

"We got it yesterday morning, sir."

"Good enough! And how was the request signed?"

The clerk consulted a file of messages. Signed 'Strecko,' sir," he replied. "Rather unusual signature, but we made the reservation, nevertheless."

"Perfectly all right," Marpe told him. "But I do not want the room; I want another."

"It is a good room, Mr. Marpe."

"Not objecting to it on the grounds that it might not be suitable," Marpe hastened to assure him. "I am on government business. I may have active enemies. That room was assigned to me twenty-four hours ago. Many persons may have learned that I am to have that room."

"Just as you please, Mr. Marpe. I'll give you another."

"I'll go to my room at once, and I expect a caller soon. If anybody asks for me, I'm in."

Marpe ascended in the elevator with a bellhop and was conducted to the room that had been assigned him. The bellhop withdrew. Creighton Marpe made a swift inspection of the closet and bath, finding them both empty. Then he examined the room itself, and became assured that everything was as it should be. After that he paced the floor from one corner of the room to another, waiting.

The telephone rang, and Marpe darted across to it.

"Mr. Marpe?" a man's voice rang.

"Yes."

"Captain Makker speaking."

"Come right up, Captain."

Marpe replaced the telephone receiver on its hook and took up a position in the middle of the room. Once more he glanced around like a man surveying the scene of an impending battle.

He heard an elevator door clang in the distance, and moved swiftly across the room to the door, which he unlocked. His hand went into his coat pocket and clutched the automatic that was there, holding it ready for instant use.

A knock on the door.

"Come in!" Marpe called.

The door was opened, and a man stood framed in it. "You are Mr. Marpe?" he asked.

"I am, yes. And you — ?"

"Captain Makker."

"Ah! Come right on in, Captain, and close the door behind you, please," Marpe instructed. "Have to be a bit careful, you know."

"Naturally," his caller said. "I don't blame you at all for being careful."

"And so, being careful, we'll have you turn the key in the lock of that door, please," Marpe said. "Thank you! Sit down there by the table, now."

Marpe walked around to the other side of the table and stood looking down at him. "You are not in uniform, Captain," he said.

"It would have been conspicuous. I thought it best not to wear one."

"Undoubtedly it was best. There is a penalty for impersonating an officer of the United States Army."

"But how could that apply to me?" the other asked, looking up at him quickly.

"Steady, sir!" Marpe warned. "You'll notice that my right hand is in my pocket. You are covered with an automatic."

"Well, upon my word! This is a reception that I did not expect."

"I dare say. But we have to be careful," Marpe told him. "Got something for me?"

"When I hear a hear a certain password, Mr. Marpe."

"Um! It would be better, under the circumstances, if you spoke that password first," Marpe said. "Just suppose, for the sake of argument, that you are not Captain Makker, but one of the enemy. I speak the password, you get it —"

"But how do I know that you are Creighton Marpe? One of the enemy might have registered under that name in the hope of getting what I have to deliver."

"I know that I am Marpe, you see; but I do not know that you are Captain Makker."

"Oh, well, I guess that is all right! I have a sealed document for you, Mr. Marpe. Here it is."

He brought it from an inside pocket of his waistcoat and put it down on the table. It was an envelope of very thin paper, about five inches square.

"Very good!" Marpe said. "I am to take this thing and get it to New York as swiftly as possible, and put it in the hand of a certain gentleman there."

"That is my understanding. I'll be going, then. You'll be wanting to make your arrangements for the return trip. How do you return, Mr. Marpe?"

"Nobody knows that except myself."

"Beg pardon! Shouldn't have asked. Well, glad to have met you, Marpe. Hope to meet you again when we can have time to chin together."

"Just a moment!" Marpe said. "Sit down again!"

"Beg pardon?"

"I said for you to sit down. Before my trigger finger gets nervous and contracts. That's it. Your hands flat on the table, please."

"I must say —"

"Say nothing! I'll do the talking," Creighton Marpe told him. "Man, your game is raw!"

"What do you mean? Do you realize how you are acting, what you are saying?"

"Certainly! You are not Captain Makker. I have seen a recent photograph of him. Just sit still and do not make a move, if you value your health. We'll have a look at this document you brought me."

Marpe, ever alert, ripped the envelope open and took out several sheets of thin paper.

"Blank!" he said. "Just as I expected, sir. You believed that I would accept this thing and hurry away, back to New York. With me out of the way, the real Captain Makker could not deliver the genuine document. There would be a break in the plans, and you people might have a change to get the thing from Makker. How many more of you are in the hall?"

"You seem to know everything," the other said. "Well, what are you going to do about it?"

"What have you done with Makker?"

"I do not know what has been done with him, if anything," came the reply. "This was just a trick to get to you before Makker did, get you out of the way."

"I should smash you in the nose," Creighton Marpe told him. "But I have neither the time nor inclination for barroom brawls, so to speak. You appreciate the fact that I could shoot you, say that you intruded here and tried a holdup, or something like that?"

Color drained from the other's face. "I — I suppose that you could," he said.

"You people certainly are eager to get that document, whatever it is. I do not know what it is, nor does my Chief. But I have orders to carry the thing to New York, and I am going to do just that. Now you tell me something — how many men are prowling around in the hall outside, hoping to get at me and steal my credentials?"

"I am not talking."

"Didn't expect you to," Marpe said. "However, when you see them again, just tell them that it won't do any good to try to get credentials from me. They couldn't do it. I think that I'll keep you here until I hear from Captain Makker. If anything happened to him, I can deal with you."

"What do you think has happened to him?"

"To be truthful, I do not think that anything much has happened to him, unless he is an utter fool. I do not think he'd come alone from Fort Leavenworth to deliver that document to me. But possibly you people have managed to delay him."

"That's it. Might as well confess. He was to be delayed until I had the chance to hand you that bogus letter and get you started back to New York."

"No doubt you were ready for me in that other room — the room that was reserved for me."

"Naturally."

"Uh-huh! Thought as much," Marpe said.

"You are not yet safe back in New York. You've got a job ahead of you — to get that document, get it to New York, and deliver it safely to a certain person."

"Very simple task," Marpe assured him. "Merely a matter of hours. Steady, there! Hands on the table!"

Creighton Marpe whirled suddenly to one side as he spoke. He had noticed a slight contraction of the other's eyelids. And now he discovered the reason for it.

The door of the room adjoining had been unlocked and opened. A man was creeping upon him. But now the intruder came to an abrupt stop as Marpe drew the automatic from his pocket.

"Steady, both of you!" he warned. "Close that door — you! Come over to the table and sit down. Hands flat! It occurs to me that I may have some target practice here yet."

They sat side by side and glowered at him, two middle-aged men of the type Creighton Marpe expected to find arrayed against him. He stepped across to the door, still alert, and propped a chair beneath the knob.

"Only two doors, thank heavens!" Marpe said. "You gentlemen are rather persistent, aren't you? Steady, now, while I use the telephone." He stepped back to the instrument and put the receiver to his ear.

"Get the house detective up here quick!" he snapped into the transmitter.

Replacing the receiver, he approached the table again.

"I simply cannot be bothered anymore by you men," he told his prisoners. "Expecting a caller, you know. If isn't at all gentlemanly of you to annoy me in this manner."

"Oh, we'll go!" said the latest arrival.

"I know that. You'll go in charge of the house officer. And possibly you'll be detained for a time, at least until I am sure that nothing has happened to Captain Makker."

Once more there came a knock on the door.

"Who's there?" Marpe questioned.

"House detective, Mr. Marpe!"

"One moment, please!" Marpe, watching his prisoners, went across the room to the door. There was a smile upon his face and it was a peculiar sort of smile. He turned the key and unlocked the door and stepped back swiftly. "Come in!" he called.

The door was opened and a man entered. And the instant he had done so Creighton Marpe slammed the door shut and poked the muzzle of his automatic into the man's ribs.

"Up with your hands!" he snapped. "House detective, are you? One of the gang waiting in the hall, you mean. You heard me telephone and thought that you'd get to me before the house officer arrived. Keep those hands up!"

"You — why — I'm the house officer!"

"If you are, we'll know it later. But I think that you're not. You see, your friends at the table are not very clever. When you spoke and said that you were the house officer, they betrayed in their faces that they knew your voice, and that it was the voice of a friend. Stand right there against the wall, please, and keep your hands up. I feel quite flattered, gentlemen. It appears that they have sent an army against me."

Again there came a knock at the door.

"Who is it?" Marpe demanded.

"House officer, sir."

"Come right in."

Once more a man entered the room. His eyes opened wide at what he saw.

"Ah! Here we have the real house officer," Marpe said. "I spotted him in the lobby when I entered the hotel. Can always tell a hotel detective. And that is another reason why I did not accept the fake one."

CHAPTER VII

THE BACK TRAIL

"What's all this?" the house officer asked.

"Have you been informed as to my business?" Marpe wanted to know.

"Yes, Mr. Marpe."

"Good! These gentlemen are attempting to molest me. Just take them away, so I'll not be annoyed by them anymore."

"Want me to make charges against them?"

"Keep them in the manager's office for a time, until I tell you what to do."

"Very well, sir. I'll telephone for help."

Marpe watched the three while the officer telephoned. Another house detective appeared, and an assistant manager.

The men were searched, and weapons taken from them, and they were led away. The assistant manager locked the door that had been opened and was profuse in his apologies.

Marpe was left alone once more. He touched match to cigarette and paced the floor and smoked. Luncheon hour came, and he had something to eat in his room, and was very careful about it, indulging only in a salad that he knew could not have been doctored, plain bread, and water.

He sent down for railroad time tables and consulted them. All he was waiting for now was Captain Makker and the document he was to carry. The instant he got the latter, he would make arrangements for the return trip to New York.

And finally, when he felt that he could endure the delay no longer, he called the army post at Fort Leavenworth by telephone and got the commanding officer on the wire.

"What about Captain Makker?" Marpe asked, after establishing his identity. "I am waiting for him."

"He should be there soon, Mr. Marpe," came the reply. "He started once with a decoy document. They mussed him up a bit and got it away from him. We only hope that they'll think they have the real one."

Marpe chuckled at that. The Army was a bit clever, too, he told himself. He paced the floor some more, not exactly nervous, but restive. Once more the telephone rang.

"Hello!" Marpe called.

"Captain Makker speaking."

"Come right up to the room, Captain. I am waiting for you."

And again Creighton Marpe stood to one side of the door and called for the man who knocked to enter. He knew at the first glance that this was the genuine Captain Makker.

"I've been having all sorts of fun, Captain," Marpe said. "A fellow impersonated you — unsuccessfully. A couple of others tried to be clever also, and failed."

You have nothing on me," the captain replied. "I was waylaid and knocked out, and papers stolen from me. But a couple of my friends who happened to be near and watching got the men who got me. Just marked them up a bit."

"We'd better conduct the remainder of our conversation

in whispers," Marpe said. "The enemy is very active here-abouts. Have you a certain password?"

"Yes. *Feliz* — You may give me the remainder."

"*¡Aventura!*"

"Fair enough! Here is what you came for."

Captain Makker put a small package down upon the table. It was an envelope about six inches square, of very thin opaque paper, and there was an official seal on it.

"Well, now, that looks like the real thing," Marpe observed. "Not much to cause all this fuss, is it?"

"You don't know what it is?" Captain Makker asked.

"Haven't the slightest idea."

"Nor have I."

"How's that?" Marpe gasped. "What is the confound thing, anyway?"

"I know that it is in code, whatever it is — but sometimes codes are deciphered by the wrong persons."

"I imagined that it was some army stuff you men at Leavenworth had concocted."

"But it isn't. Leavenworth is only a relay station, so to speak," Captain Makker explained. "That thing came to us from the west, presumably the Pacific Coast. You are to carry it on. I do not know what it is, but it sure has had our people worried. We're glad to be rid of it. Six officers in civilian attire were in my neighborhood when I brought it here. Two are outside in the hall now. That's what we think of it."

"Huh! And I've got to carry the thing alone, without any army to guard me," Creighton Marpe said. "With that whole outfit against me, too. Well, makes no difference what it is. None of my business. I've got orders to deliver it to a certain man in New York, and that's all it means to me. Captain, will you be kind enough to wait here for me?"

Creighton Marpe went into the bathroom and closed the door. He was gone about ten minutes. When he emerged, he was grinning like a schoolboy.

"Just tucking the thing away so I can carry it safely," he reported. "And now, Captain Makker, I am going to ask you to do something a bit unethical, as it were."

"What's that?"

"I am going to jump a board bill," Marpe said. "I'll ask you to pay it for me later, however, and here is plenty of money with which to do it. What I mean is, I am going to sneak out of this hotel and leave the enemy holding the sack, if you catch my meaning. And I want you to remain here for at least half and hour after I am gone, and then go downstairs and pay my bill for me."

"I understand, Marpe. Good idea!"

"I'll do some telephoning first, and let us hope that the enemy hears me."

Marpe went to the telephone, consulted the directory, and then called a ticket office.

"I want a lower to Chicago," said he, "on the five o'clock train. Name is Marpe. Yes, sir, I'll claim it at the station in half an hour."

He was smiling as he returned to the table and conducted the conversation in whispers.

"That will cause them to get active, if they heard it," he told the captain.

"But I don't understand. You're tipping them off to what train you'll take."

"Nothing like it! I do not intend to take that train. I am not going to Chicago at all. Nor am I going to catch a train at the Union Station."

He got his bag, put on his hat, and hurried to one of the windows.

"Talk about something, in fairly loud tones," he instructed, speaking in whispers himself.

Captain Makker commenced talking, telling of an incident at Fort Leavenworth, speaking in a loud voice and laughing raucously. And while he did that Creighton Marpe opened the window, making very little noise about it.

"Now, keep muttering," he said, as he shook the captain's hand. "Try to make it sound like a conversation. You grasp the idea? You may have a couple of friends in the hall, but some of the enemy may be in an adjoining room. Goodbye, Captain, and I hope that we meet again."

Creighton Marpe got out upon a fire-escape landing and went swiftly down the ladder to the floor below. He glanced through the window there and saw an empty room. He opened the window and got inside, went to the telephone, spoke in low tones, and asked that one of the house officers be hurried up to him.

The officer was there almost immediately, and Marpe let him in.

"I wondered who was calling from this room," the detective said. "Tried to tell the switchboard girl that she had made a mistake, since this room was not occupied."

"I'm sneaking out," Marpe said, grinning. "Captain Makker will pay my bill in half an hour or so. I want you to help me get out without being seen."

"Come along with me, Mr. Marpe. It is only a step to one of the service elevators."

Marpe followed the house officer into the hall and along it for a short distance, where they disappeared through a door. A moment later, they were in the service elevator and descending to the basement. Arriving there, the officer conducted Marpe to an alley door, and left him there while he went out and got a taxicab and had it ready at the mouth of the alley. Marpe scurried out and got into the cab.

But he did not drive to the Union Station. He went swiftly away from the central part of the city, and finally reached a suburban railroad station. There he dismissed the taxi and hurried into the depot.

And presently a train thundered in, and Creighton Marpe got aboard. He sought the Pullman conductor and acquired a berth. He was on a train bound for St. Louis instead of one going to Chicago, and at St. Louis he could transfer to a New York train.

Making himself comfortable in the seat Marpe relaxed. He was doubly alert and on guard, now that he was carrying that precious document. He could go, without sleep until he reached New York, if necessary, and he probably would.

He allowed himself to dream a bit of Alla Stimney now. He was eager for her to quit the Service, but she did not want to do so while he remained in it. And he hated to give it up, even to marry Alla Stimney. He loved the thrill of it, the excitement and adventure, the pitting of wits against clever foes.

He felt that he was safe, now that he had escaped the enemy. He knew that there might be a bad moment in New York. They would be watching Major Sinlon, probably, and would make a last effort to get that document. But that was something to worry about when the time came.

The hours passed slowly for Marpe. He read and he smoked, and he watched the scenery through the window until the darkness came. He dined carefully and well. This train was due in St. Louis about midnight, and there was an excellent New York connection. He would make that, he promised himself, and settled down to the last lap of the journey.

As the train pulled into St. Louis, Marpe picked up his bag after motioning the porter aside, and prepared to get off. He wanted to get a compartment on the New York train, if it was possible. He sprang to the platform and hurried along it in the midst of a horde of passengers. He passed through the exit gate and went speedily toward the ticket office. If he made this connection, he would have less than twenty minutes in St. Louis.

He had no trouble getting his compartment. Taking his ticket and change, he turned away from the window — and came face to face with Lenserg.

"Ha. The man who changes rooms," said Lenserg.

Marpe was startled, though he did not betray it.

"It appears that I run across you every now and then," Marpe said. "Airplane again?"

"Surely! You are not so clever as you think, Mr. Marpe. We had men watching every train, and when you were located on the St. Louis train my man wired back to me. So I came ahead to wait for you."

"You are getting to be a confounded nuisance," Marpe informed him. "I feel inclined to adopt stringent measures regarding you. I cannot be annoyed much more without losing my temper."

"You haven't completed your mission yet, Marpe."

"Merely a matter of time," Marpe assured him. "I suppose you saw me buy my tickets?"

"Yes. I know that you got a compartment, too."

"Going to travel on the same train."

"Possibly."

"Uh-huh! And about how many little playmates are going to be along?" Marpe asked.

"How many have you?" Lenserg countered.

"Have you spotted any?" Marpe wanted to know. "If you haven't anything more important to do, you might do that — try to spot them."

He turned away abruptly and made for the gate, knowing well that Lenserg was close behind him. Lenserg continued to follow closely as Marpe walked alongside the train, searching for the car in which he had the compartment. It was rather annoying, but Marpe was lightly humming a little air as he mounted the steps in the wake of a porter. He beheld Lenserg making for the Pullman conductor, and guessed that the enemy did not have a reservation, and was compelled to get one at the last moment.

Marpe went into his compartment and closed the door. He opened a window and watched Lenserg conduct negotiations with the Pullman conductor. He saw Lenserg get into a car some distance ahead.

Then Creighton Marpe violated the rules of the railroad company. Picking up his bag, he left the compartment and went into the vestibule, and when the porter was not looking he opened the door and trap on the off side. He dropped down and walked the next track toward the rear of the train.

As he came to the end, the train started. It went without him — but it carried Lenserg.

CHAPTER VIII

TRAPPED

Creighton Marpe returned to the station. There were other trains for New York, and he had to wait only an hour to catch the next. He purchased a compartment and another ticket, turning in the old one. The ticket agent lifted his eyebrows at him.

"Government business — no explanations are necessary,"

Marpe said. He made his getaway on that train, made himself comfortable in the compartment, and wondered what Lenserg was doing. He did not anticipate any more trouble until he reached New York. But he would not relax vigilance.

The following day, Creighton Marpe sacrificed speed for safety. He lost a couple of hours by leaving the train at a town in Ohio and catching another on a different railroad. He encountered no opposition. None of his enemies seemed to be around, and he hoped that he had shaken them off.

But they would be massed and waiting for him in New York, and especially at the Hotel Magnificent, he supposed. They undoubtedly had learned of the room he had reserved there several days before, and probably had made certain plans.

And when New York was reached, he did not go into the Grand Central Terminal, but left the train at a suburban depot. Nor did he go to his rooms. He engaged a cab and hurried to the Hotel Magnificent.

He reported his arrival immediately to the clerk and claimed his room, but he did not go up to it. He checked his bag at the parcel stand and went to sit in an easy chair in the lobby not far from the information desk.

"Hope that I don't have to wait here all day to get some action," he mused.

The ever-changing lobby crowd was all about him, engulfing the chair he was occupying. Creighton Marpe watched it come and go. He did not see any known enemies, nor did he see any known friends. But he made a close observation of every person who approached the information desk.

And then he saw Alla Stimney. The flickering of her eyelids told Marpe that she was surprised to see him then and there. He started to get to his feet, but once more she made that little signal — that he was not to recognize her.

Marpe wondered at that. She seemed to be alone, to be waiting for somebody. She moved slowly through the crowd, and finally sat down at a distance.

Marpe divided his attention now between Alla Stimney and the information desk. And after a time he saw a man stop in front of Alla Stimney and engage her in conversation. The man was Herman Carlmurg.

Marpe remembered Herman, and that Alla had tapped him a message that the man was one of their foes. What was she doing; what sort of game she was playing, Marpe could not guess. He caught her eye, and again she flashed him the message that he was not to recognize her.

However, he did get up and moved slowly around the lobby, and finally came to a stop a few feet from her, where he turned to look over the crowd.

"I am sorry that our luncheon engagement must wait, dear lady," Herman Carlmurg was telling her. "I am wondering if we cannot make it an hour from now. Can't you shop, or something?"

"You are not very gallant," Alla told him.

"I appreciate that fact, and so I'll have to explain. I have been waiting for several days to see a man on very important business. He has just got to the hotel, and I must interview him at once. It should not take me more than an hour."

"I'll wait around the lobby," she said. "If you'll kindly get me a magazine —"

Herman smiled at her and hurried toward the newsstand. Marpe moved a couple of steps nearly, but did not even look down at her.

"Creighton! Don't turn, but listen!" he heard her say in guarded tones. "He is one of them. I have been trying to learn their plans but have not been able to do so. But I am quite sure that they have planned something."

"Do you know Major Sinlon by sight?" Marpe asked.

"Yes," she replied.

"He probably will go to the information desk when he comes in, to see whether I have arrived," Marpe said. "Watch for him. Hold him here in the lobby until I have you paged."

He moved away quickly then, for Herman Carlmurg was coming back toward her with a couple of magazines in his hand. Mr. Carlmurg was much interested in Alla Stimney, Marpe thought, with a pang of jealousy, but had not been interested enough to betray his plans to her.

Marpe went to the parcel counter and got his bag. He gave

it to the bellhop, and they ascended to the room Marpe had reserved.

As soon as the boy had gone, Marpe made a swift inspection of that room. The closet and bathroom looked innocent enough. There was a door that opened into an adjoining room, and Marpe propped a chair beneath that knob of that. He made sure, then, that his automatic was ready for use, and waited.

The telephone rang. Marpe answered.

"Is this Mr. Marpe?" a man's voice demanded.

"It is, yes."

"Major Sinlon calling. Shall I come right up?"

"Please, Major!"

Creighton Marpe replaced the telephone receiver and hurried across to the hall door. He opened it and peered out into an empty hall. He went out, closed the door behind him, and darted twenty feet to a cross hall and disappeared from view.

He did not have long to wait until a man left the elevator and came briskly along the hall. He stopped in front of the door of Marpe's room and knocked. When he got no answer, the knock was repeated. He seemed puzzled when the door was not opened for him. Out went a hand to try the knob. He found the door unlocked, and opened it.

Marpe slipped quickly along the hall, then, and into the room behind the other. The intruder whirled as Marpe stared to close the door.

"Ah! You are Mr. Marpe?" he asked.

"I am, yes. May I ask by what right you open the door to my room and enter?"

"I just telephoned you from the lobby, and you told me to come up. When you did not answer my knock, I was afraid that — that something had happened to you."

"Oh! You are Major Sinlon?"

"Certainly! I have come for — well, you know what."

Marpe had closed the door, and now he turned the key in the lock and motioned his guest toward a chair. The other sat down.

"I am glad that you got through with it, Mr. Marpe," he said. "We have been worried."

"No doubt," Marpe told him. "Just what is it that you are speaking about?"

"Cautious, aren't you? You are to be complimented on that. It pays to be cautious and alert in this sort of affair."

"True words!" Marpe told him.

"What I am after is a certain document that you got from Captain Makker in Kansas City and have brought to me."

"No doubt that is what you want," Marpe told him. "But how do I know you are the man supposed to receive it?"

"Still cautious? Well, I do not blame you. I am Major Sinlon, I say."

"There is a certain password —"

"Surely! *Feliz Aventuro.*"

"I beg your pardon? Say it slowly, please."

"*Feliz Aventuro,*" the other replied.

"Would you mind spelling it for me, slowly and carefully?"

The other did so, and repeated the spelling at Marpe's request.

"And are you satisfied, Mr. Marpe?" he wanted to know.

"Yes, I am satisfied — that you are an impostor!" said Marpe.

"What is this, sir? Are you inclined to be facetious? Kindly remember that this is a serious business."

"Very serious," Marpe told him. "So serious that you, sir, are going to sit perfectly still until we got into the matter." Marpe brought forth his automatic, and the expression in his face was that of a grim and determined man.

"Why all this melodrama?" the other demanded. "Have I not given the password?"

"You have given it to me wrong."

"That is the one given me."

"Your Spanish is rotten," Marpe told him. "You said *Feliz Aventuro*. The last letter, my dear sir, is an 'a' and not an 'o.' Lenserg should have sent a man who knows Spanish."

"Why you —"

"Careful! You make a move, and this little toy I am holding will bark at you."

"You are making a mistake, Mr. Marpe. Your superiors shall learn of this."

"If they do, I'll probably have my salary raised," Marpe said.

"I may have made a slight mistake."

"It was not a slight one."

"An easy one to make. I do not know Spanish. And because I get one little letter wrong —"

"That's only one little item. Major Sinlon is a graduate of West Point and certainly studied Spanish there. I have seen the major's photograph, and you do not resemble it in the slightest degree. More over, I happen to know that your name is Herman Carlmurg! By the way, has Lenserg got back to town yet?"

Herman Carlmurg sat back in his chair, wrath showing in his face as Marpe laughed at him.

"Very good, Mr. Marpe!" he said. "You take another trick in the game. But the game is not yet ended."

"It is for you, I fear."

"What are you going to do? Turn me over to the police?"

"That isn't being done under the circumstances," Marpe said. "But I'd advise you to sit still and not try any funny tricks, or I may turn you over to some hospital."

"For what are we waiting?"

"To see whether Lenserg or any of the others show up," said Marpe. "I have a lot of fun with Lenserg. I understood that he was quite a dangerous person, but I have not found him so."

"As I said a moment ago, the game is not ended."

"I heard you then, and I hear you now."

"You are of the opinion, sir, that you hold the winning hand. But you do not. Let me tell you something — you'll hand that document to me, or you'll never leave his room alive!"

"Isn't that threat rather preposterous?"

"I think not. You have walked into a trap, Mr. Marpe. If you will look at the wall to your left, just beneath the picture, you will see a hole in the wall. It has been there for a couple of days, ever since we engaged the adjoining room. There was a plug in the hole, but you'll notice that it had been withdrawn, and the muzzle of an automatic is through that hole now, Mr.

Marpe, covering you effectually. Drop your gun, or my friend will shoot!"

CHAPTER IX

A DECISION TO BE MADE

Herman Carlmurg was speaking the truth. Marpe saw instantly that whoever was hold that weapon could fire and get him before he could spring far enough to one side to avoid the bullet. He had been trapped neatly.

But he had rather expected that. He had not known what sort of a trap it would be, but he judged that the enemy had had time to prepare one.

"You see?" Carlmurg was saying. "The game is not ended."

"So it seems," Marpe admitted.

"Drop the gun instantly!"

Marpe allowed his automatic to drop to the carpet.

"Stand back!"

Marpe stood back. Herman Carlmurg got up, stepped forward quickly, and picked up the gun.

"Now you may sit down, Mr. Marpe, and keep your hands on the table before you," Carlmurg instructed. "It probably is not necessary to inform you that I'll shoot if you make a hostile move. We are playing for big stakes, remember."

"I do not know anything about it," Marpe complained. "I don't even know what that document is. What's the next move?"

"Sit still. We will make the next move," Carlmurg said.

As he finished speaking, he stepped to the door and unlocked it. Marpe noticed that the muzzle of the automatic no longer menaced him from the hole in the wall. In a moment somebody knocked at the door, and Carlmurg moved back to it, continually watching Marpe, and opened it a crack and peered out. An instant later, Lenserg was in the room.

"You see me again, Marpe," Lenserg said. "Didn't expect that, did you? You have led us a merry chase and I admire you for it, but we have you now, here at the end of the trail. I hope that you will be sensible."

"Just how am I to be sensible?" Marpe asked.

"You know what we want. Give it to us, and you may go."

"Now, Lenserg, you know the game better than that! It wouldn't be playing it if I handed you what you want without any argument or an attempt to outwit you."

"I can understand that, Marpe. You want to make it look right to your chief. We're willing to bind and gag you and leave you here. Whatever story you tell, we'll not contradict it. You may say that half a dozen men jumped you, if you like."

"Oh, I couldn't be so deceitful, though half a dozen or more have jumped me since I was given this assignment," Marpe replied.

"Are you going to hand us that paper?"

"I couldn't think of doing such a thing."

"Want us to find it and take it off you — that it? So you'll be able to say that you didn't give it up? Well, I can't blame you. It doesn't look good to fail."

"*Feliz adventua* — happy adventure," Marpe said.

"You are playing for time, but it won't do you any good," Lenserg said. "You watch him, Carlmurg, and I'll get that document."

"You won't find it," Marpe declared. "Think that I am an unsophisticated fool to pack such a thing around where it could be found readily?"

"You brought it here with you, expecting to hand it over to Major Sinlon, so it is here."

"Not necessarily. And the major is about due to telephone this room, by the way."

"If he does, the call will not be answered," Lenserg said. "Stand up, Marpe, for I am going to search you."

"It's a useless and criminal waste of time, Lenserg. However, if you insist —"

Creighton Marpe stood up. Lenserg stripped off his coat and examined it thoroughly and tossed it aside. The waistcoat came next, and yielded nothing.

"Strip!" Lenserg ordered.

"Oh, I say!" Marpe protested. "I'm telling you that you won't find it on me."

"We are not playing now. Do as I say!"

Marpe realized that he was dealing with desperate men. He removed his garments one at a time, and Lenserg examined them well while Herman Carlmurg watched him and covered him with his own automatic pistol. Finally he was down to his athletic underwear, which did not take much searching.

"Nothing!" Lenserg said.

"How about his traveling bag?" Carlmurg suggested.

Lenserg unlocked the bag and tumbled out its contents. There was nothing unusual about them, just the ordinary traveling things. Lenserg even ripped out the lining and examined the bag for a false bottom or side.

"Nothing!" he reported.

"Make him talk!" Carlmurg snapped.

"I haven't a thing to say," Marpe told them. "I informed you that you couldn't find the thing on me, and you wouldn't believe it. You've had all your work for nothing."

"But you are going to talk. You are going to tell me where to find that document," Lenserg said, his eyes flaming. "It is death for you if you do not. If we have to fail and suffer the consequences, you'll pay for it, Marpe!"

"What can I say?" Marpe asked.

"You brought it here from Kansas City, didn't you?"

"I did, to give to Major Sinlon, as you know."

"But you have not given it to Major Sinlon. We know where Major Sinlon was when you came upstairs. You had not met him since getting back to the city. You talk, Marpe!"

But Creighton Marpe had thought of a way out now. He gulped and pretended to hesitate, and looked up quickly when Lenserg stepped forward menacingly.

"Just suppose," Marpe said, "that I met a friend in the lobby, and that this friend is in the Service. Suppose, also, that I was a bit afraid that I might encounter trouble in this room. Wouldn't it have been the wise thing for me to hand that document to my friend with orders to wait around the lobby until I communicated again?"

"So that's it!" Lenserg exclaimed. "And your friend —"

"A lady."

"So? We want that document, Marpe, and intend to have it. So think fast! Who is the lady?"

"Her name is Alla Stimney."

"What?" Carlmurg cried.

"Exactly," Marpe said, smiling despite his predicament. "You are acquainted with her, Mr. Carlmurg? She has been rather clever, hasn't she, keeping tabs on you? But I scarcely think that you'll go down into the lobby and seize her and make her surrender that paper."

"You never gave it to her, I was with her a short time ago."

"I know it. You left her for a moment to go and buy her some magazines," Marpe said, grinning.

Herman Carlmurg muttered a curse.

"We'll get her up here!" Lenserg said.

"You may depend on one thing, gentlemen — I'll let you shoot me before I have her up here to be affronted, possibly harmed. If you are men of honor, and will give me your word that she will not be molested —"

"Gladly!" Lenserg said. "We do not fight women. All we want is that document."

"She will come to the telephone if I have her paged."

"Then have her paged. Ask her to come to this room at once," Lenserg said.

"Let me get into my clothes," Marpe said.

He thought that he saw a way out now. He dressed as swiftly as possible. He made himself presentable, and then, while Lenserg and Carlmurg watched closely, he crossed the room and sat down at the telephone.

"I wish to have Alla Stimney paged, please," he said. "She is somewhere in the lobby. I'll hold the wire."

With the receiver at his ear, Creighton Marpe reached out in a manner quite natural and picked up a pen from the desk. He tapped the desk with it nervously, tapped his teeth with it, tapped the telephone transmitter. And he began talking to Lenserg and Carlmurg in a rather loud voice.

"Understand, I won't have her hurt," he said. "If you use rough tactics, I'll get you if it takes me years! I'll tell you confidentially that I am interested in the lady above and beyond the fact that we are in the same line of work."

"Do not worry about that," Lenserg said. "You'll do her a favor by telling her to hand that document to us. When she answers that call, tell her to get up her at once."

Creighton Marpe said something more to them, spoke in such a voice that they did not hear Alla Stimney when she called "hello!" into the telephone transmitter downstairs. But Marpe heard her and knew that she was listening.

And, in a manner quite natural, he tapped the transmitter with the penholder, sending dots and dashes to her:

H — E — L — P.

And then he spoke.

"That you, Alla? Can you hear me — and understand?"

"Yes — I understand," she replied.

"Please come up to my room at once. It is Number 675. At once, that's the girl!"

He returned the receiver to the hook and turned to face them.

"You remember — no rough stuff!" he warned.

"She is a wonderful woman. She had me fooled completely," Herman Carlmurg admitted. "I admire her. I give you my word that she'll not be insulted or bothered in any way. We'll get that paper, detain you both for a short time, that is all."

"If Major Sinlon comes —"

"If he calls, nobody will answer the telephone, and he will wait and call again — too late," Lenserg said. "Marpe, I'm feeling pretty good about this. You have quite a reputation; it isn't everybody who can outwit you. But a man can't win all the time."

"I suppose not," Marpe replied.

He was doing some rapid thinking as Lenserg talked. He hoped that Alla had understood fully, that Major Sinlon was with her, and that these men could be outwitted in the end.

Carlmurg went across the room and unlocked the door.

"When she knocks, you'll call to her to enter," he told Marpe. "Let's have it over with as quickly as possible. No use in fighting after the war is ended."

And so they waited for a few minutes longer, Marpe sitting at the little desk and tapping it nervously. He got out a cigarette, lit it, and blew a cloud of smoke toward the ceiling.

"A lot of fuss about a piece of paper," he said. "I think that I'll get some prosaic sort of job."

"Don't let one failure discourage you," Carlmurg advised. "You have had some great successes. You went up against stiff opposition this time. I am rather surprised that you were not given a lot of help."

"It's a compliment to me that I wasn't, I suppose," Marpe said. "But it might have been better if I'd had a small army around me — as you did."

A knock on the door. Both Carlmurg and Lenserg were on their feet and moving to either side of that door instantly. They motioned to Marpe.

"Come in!" he called.

She opened the door and stepped inside. She gasped when she saw Carlmurg and Lenserg, and would have retreated, but Lenserg closed the door behind her.

"What — what is it?" Alla Stimney gasped.

"First, dear lady, allow me to compliment you," Herman Carlmurg told her. "You fooled me nicely. It is a wonder that I did not tell you secrets."

"But — I don't understand. What is it, Creighton?" she asked Marpe. "You told me to come up here —"

"He was compelled to do so, Miss Stimney," Lenserg put in. "We forced him to reveal that he had given you a certain document for safe-keeping. We want that document, so we had him tell you to come up. Isn't that right, Marpe?"

"That's right," Marpe replied. "You are at liberty to give them any document you have, Alla. They seem to think that they've got us licked this time. As one of these gentlemen told me a few minutes ago, we can't win always."

"How very ridiculous all this is!" she said. "I haven't any document."

"It will avail you nothing to play for time," Carlmurg told her. "We have no wish to resort to violence. But, if we are compelled to do so — ! It would be the part of wisdom for you to hand us that paper at once."

"I have no paper. Which one do you mean?"

"The one Mr. Marpe carried from Kansas City," Lenserg said.

"But I haven't it. I never have had it."

Carlmurg whirled toward Marpe. "You told us that you gave it to her," he accused.

"I believe that I did say so," Marpe replied.

"It was a lie?"

"Oh, do not call it that, please! Just say that it was a subterfuge," Creighton Marpe begged.

"What was your object?"

"To gain time," Marpe replied.

"And where, then, is the document?".

"Sorry, but I must refuse to tell you that."

"You think that you are so very clever, eh? On the contrary, my dear sir! We have the lady here now, and you have professed a sentimental interest in her. So we have a grip on you, Mr. Marpe! You would dislike to have anything happen to the lady, eh?"

"If you dare —"

"We are desperate men, Marpe. We intend to have that paper. Tell us at once where it is, or —"

"Or what?" Marpe asked.

"Miss Stimney is entirely in our hands, Marpe!"

For a moment, Creighton Marpe had a horrible fear. He glanced at Alla Stimney, but could read no message in her face. He could produce that document despite the fact that they had not found it when they had searched him so well a few minutes ago.

But he did not want to surrender it. And he did not want harm to come to Alla. It was a difficult decision to make. And now there flashed into his mind the words of his Chief: "If there ever comes a time when you must choose between the Service and your sweetheart, you will remember that the Service comes first!"

"Talk!" Lenserg snapped at him in a hard voice.

CHAPTER X

GOODS DELIVERED

Marpe looked at Alla again.

"Do your duty, Creighton, and do not think of me," she said.

"Why be foolish?" Lenserg asked. "Would it not be better to give us what we want? There is no way out. Let us have it at once, Marpe. No more of your subterfuges."

"It is a difficult decision to make," Marpe said.

"The Service comes first, Creighton," Alla Stimney spoke up. "Do not forget that."

"But you, Alla —"

"I would despise you if you thought otherwise."

"Very well!" He faced Lenserg again. "You won't learn anything from me," he continued. "But if you offer harm to Miss Stimney you'll regret it. I'll hunt you down as I would hunt mad dogs. I'll quit the Service and go on your trail!"

"Don't waste time making threats," Carlmurg interrupted. "Are you going to talk and tell us where that document is? I am asking you for the last time."

"And I am answering the same — you'll learn nothing from me," Marpe said.

Carlmurg sprang toward him angrily. Lenserg seized Alla Stimney roughly by the arm.

Then there came an interruption that startled all of them, save perhaps Alla Stimney. The hall door crashed in and men spilled into the room. The door that led to the adjoining room was crashed in also, and more men entered. There was a quick rush. Carlmurg whirled angrily, was off guard for an instant, and Marpe was upon him and knocked the pistol from his hand. Lenserg found himself in the grip of two men.

Major Sinlon suddenly stood in the center of the room.

"Good!" he snapped. "Get them securely! Get those doors shut, some of you men!"

Creighton Marpe was just commencing to visualize what had happened. He saw half a dozen army officers in uniform. He saw other men that he knew were police officers and hotel employees. And then Major Sinlon was clasping him by the hand.

"Good boy, Marpe!" he snapped. "Was with Miss Stimney when you called for help. We made our arrangements swiftly. These officers were with me, as a sort of escort for that document you are supposed to have brought me. So here we are!"

"Glad to see you, Major!" Marpe said, grinning.

"Give me that confounded thing and relieve yourself of a lot of anxiety. Miss Stimney will tell you that I am Sinlon."

"I've seen your photograph, Major. But there was a little password —"

"I'll whisper it in your ear." The major did so.

"Good enough!" Marpe said. "You want that rare document now? These men searched me, but they didn't find it."

"Want to get the thing privately?"

"That's not necessary. I never use the same hiding place twice," replied the man who changed rooms.

He sat down and removed his right shoe. At the edge of the sole, he found and touched a tiny spring. The sole came away. And there, in a hollow space not more than an eighth of an inch deep, folded neatly, was the precious paper.

Marpe arose and handed it to Major Sinlon. Lenserg and Carlmurg growled oaths.

"They might have examined the heels," Marpe said. "Hollow heels are old stuff. But the sole was different. And now, if you don't mind, I am going to take Alla to lunch. She had a date with Carlmurg, but she won't be able to keep it now."

ETERNAL ASSETS

I

Leaning far back in the chair, Sherman Krale propped his feet on the corner of the desk, laced his fingers behind his head, yawned, squinted his eyes, and glanced at the calendar before him on the wall.

The office was a dingy one, not because Sherman Krale had little of the world's goods — indeed, he was comfortably well off, and most men knew it — but because Sherman Krale, years before, had furnished that office to suit himself, and never had cared to change its arrangement. Years before, when Sherman Krale had first taken that office, it had been in the finest building of the city. Since then the city had grown away from there, and a part of the building now was given over to manufacturing enterprises. But Sherman Krale remained. He felt comfortable and settled. If any man wanted to find Sherman Krale, that man knew where to find him.

In the front office was Miss Miggins. She had been a girl just out of business college when Sherman Krale had engaged her years ago to do his typing. Save for a vacation of ten days or two weeks each year, she had never left him. Sherman Krale had remained a bachelor, and Miss Miggins had remained unmarried. Her employer had seen to it that her savings were regularly and securely invested. Miss Miggins could have retired, but she did not. She was as much a part of the establishment of Sherman Krale as the battered desk upon which he now rested his feet.

At the outset Krale had hung out a lawyer's shingle. He was a good attorney, too, and known to be absolutely honest, refusing cases that did not appeal to him, accepting many where there would be no fee. There were important committees on which he had served, and honorable offices to which he had been elected. Sherman Krale was of the old-fashioned, shabby sort, with law in his head as well as in the books in his office.

In addition to being a lawyer, he was a criminologist. He dabbled in chemistry and electricity, and loved to solve mysteries, both those of human motives and acts, and those of unexplored fields of science.

The door opened softly, and Miss Miggins stepped into the inner office. She was tall, thin, with straight hair severely combed flat, and wore huge spectacles.

"Well, Miss Miggins?" asked Sherman Krale. He had always called her that. It is doubtful whether he had ever called her by her first name, though she had worked for him twenty years.

"Chief of Police Slade to see you, Mr. Krale," Miss Miggins said.

"Show the chief in," said Mr. Krale.

It was their regular ceremony when a caller or client appeared. Sherman Krale would not have varied it had the President of the United States, himself, come to the office.

Miss Miggins retired and almost immediately ushered in Chief Slade. He was a middle-aged, fat man, very competent in his position, which he had held for years despite changing political conditions.

Krale did not take his feet down from the desk or remove his hands from the back of his head.

"Find a chair, chief, and make yourself comfortable," he said. "Nice day!"

The chief sat down. "It's a nice day as far as the weather is concerned," he admitted.

"You seem all fussed up about something, Slade."

"I am," the chief replied. "But I don't think anything in the world could fuss you up, Krale."

"No particular sense in getting fussed up," Sherman Krale said. "A man's brain doesn't do its best work when he's fussed up."

"Speaking of brains, I've come to give yours a test."

Sherman Krale put his feet on the floor, removed his hands from the back of his head, and bent forward in his chair. He extracted a cigar from his vest pocket, struck a match, and drew a puff, glancing across at the chief questioningly.

"I came away down here to your old office to get you to help me out," Slade said.

"I'm always willing to oblige. But I haven't noticed any unsolved mysteries in the daily papers."

"This one hasn't been in the papers, and for very good reasons. The department is up a tree. Tried and true police methods won't work in this case."

"Is it an important affair?"

"It is," the chief replied. "You know Morgan Eldinton, I suppose?"

Sherman Krale blinked his eyes rapidly. "Of course," he said. "He's been in town as long as I have. Somebody trying to blackmail Eldinton, or something like that?"

"Nope!" said Chief Slade. "Eldinton, on the other hand, is turning crook."

Sherman Krale showed sudden interest. "That is a surprising statement," he said, "I always have suspected that Eldinton is none too scrupulous in business affairs, but he has always managed to stay inside the law."

"Eldinton made a fortune with his contracting company," Chief Slade said. "For the last few years he has done nothing."

"He hasn't had to do anything, having a fortune," Sherman Krale declared.

"But the fortune has disappeared," the chief reported. "Eldinton, like many men before him, has been bucking the market. And he has discovered that there are financiers wiser than he."

"Humph!" Krale said with a grunt. "I thought he had too much sense for that."

"He's down to his last two thousand dollars, as I happen to know. He has always lived high. And now the crook strain in him is showing itself. He's resorting to underhand means of making that two thousand last."

"Let's hear about it," said Krale.

"It is a surprising story, but if is true. And the department isn't able to touch him. Eldinton carries around with him an ordinary pocket check book. He is well known, and very few men are aware that his fortune is gone. He can cash a check anywhere. You'd cash one for him, wouldn't you?"

"I suppose so."

"There you are! He can go into any café or store and cash a check. And he's been cashing them regularly."

"Slade, have you come here to bother me with an ordinary, common, short-check man?" Krale demanded.

"I have not, and you know I wouldn't do a thing like that. You listen to me, Krale. This will interest you. Eldinton writes a check for a hundred — say. He cashes it, and some cashier puts it in a drawer. Making up the bank deposit slip later, that cashier finds a blank check, not a scrap of writing on it, and her cash is a hundred short."

"Huh!" Krale said, grunting.

"Eldinton always cashes the checks when there is nobody else around, no witnesses. If his attention is called to the matter, he declares that he never cashed one, or else that the cashier has misplaced it, or that it has been stolen and a blank put in its place."

"I commence to see," said Krale.

"The thing isn't made public, of course. Eldinton goes right on cashing checks, the checks go blank afterward and are never presented at the bank, and his two thousand remains untouched while he continues to live like a prince."

"What I'd call eternal assets," Krale said, chuckling.

"I understand it, of course — disappearing ink."

"Uh-huh!" said Krale. "A very easy thing to make. But though the ink fades and disappears, under a microscope the paper should show scratches."

"Give me credit for having thought of that!" Slade retorted. "But there are no scratches. He uses a soft-pointed gold pen, I suppose, and blots quickly. Oh, I had him at headquarters, Krale. He gave me the laugh. And he's got us!"

"The remedy," Krale said, "would be to have those checks remain good and pile up, and catch him with a short one."

"That's what I want to do," the chief declared. "I want to catch the scoundrel short and send him up. But I can't think of a way out. It's a new game. He'll keep on playing it as long as he doesn't do it in the same place twice. And there are thousands of places in the city where he can cash a check. We can't talk right out, for he'd jump us for libel, and I couldn't produce proof of his dishonesty."

Sherman Krale threw back his head and laughed. "He seems to have you, chief," he said.

"And so I have come to you. Can you help us, Krale? Is there some way out?"

Sherman Krale seemed to be thinking deeply for a moment. After a time he chuckled. "It is a very simple matter," he said. "Just leave it to me. The scoundrel should be jailed, of course. This case appeals to me, chief, I know half a dozen worthy persons this Eldinton has swindled in such a manner that he could not be touched. Just leave it to me. I'll get you on the telephone when I have everything ready."

Chief Slade thanked him and retired. Sherman Krale thought for a few minutes longer, and then touched a button that summoned Miss Miggins.

"Miss Miggins," he said, "you remember that young, tough-looking scoundrel who does a bit of work for me now and then? I refer to the fellow generally called 'Bull' Carten."

"Yes, Mr. Krale."

"Can you get in touch with him?"

"Yes, sir."

"Send word, please, for him to see me here as soon as possible."

II.

Morgan Eldinton, having just cashed another check that he knew would fade into nothingness within a few hours, left a café and strolled up the street. He had dined well. It was a pleasant evening, and the street was thronged with hurrying theatergoers. But Mr. Eldinton decided not to attend the play.

He was worried over his financial condition, and thought it best to take a long walk and think things out. The game he was playing could not last forever, and he knew it. It was only a sort of stop-gap. How could he turn his two thousand into many thousands? His contracting business had dwindled to nothing. Though he still maintained his offices, he had dropped his staff. To form another staff, gather clerks and superintendents and foremen, purchase materials, put up certified checks, and make bids for decent contracts required a great deal more than a paltry two thousand.

Thinking of his problem Mr. Eldinton walked slowly toward the nearest residence district, went along a tree-bordered boulevard where patches of moonlight alternated with patches of darkness, and finally passed close to a park where there were lonely stretches shadowed by clumps of underbrush.

No one else was in sight. Eldinton walked leisurely, intending to approach another boulevard and return downtown to his club. He came, in time, to a dark stretch beneath overhanging trees, where the moonlight was obscured. Out of the dark, a blow descended. Morgan Eldinton uttered a single groan and then stretched his length on the ground at the edge of the walk.

A figure stooped over him. Deft fingers went through his pockets. They removed currency and silver change, a watch, even a fountain pen. And then, leaving Mr. Eldinton there, slowly to regain consciousness and nurse his sore head, Mr. Bull Carten slipped like a shadow through the trees and was gone.

Some time later Eldinton came back to earth, investigated his pockets, and growled.

"Common thug!" he said. "I shall report it to the police!"

An hour afterward Sherman Krale received Bull Carten in his office.

"It desolates me to have to resort to such means, Carten," Krale said, "but there are times when — er — we must fight fire with fire. You may retain the watch and money. All that I desire is the fountain pen."

Carten grinned and slipped out of the office building. Sherman Krale grinned too, but for quite a different reason. He left his private office and entered a tiny room in the rear of the suite, where he had a sort of chemical laboratory. Far into the night he worked.

III.

Mr. Eldinton was a sort of hero for two days because of the holdup. The blow on his head healed, he stepped abroad again, and once more commenced passing his fading checks and playing on his eternal assets. He was not aware of the fact that Sherman Krale and a city detective shadowed him continually during the afternoons and evenings, but such was the case.

On the evening of the first day of the shadowing, Mr. Eldinton cashed a check for one hundred dollars at a prominent hotel. As soon as he turned away from the cashier's window, Sherman Krale and the detective approached it.

"Let me see that check," the detective commanded, showing his shield.

The cashier obliged immediately, and the hotel manager approached. "That was Morgan Eldinton," said the manager. "He often cashes checks here. Surely he's all right!"

The detective grinned and Mr. Krale grunted. They went into the manager's office, taking the check with them. Mr. Krale took from his coat pocket a metal box about the size of a bank note. He opened the lid, and the others saw that the box was filled with some sort of liquid. Sherman Krale gave the check a bath, as a man bathes a photographic print.

"Let it get dry," said Krale, "and then put it through the bank in the regular way. And say nothing about it, please."

The mystified manager promised. Sherman Krale made an entry in a notebook, then he and the detective went forth, still on the trail of Morgan Eldinton.

Eldinton wrote checks often, and spent the money as fast as he got it, letting his two thousand balance remain in the bank. Sherman Krale gave check after check a bath, and continued on his way, making note of each check in his memorandum book.

Then there came an evening when, having bathed a check Eldinton had passed at a cigar store, Sherman Krale did a lot of figuring and looked at the detective and grinned.

"Got him!" Krale exclaimed. "Report to Chief Slade, and tell him to call me tomorrow."

It was the middle of the following afternoon when Sherman Krale answered a summons from the chief and entered the latter's office at police headquarters to find Morgan Eldinton there. The contractor was in an ugly mood.

"I want to know what this nonsense means, Slade!" he said. "And what has Sherman Krale to do with it?"

"Mr. Krale has been aiding my department," the chief replied. "I wanted him here before I went into details. Eldinton, I have received a complaint against you!"

"Yes?" Eldinton said, sneering. "What is the nature of it?"

"Giving bogus checks. Writing checks when you were aware that you did not have enough money in the bank to cover them."

"Preposterous!" Eldinton exclaimed.

"Oh, no, it isn't preposterous at all! I know a great deal about you, Eldinton. I know all about the fading ink, and know that your assets were down to two thousand dollars. You've drained that two thousand out of the bank and have kept on writing checks. I have three — the last three you wrote — returned by your bank. The losers insist on prosecuting you — and it looks pretty bad for you, Eldinton. You can't be dishonest forever and get away with it. Here are the checks, if you care to see them."

Eldinton's eyes bulged. "But — but —" he stammered.

"I presume you believed that the ink had faded, as it did on the others. But it happens, Eldinton, that all the checks you have written the past week have endured and have gone through the bank. That's why your account dwindled, and why these checks are bogus."

"Oh, you are caught, Eldinton," Krale said. "And you richly deserve it. You've swindled widows and orphans for years, and have hidden behind the law each time. It was a trick that caught you. I hope the judge gives you ten years!"

"But —" Eldinton seemed to be mystified yet.

"Every poison has its antidote," Sherman Krale said, in his smooth voice. "There are such things as reactions in chemistry. You had an ink that faded after a short time, Eldinton. All any chemist needed was some of that ink to study and analyze, and he could make a bath that would set it instantly. We bathed your checks, Eldinton. Very simple."

"You!" Eldinton gasped out. "But how — how did you get some of my fading ink?"

"A mere detail!" Sherman Krale said.

He smiled as he spoke. He was thinking of Bull Carter and the purloined fountain pen.

INITIATING NOGGINS

"Noggins!" the chief of detectives exclaimed. "The justly celebrated and far-famed police department must have signed up some prehistoric monster. The town is full of potential fly cops, the city directory is filled with nothing but names; and I draw a prize like this. Noggins! Who in the high water ever heard of a crackajack detective by the name of Noggins? That's a cognomen for a sleuth, that is! For a regular, honest-to-court, courageous, go-and-get-'em fly bull, give me a man with a name like Noggins!"

The chief of detectives paused to draw breath, and the desk sergeant turned aside for a moment to hide a grin, knowing better than to let the chief see it in his present state of mind,

"Tell me the worst," the chief demanded.

"That prehistoric-monster idea won't do, chief," the desk sergeant said.

"Isn't he a monster?"

"Nothing like!"

"Well, tell me about him. Don't stand there on one foot stretching your wings. Unravel your silent tongue, and let's get at the root of the matter."

"Mr. Noggins," the desk sergeant answered, "is a man about five feet and five inches high and not more than a foot thick either way. His shoulders are stooped, his complexion looks like talcum powder, he blinks his eyes, and he is mild. I may say that he is mild to an extreme. That is Noggins."

"Are you telling me the truth?" the chief demanded.

"Yes, sir."

"Well, who is playing the merry jest? When do we laugh? Why does this bird that you have described so aptly get a place on the detective force?"

"Examination," said the desk sergeant.

"How'd he get to be a policeman in the first place?"

"Managed to pass the physical and got put into the clerical department," the desk sergeant explained. "For three or four years he kept records."

"Bookkeeper type, is he?"

"Only more so," said the sergeant. "Then he said that the indoor work was too confining, and somebody got him put into uniform and transferred to a day beat on the well-known outskirts. He plucked daisies there in summer and helped suburbanites clean the snow off their walks in winter. One afternoon somebody swiped a diamond ring from a dresser drawer, and Noggins was called in by an irate housewife. He happened to see the hired girl trying to hide the thing in the flour bin, made the pinch, and straightaway got the idea he was a detective."

"Don't pause in your clever recital," the chief of detectives said grimly. "I am firmly braced in my chair, there is water in the cooler in the corner, and I am determined to hear the worst. Intrepid and staunch and courageous — that's me!"

"Well, he managed to come to the attention of —"

"That's enough!" exclaimed the harassed chief. "He came to the attention of somebody with a pull — some amateur politician who loves to play in the police department's back yard. I wish some of those guys would monkey with the fire department once in a while, or pick on the street-cleaning department, or have fell designs on the city clerk's office. But no! The police department is the official goat. Proceed, sergeant. I am determined to listen to the entire story."

"Well, when the vacancies occurred in the detective squad, and the usual examinations of patrolmen were held to pick those for promotion, Noggins put in his bid."

"Naturally," said the chief. "Every time there is an examination for detectives nine-tenths of the patrolmen take it. Why in the name of all that's sensible they want to be detectives is more than I can figure out. The extra pay isn't worth the extra worry. But we asked to have only five new detectives accredited to us, and I'll bet half a hundred took the examination."

"Sixty-four, and thirty-one passed with flying colors, as they have it," said the sergeant.

"All right! And from that eligible list five had to be picked. Now tell me this: Why did one of the five have to be a man with a name like Noggins?"

"The report says as how he gives indication of showing aptitude for the work."

"Aptitude!" The chief of detectives growled. "Is that all he's got?"

"All I can see," the sergeant replied.

"I related a few facts about his physical appearance. I may say, also, that he appears to be afflicted with chronic laziness."

"By Jupiter, we can take that out of him!"

"Nothing seems to fluster him at all, chief. He's a mighty meek man; one of these live-and-let-live boys. He's got a voice like a baby doll with the asthma. I suppose he carries the regulation gun, but I'll bet he's afraid to keep it loaded."

"One of these brains-over-brawn youths, eh?" the chief asked.

"Something like that," the sergeant admitted.

"And I'm to make a detective out of him?"

"He's already one — his appointment says so."

The chief snorted. For an instant his face turned purple, and the sergeant glanced toward the water cooler in the corner. But the chief regained his composure.

"Our business is one long succession of shocks," he said weakly. "I'll be glad when I get pensioned. Is this paragon of the detective service anywhere near headquarters?"

"Yes, sir. He is waiting to see you now, with the other four new ones."

"I suppose he'll want to be assigned to all the difficult homicide cases right away."

"They generally do," replied the sergeant.

The chief of detectives gulped and straightened himself in his desk chair,

"Send him in!" he commanded. "Send him in to me, sergeant, and be sure that the door to the outer office is closed afterward. If you happen to hear a shot or what sounds like a man being strangled to death, pay no attention to it until I have had time to make my getaway. I'll expect that much from you in the name of our longstanding friendship. Send me this

Noggins, sergeant — this daisy-picking sleuth, this brain marvel, this intellectual giant, this flamboyant fly cop, this — Send him in to me — and may Heaven have mercy on us both!"

The desk sergeant retired speedily, bubbling with wild laughter. But he knew that the chief of detectives was not to be blamed too much. He had many things with which to contend. Newspapers antagonistic to the city administration had been saying sarcastic things about that branch of the department.

"If a citizen loses a lead pencil and one of my boys doesn't find it inside half an hour, we are a bunch of dizzy incompetents," the chief had said the day before.

And there was a sort of political mix-up, of course, and the best men were kept walking beats, and those the chief called imbeciles were accredited to the detective branch. The chief simply had to make the best of it. It was one of the drawbacks of his office.

There had been five vacancies for some time, and finally the chief had prevailed upon those higher up to fill them, since he needed the men badly. And now they had sent him Noggins.

He never had seen Noggins, as far as he knew. He simply had taken a dislike to the name and the description of the man as given by the desk sergeant, and his heart was bitter because he believed that Noggins had been picked in the place of a better man because of political preference. The chief of detectives was an honest officer and believed in promoting men for merit only.

The door opened quietly, and the chief glanced up from a report he had been reading. He knew without asking that the man before him was Noggins. The new detective was meek and mild, as the desk sergeant had said. He seemed to be apologizing silently for existing and cluttering up the world.

He was a sort of colorless man. In a group of four he would have passed unnoticed. With Noggins, being inconspicuous was nothing less than an art. He stood just inside the door, hat in hand, bowing to the chief. His face was flushed slightly, as though he feared to be alone in the presence of a great man.

"I — I am Noggins, sir," he said, in a thin voice.

The chief of detectives whirled around in his chair and looked him over. "Sit down!" he commanded; and Noggins sat down, thankfully, gladly, having felt weak in the knees.

The chief cleared his throat and made an attempt to look through Noggins. But, the first shock over, Noggins seemed to have retired into his shell.

"I understand that you have been transferred to the detective branch, Noggins," the chief said.

"Yes, sir."

"Heaven knows why you picked out that branch!"

"I — I fancy I'll like the work, sir," Noggins said.

"That is because you are not acquainted with it. Unraveling mysteries and running down desperate master criminals is a small part of the work of this department, Noggins. The few experienced men, the few who have a natural ability, I may say, attend to the sensational cases when we have them. And the other men attend to the mass of routine. You may have to be confined to routine for years, with never a thrill. There is no thrill making the rounds of the pawnshops and gathering lists of articles pawned, and in going over them in an effort to locate stolen property."

"I can work and wait, sir," Noggins said.

"You're not very much physically," the chief suggested, not without some malice.

"I realize that, sir."

"Who is your particular friend?"

"Sir?"

"Politically."

"Oh! I understand what you mean. Why, I haven't any pticular friend politically, sir. I haven't a pull, if that is what you mean. It has taken me several years to get assigned to the detective branch."

"No pull?" The chief gasped. "Then how in the name of justice did you get picked out of the bunch of eligibles?"

"I don't know, sir, unless I just happened to make an impression on the examining board," Noggins said.

The chief grunted. He could not imagine Noggins making an impression on anything or anybody. Was there something peculiar about Noggins? Was there really something to the man? The chief hoped so, though he doubted it. He became the superior officer again.

"I expect strict obedience to orders, a continual alertness."

"Yes, sir."

"You'll find me ready and willing to reward merit and hard work at all times, Noggins, and equally ready and willing to punish any breach of discipline."

"Yes, sir."

"I'm going to pair you with Detective Merriwale, and you'll work on the first night shift. Merriwale has been in the service for several years and will show you the ropes. Pay a bit of attention to him, Noggins, for he knows things."

"I'll be glad to listen to him and to learn, sir."

"Um ! Very well!"

The chief grunted and waved a hand in the general direction of the door, and Detective Noggins realized that he was being dismissed. He got up, bowed again, stumbled to the door, and disappeared.

"Detective!" the chief said under his breath, then snorted.

II

Three weeks later Detective Merriwale appeared at a late hour to make a private report to his chief regarding the activities of a pawnbroker suspected of being a "fence." The report having been made to the chief's satisfaction, he offered Detective Merriwale a big, black cigar.

"And how is this man Noggins?" the chief asked. "You haven't said anything about him."

"Noggins isn't a man you think about a great deal," Merriwale replied. "Half the time I don't know he is around. I don't think his brain functions — if he's got a brain."

"Well, tell me about him."

"Nothing to tell, chief. He isn't a bad scout, though. He listens to what I tell him, all right, and gradually he is gathering a bit of information from here and there. But if we wait for this Noggins to set the world afire we needn't take out any extra insurance for some time yet."

"Like that, eh?"

"He's a willing cuss. He's always ready to do the tedious work. He'll copy pawnbroker's lists with a cheerful grin and let me go on about my business."

"Not much life to him?"

"Not any."

"Did you ever see an indication of that unusual aptitude for the work that the examining board found in him?"

"I think he always leaves it home when he reports for work," said Detective Merriwale, grinning at his superior. "Noggins just follows around at my heels and says little or nothing unless I speak first."

"He's probably waiting for a big case," the chief said, grinning himself. "When the city is startled by some sensational crime then Mr. Noggins will show that natural aptitude of which we speak."

"Don't make me laugh," Merriwale warned. "But he's all right to work with in the ordinary run of things. He does the grind and makes it easy for me. But if I ever run up against a real case again, chief, for Heaven's sake give me a different partner — one with some brains and initiative."

Merriwale left the office, found Noggins, and they went out together on their regular rounds. At present their detective work consisted of nothing more exciting or interesting than making a few inquiries regarding a man who had just opened up a new secondhand store. Having assured themselves that he was honest and did not intend to traffic in the swag of thieves, Merriwale and Noggins stopped into a little restaurant for coffee and rolls, then drifted aimlessly up the street toward headquarters. They were to be office men tonight during the last period — which meant sitting around smoking and looking at year-old magazines in the detectives' room.

But the unexpected always happens at police headquarters. One hour before time for reporting off the desk sergeant called them.

"Burglar killed," he explained. "Sylvester G. Coolin did it. Captain says for you to go up and take a look and have the body cared for. Clean up the whole thing."

Merriwale led the way to the street and engaged a taxicab. Merriwale was the sort of officer who always engaged a taxicab when he thought it would be tolerated by the chief.

"Imagine old Coolin plugging a burglar," he said to Noggins.

"Coolin is the millionaire, isn't he?"

"He is — *the* millionaire," Merriwale replied. "Funny old coot, too. I met him once; spent a couple of hours with him when his house was gone through. He's been watching for burglars ever since. Well, I suppose he got one."

"I know his house," Noggins remarked.

"Some house, too. He's an old widower, and he lives in that marble palace with a cook and a butler. Doesn't even have a chauffeur, nor a car for one to drive. Hires taxicabs when he wants to motor. Gets an outside gardener to fix up the lawn now and then and hires a couple of women to come in once a week and clean. He's got fifty millions if he's got a cent."

"Retired, isn't he?" Noggins asked.

"Retired as far as manufacturing is concerned. That's where he made his pile — bringing out some patent. But he makes his money work, you can bet — stocks and bonds and things like that; close-fisted old coot, but powerful. Whenever you run across a man like that, Noggins, be nice to him. You never know when he may be able to give you a boost. I suppose he's plugged this burglar and is all fussed up about it. We'll take a glance around, tell him he did just right, clean up the mess, get the body away, assure him that he will not be troubled except to tell the tale at the inquest, and he'll be grateful."

The taxicab was now in that section of the city devoted to imposing residences, and after a time it drew up to the curb, and Merriwale and Noggins got out. Merriwale told the chauffeur to wait and led the way through the big bronze gate, up the walk and steps, and to the front door of the Coolin mansion. Merriwale rang, and the door was opened by the butler, an old man whose face wore a frightened look.

"Police officers," Merriwale explained. Merriwale always took the lead, and Noggins tagged along behind, filling in the picture and doing little else. But Noggins appeared to be a bit more excited than usual. He supposed that it was an ordinary case, but it was the first since he had been assigned to the detective service. It was better, at least, than gathering pawn-shop reports. Maybe he would be a witness at the inquest.

"This way, gentlemen," the old butler said. "It is a terrible affair, but I suppose a man who breaks into the house of another must be ready to take the consequences."

Merriwale made no reply, and so Noggins kept silent. The butler led them to the library, a gigantic room filled with books and works of art and rare tapestries. Sylvester G. Coolin sat before a mahogany table at one end of the room. His face was white, and he was trembling.

"I am glad that you have come," he said to Merriwale. "This thing has rather unnerved me."

"I don't doubt it, sir," Merriwale replied. "But don't let it bother you too much."

"Over — over there," Coolin indicated, pointing toward the other end of the room. "I — I had the butler put that rug over the body."

Merriwale stepped quickly across the room, and Noggins followed. Merriwale threw back the rug. The man was dead — there could be no denying that. A crimson stream had been flowing from a wound in his left breast, and the two detectives concluded instantly that the heart had been pierced by a bullet.

"Don't know him," said Merriwale. "And I'm supposed to know almost all of 'em, too. I've never seen that face in the rogues' gallery. Have you, Noggins?"

"No, sir."

Merriwale led the way back to where Sylvester Coolin was sitting.

"Just tell us in a few words, Mr. Coolin," he said. "We won't trouble you any more than is necessary. But I have to make a report, of course."

"My two servants had retired, and I was stretched on my bed," Coolin explained. "I am subject to insomnia and found that I could not sleep. I decided to come down to the library and get a book and go back and read until I grew sleepy. I often put myself to sleep in that way."

"I understand," Merriwale said.

"I didn't turn on any of the lights but came right down the stairs. I had on my bedroom slippers, as you see I have them on now, and so I suppose I didn't make any noise. I reached the hall door of the library and turned the knob. As I started to open the door I saw the flash of an electric torch.

"That startled me, of course, and I thought at once of burglars. My house was robbed a few years ago, you remember, and I always have feared burglars. I have some expensive art objects in this room, and generally there is a large sum in cash in my safe.

"I remembered that I had a revolver in the little den across the hall, and I slipped over and got it, and then returned. Once more I opened the door, and this time I stepped inside quickly and snapped on the lights. That — that man was kneeling before my safe, and the safe was open. He was trying to get into the strong box. Papers already were scattered over the floor; as you see them now. He was trying to get the money, of course.

"When I turned on the lights he sprang to his feet and whirled to face me. He started to reach for his hip pocket, and I fired. I was afraid that he was going to take out a gun and shoot at me. Maybe I made a mistake — possibly he didn't intend shooting, but I could not take chances."

"Certainly not," said Merriwale.

"I went over to him and made sure that he was dead, and then the butler and the cook came running down. I sent the cook back to her room; she is an old woman inclined to hysterics, and I didn't want her to see the body. Then I telephoned for the police."

"You did perfectly right," Merriwale assured him. "There can no blame attach to you, I am sure. Don't worry about it, Mr. Coolin."

"You — you know him?"

"No. Possibly he isn't a known crook, but some man

starting out to be one. We'll take his description and try to trace him, of course. Don't you worry about it at all."

"And what shall I do now?"

"I'll telephone headquarters and have the coroner notified, and the body will be removed," Merriwale explained.

"He got in through that window over there. See — it is open," Coolin said.

Merriwale and Noggins walked across the room and inspected the window. It was open from the bottom, and a man easily could have entered through it from the ground.

"Common case," Merriwale remarked. "Got in, started to loot the safe, got caught and plugged. Happens scores of times a year. Don't you worry, Mr. Coolin."

"You're very kind," Coolin said.

Merriwale went back to the body again and began going through the pockets, while Noggins stood beside him. The dead man had no weapon in his pocket, neither did he have burglar tools.

"Worked the safe by turning the knob," Merriwale whispered. "Between you and me, Noggins, that isn't much of a safe, except for looks. A child could open it."

"Yes, sir," Noggins said.

The dead man's pockets offered nothing in the way of identification. A knife, a few coins, a handkerchief, an empty wallet, and a common door key were all that Merriwale removed. He wrapped the other things in the handkerchief and then faced Noggins.

"It is time for us to report off duty," Merriwale said, "Noggins, do me a favor, will you? Remain here until the coroner's assistant comes, and tell him what he wants to know. I'll turn in this stuff at headquarters — no, you turn it in. Matter of fact, I want to get to bed as quickly as possible — got some business to attend to tomorrow. Do as much for you some time."

"Certainly," Noggins agreed.

He might have made the remark that Merriwale generally left him to do the obnoxious work and labor overtime, but he did not. Noggins was a meek man, and he was a novice in the service compared to Merriwale.

Once more Merriwale assured Sylvester Coolin that he should not let himself to be troubled by what had occurred, and then he took his departure. Noggins covered the dead man with the rug again and knelt before the safe and examined it. Then he went over to the window and examined that, leaned out, turned on his flashlight, and looked at the casement, inspected the lock — and grunted.

"I — I hated to have to do it," Coolin was mouthing.

Noggins made no reply. He acted as though he did not know how to handle himself before this multimillionaire. He walked slowly around the room again. His face was flushed a bit now, and he appeared to be nervous, like a man gathering courage to make a demand of a superior, or an employee about to ask for a raise in wages.

Again he knelt before the safe, and he swung back its door and looked at that. Once more he knelt beside the dead man, and now he lifted one of the hands and looked at the fingers, then lifted the other and looked at the fingers of that. Sylvester G. Coolin bent forward in his chair to watch.

The old butler came into the library again.

"How is the cook?" Coolin asked.

"She was a bit hysterical, sir, when I told her what had happened, but I prevailed upon her to remain in her room, and she is quieter now,"

"Very good, Martin. You may remain here until the coroner's men come to remove the body."

"Yes, sir."

Noggins turned slowly and regarded the butler as though he had been a freak of nature. The butler turned away; he had a feeling that Noggins was searching his mind with those peculiar eyes of his, which suddenly seemed to have taken on life.

"Everything is all right," Coolin was saying to his servant. "The other detective went to make a report and send for the coroner, and this gentleman is standing by until the coroner comes. They have been very courteous to me. Yet there was nothing to it, of course. I had to shoot."

"Of course, sir," the butler said.

Detective Noggins suddenly turned and walked across

the room to him. He raised a hand and pointed a forefinger straight at Sylvester G. Coolin.

"Coarse work!" he said.

"I beg your pardon?" Coolin gasped.

"Very coarse work!" Detective Noggins said, his face fiery red because this was a crisis of a sort. "This man is no burglar. And you did not shoot to defend yourself. You murdered him!"

III

There was an instant of silence; the butler gasped, and Sylvester Coolin's face turned while, then went red. He smashed a fist down on the table before him.

"Are you insane?" he cried. "What do you mean?"

But Noggins did not have a chance to reply at that instant. A bell rang, and the butler hurried to the door while Coolin sputtered in an attempt to talk.

The butler returned with the coroner's assistant and a doctor. Once more Noggins found himself in the background. Mr. Coolin told his story, and the coroner's assistant, eager to please such a wealthy man, accepted it at face value.

"And that fool!" Coolin cried, pointing to Noggins. "That fool has the impertinence to say that I murdered the fellow!"

"You did," Noggins said quietly.

"You are new to the force, aren't you?" the coroner's assistant asked significantly. "I understand that Detective Merriwale was here. He is an officer of experience, and I guess we can abide by his decision. I'd think twice if I were you before I'd affront such a gentleman as Mr. Coolin."

"You see," said Detective Noggins mildly, "Merriwale jumped to conclusions, as you are doing now. Just because a gentleman of Mr. Coolin's standing said that he had found a man in the act of burglary and had shot him, Merriwale was ready to believe it. But I took a look around."

"Indeed?" the coroner's assistant asked, a sneer evident in his voice.

"And it's my duty as an officer to arrest Mr. Coolin for murder and take him in."

"Take me to the police station?" Coolin cried. "You try it! I'll have you kicked off the force for this!"

"I'm not easily bluffed," Noggins said quietly. "And I don't think you'll have me kicked off the force while you're in jail charged with murder."

"But when they let me out —"

"You're not going to be let out," Noggins said firmly. "You'll probably use your money to prolong your trial, but in the end you'll either go up for life or make a trip to the electric chair."

"This is nonsense!" the coroner's assistant cried. "Noggins, you are committing professional suicide. You're cutting your throat. You must be insane to make such an accusation against a man of Mr. Coolin's standing, especially since Merriwale looked over things and decided Mr. Coolin spoke the truth."

"Maybe Merriwale was in a hurry to get to bed," Noggins offered. "He seemed to be."

"Mr. Coolin, don't worry about this imbecile," the coroner's assistant said. "I'll telephone police headquarters and get the night captain of detectives up here, and he'll soon settle things, this upstart, this amateur sleuth included."

"Of course, you can do that," Noggins said. "But you don't want to make a mistake, do you? It'd look bad if you did. Folks might say you favored Mr. Coolin because of his wealth. Why not let me explain first?"

The coroner's assistant snorted. "It'll be the best way," he told Coolin. "Let the fool explain, and we'll show him where he has some crazy idea."

"Save that fool talk until afterward," Noggins warned, with some show of anger. "If I don't convince you, then you can call me a fool, and welcome. You can call me all kinds of a fool."

"Well, what have you got to say?" the corner's man demanded. "What fool stuff have you found that you consider evidence?"

"Now we're getting down to business," Noggins said. "I'll explain just as quickly as I can. Mr. Coolin told us his story, of course. He says he couldn't sleep, and he came down here to get a book to read and found the burglar kneeling before the opened safe. He had come through that open window."

"That's the truth!" Coolin said.

Detective Noggins took up his position in the middle of the room and looked at them. Coolin was sitting before the table again, his face showing anger and a trace of fear; the coroner's assistant was sneering openly; the physician seemed to be acting in a neutral manner; and Martin, the old butler, was extremely nervous as he stood against the wall.

"Mr. Coolin said that the man reached toward his hip pocket as if to draw a revolver," Noggins said. "If you'll look at his trousers you'll see that they're an old pair of dress trousers. I suppose the poor devil bought them at a second-hand store. The point is, they haven't any hip pockets."

"Probably made that move to frighten me," Coolin said.

"'That's possible," Noggins admitted. "So we'll consider some other things. There is a strong lock on that window. I wonder if it was locked."

"It was, sir," the butler said. "I see to the windows myself."

"Sure of that?"

"Absolutely, sir."

"The thief pried it open," Coolin said loudly. "There's a scratch on the casement, if you look to see."

"When did you see that?" Noggins asked.

"After I had telephoned the police I went over and looked. He just pried the window open."

"I'll admit that there is a scratch on the windowsill," Noggins said. "But it isn't a deep scratch, not deep enough for a jimmy. And the window lock was not snapped. That's funny, isn't it? The butler is sure it was locked, and if it had been pried open the lock would be ruined. But it was just unlocked.

"Right beneath the window is a flower bed, with soft earth. Take a look, Mr. Coroner's Assistant, and you'll see that the flower bed is ten feet wide and twenty long. A man couldn't get to that window without stepping on it. And when I flashed my torch over it, I failed to see a single footprint."

"Oh, maybe he got in some other way," Coolin said.

"Sure," the coroner's assistant added. "He probably opened the window on this side, for a quick get-away."

"Then why didn't he make his quick get-away instead of pulling a bluff that he had a gun?" Noggins demanded. "Mr. Coolin says he was in front of the safe, and the safe is only one jump from the open window."

"I — I shot as soon as he reached for his hip. He didn't have time to get to the window," Coolin said.

"Any more marvelous deductions?" the coroner's assistant wanted to know.

"A few," Noggins admitted. "The dead man had no tools with him. He might have been able to open the safe door without them, but how did he expect to get inside the strong box? Mr. Coolin says he was at work on the strong box. We are to take it for granted, I suppose, that he was after coin or things that could be turned into coin. And right there in the lower compartment of the safe is a jewel box with some rare old jewels in it. Wouldn't he have looked into that first? And wouldn't he have slipped the jewels into his pocket before tackling the strong box? He was a funny burglar, it seems to me. How did he get in? Not by that window!"

"He may have had a key to the front door," the coroner's assistant said.

"Well, it isn't in the door now, and it isn't any place in the hall. And he's got only one key on him, and I can tell at a glance that it won't fit the lock on the front door. It's an old-fashioned key, and your front-door lock calls for a flat one."

"He got in some way," Coolin said, snarling.

"Certainly he did," said Detective Noggins. "I have an idea he came in by the front door — and that you let him in."

"I'd be likely to let a stranger in at a late hour at night!" Coolin said.

"Stranger, was he?"

"I certainly never saw him before," Coolin declared. "If he came in through the front door he must have had a key. Maybe he tossed it away after he unlocked the door."

"When we came, and the butler answered our ring, I heard him shoot a bolt on that front door," Noggins said. "I always make it a point to watch for little things like that. If the burglar came through that door he wouldn't throw away the key and then bolt the door, would he? What sense would there be in that? Any self-respecting burglar would leave the door unlocked for another chance at a get-away."

"I found him in front of the safe. He reached for his hip pocket and I shot him. And that's all there is to it!" Coolin declared, showing greater anger. "And I don't want to listen to much more of your foolishness."

"I'm not done yet," Noggins said mildly. "As a matter of fact, the burglar was knocked on the head before he was shot. He's got a big lump on the back of his head, and there's a cut there, too. And that poker over by the fireplace has a stain on the knob handle. That looks funny, doesn't it?"

The coroner's assistant went over and examined the body and then examined the poker. He looked across at Noggins with sudden interest and something like respect.

"It looks to me, Mr. Coolin," Detective Noggins continued, "that this man came here at midnight on your invitation, say to settle some controversy. You decoyed him into the library; you quarreled with him, struck him over the head with the poker, and then, to silence him forever, fired a shot into his body and made up the story that you had killed a burglar."

"Of all the nonsense —" Coolin began.

"The shot aroused the servants, of course. Between the time you struck him and shot him you opened the window and made that scratch on the sill, and then you opened the safe and scattered a few papers around to make it look good. The scratch on the sill was made with those coal tongs — there's a bit of chipped wood and green paint on them yet."

The coroner's assistant made another swift examination and nodded approval.

"And it is a cinch that the safe was opened after the man was struck down," added Noggins.

"How did you know that?" Coolin cried.

"Thanks — I only suspected it before you spoke," said Detective Noggins.

Coolin's face turned white again.

"I — this is preposterous, and I'll not say another word," he exclaimed. "I'll have you kicked off the force for this. I want that body taken away immediately, and I want all of you to clear out of here. I've had about all I can endure."

"But I've put you under arrest for murder, and you'll have to go to the station," Noggins protested. "Oh, I'll take all the responsibility."

"You fool!"

"Maybe. I'm only a new man to the detective department, but I've got eyes and ears. And this was awfully coarse work, Coolin! Merriwale didn't consider your guilt, of course. He couldn't conceive of a man of your wealth murdering a poor chap — and he was afraid to offend you. He took the quickest way to the end — decided you simply had shot a burglar."

"That's all I —"

"Trying to keep it up, Coolin, in the face of the evidence? Not a chance!" Detective Noggins declared. "I'm not done yet. You said that he was standing there in front of the safe, reaching for his hip pocket —"

"He was! And I thought he was drawing a gun, and so I shot."

"You made one little mistake, Coolin. You shot him while he was stretched on the floor after you had knocked him down — bent over him and —"

"That's not so! How could you prove such a preposterous thing?"

"Simply enough," Noggins said. "I moved the body a bit while I was examining it. That's a powerful automatic you used, Coolin, The bullet went entirely through the body, you see, and *into the floor!* If he had been standing as you said the bullet, going through him, would have struck the wall. And then —"

Sylvester G. Coolin gave a shriek.

"You're a devil — a devil!" he cried.

IV

Late the following afternoon the chief of detectives looked up from his desk and into the face of Detective Merriwale.

"You're in a rut, Merriwale, and you'd better wake up and get out of it," the chief said. "You made a pretty bad mistake last night. If it hadn't been for this Noggins nobody would have suspected that Coolin hadn't told the truth. And all Noggins did was to make an investigation instead of taking it for granted that a millionaire could do no wrong.

"Coolin has confessed. He founded his fortune on an invention he stole from an inventor. The man he killed was the inventor's son. He knew all about it, and a few years ago Coolin had him railroaded to prison. When he got out he collected proof and demanded that Coolin hand over the major part of his fortune. Coolin got him to come to the house after the servants had retired, deliberately killed him after the man had refused to settle for a small sum, and tried to make good his story that he had shot a burglar.

"As it is, we are getting credit for being a courageous police department that isn't afraid to tack guilt on a powerful man — thanks to Noggins. You want to wake up, Merriwale. As for Noggins, he gets assigned to the homicide squad this afternoon, and he stays there, too. Noggins is some proper name for a detective. I'll tell the world that it is!"

FORBEARANCE

CHAPTER I

DAD MEEK ARRIVES

There was nothing impressive in the appearance of the light motor-truck's body, but the chassis was of foreign make; and the man who bent over the wheel, chuckling as he drove, wore a Stetson that was the most expensive procurable, and soft, laced boots that had been made to order. His name was Lates, and he was a raisin king — a man who held that wise economy meant buying the best of everything and keeping modern in every particular.

Lates had made half a million by forcing raisin grapes to grow where scarcely anything had grown before, and by controlling the crops of his neighbors. He was a driver of men, himself included, yet he loved nothing better than a little joke. Hence, as the truck sped over the oiled California highway, Lates took his eyes from the road long enough to glance back behind the seat. His chuckle changed to a soft laugh as he faced ahead again and took a sharp curve in the road on the high.

Here the thoroughfare was lined on the one side by giant eucalyptus trees, behind which were Lates's raisin fields, and on the other by a high, metal fence, beyond which were countless rows of little houses fronted by pens in which countless thousands of chickens cackled and sang their lives away.

"Right here's where I put one over on Bill Roach," quoth Lates, and, without slackening speed, he swung from the highway and through a wide iron gate that had been left open, and the truck charged up the private drive that led to the Roach mansion and the neat concrete office building of the National Poultry Farm.

The driveway was lined with palms, with here and there a magnolia, and it curved gracefully for more than three hundred yards from the gate to Roach's front door. An approaching vehicle could not be seen until it was within fifty yards of the house; hence, Lates decided, his should be heard. He manipulated levers and buttons to make noise and smoke.

Therefore Roach, sitting before his desk in the office building, discerned the roaring of a motor and had his ears tortured by the continual honk of an auto horn. With a roar of rage he got up, clamped his teeth down upon his lifeless cigar, put his hat on the back of his head, and strode wrathfully across the room to the door.

To Roach, the presence of a motor car on his private driveway was second only to the unpardonable insult. Roach's chickens and eggs went to market behind the finest teams in California; and when he rode or drove abroad, either on business or with his daughter Betty, he used horseflesh that would have delighted the critical judges of a fashionable stock show.

His love of horses, remaining from the old Texas days when he had dealt in cattle instead of fowls, was in an inverse ratio to his hatred of all sorts of automobiles. And now, past the house and down toward the office building, came the Lates truck in a tempest of noise and smoke, scattering noxious fumes behind it. The horn gave a last derisive honk as the machine was swung to a stop before the office door.

"Greetings!" called the raisin king.

"Lates, how many times have I told you to keep that blamed stink wagon off my ranch?" Roach demanded. "Any time you feel like making a social call, I'll send one of my men over with a rig to get you."

"He'd have to start yesterday to get me here by tomorrow," Lates responded. "You can't depend much on a horse."

"You — What's that! Why, dang your ornery hide —"

"You'll wake up some day, Bill. You're losin' money every minute. One of the Fresno commission men was tellin' me today that you sent a load of fresh eggs last week and they all spoiled on the road — and it's only nine miles at that."

"Why, dang your —"

"Don't get sore, Bill! As long as you stick to horses, you can't expect to send in a shipment of spring fresh without havin' 'em be old settin' hens when they arrive. You'll get around to autos one of these years — when you get over your nap."

"Before I litter up this ranch with a stink wagon I'll — Say, did you drive that infernal Big Ben in here just to start th' old argument? If I ever *did* lose my senses enough to have one of them things around, I'd spend a few dollars and get one that didn't sound like an alfalfa planter and smoke like a burnin' oil well!"

"Is that so?" Lates exploded. "This little machine came across th' ocean and she set me back more than three thousand bucks. She's built like a watch —"

"There are watches *and* watches."

"I can start right now and run backwards and be halfway to Los Angeles before you can even get a bridle on one of them old cab horses of yours. A Fresno commission man was askin' me today if you was runnin' a pasture ranch for broken-down and pensioned fire-department nags. He —"

"Yeh?" Roach interrupted. "There's entirely too many commission men in Fresno, anyway. There'll be one less when I get hold of th' lyin' reprobate!"

"He said old Bill Roach must have a kind heart, takin' care of bunches of skin and bone that had been worked to death."

"Yeh?"

"If it wasn't that, he said, then you was gettin' ready to start a big soap factory and was buyin' up old stock to make grease."

"You was mighty tarnation glad to have some of that old stock pull one of your tin cans out of th' mud up in th' hills last spring."

"Nothin' th' matter — just run out of gas."

"Yeh? Did you ever see a horse stop an' lay down 'cause he didn't have a bunch o' hay to chew on? What are you burnin' in that old furnace, anyway — crude oil? You're smokin' up the place. I'll bet I've got five thousand hens chokin' to death this minute. Dang you, Lates — you an' your old stump blaster —"

"Father!"

Miss Betty Roach had appeared at one end of the office building, having come down the walk from the house. Now she stood with her hands clasped behind her and stamped one tiny foot with some show of exasperation. The two old men turned sheepishly and regarded her one hundred and ten pounds of youth, health, and vivacity, and then grinned in embarrassment like schoolboys caught in a prank.

"Your father's all right, Miss Betty," Lates said. "He's just exercisin' his vocal cords."

"I heard him from the house," Betty said, walking briskly toward them. "Aren't you ashamed of yourselves, quarreling again about autos and horses? You — Not another word, father! Not another word, or into the office you go — like that!" She snapped her fingers.

"I ain't makin' any further remarks," Roach said, grinning down at her.

"As for you, Mr. Lates — didn't you promise me you'd never quarrel with father again, even if he started it?" she demanded. "You know better than to drive that truck in here when it isn't necessary."

"Great Jupiter, I forgot!" Lates exclaimed. "I come in here for a special purpose, and your paw made me forget all about it with his arguin'." He turned in the seat and looked back into the truck, and chuckled deeply. "What do you think of this?" he asked. "He's still asleep — slept through all th' noise!"

"What are you talkin' about?" Roach demanded.

"I ain't right sure what it is, but I s'pose it'd pass for a human bein'. It ain't what you'd call an imposin' sight. It don't cost a cent to take a look."

Roach and his daughter stepped forward to the truck and looked in. On the bottom was stretched a lean, lanky man of uncertain age. His clothes proclaimed him a wanderer not burdened with wealth. His face was seamed and wrinkled and covered with a stubby red beard. The nose resembled the beak of a parrot, and the chin extended itself to a point and curled up, almost meeting the nose. Just now his mouth was open, disclosing jagged, yellow teeth and letting forth a volume of sound.

"Why, dang me if I didn't think them snores of his was th' breathin' of your old stink buggy!" Roach exclaimed. "I'm apologizin', Lates. What do you intend doin' with this here animal? He looks considerable like a pestilence."

"More like an epidemic," said Lates. "There's too much of him for an ordinary pestilence. You don't care for his looks, then?"

"If he ever rode behind one of my teams, they'd run from here to th' Mexican line 'thout stoppin'."

"Think so?" Lates asked blandly.

"I can't imagine how a human bein' supposed to have some sense, like yourself, would be totin' such a thing around th' country. Is it in a trance?"

"That's just a regular beauty nap he's takin'."

"He sure needs a long one," Roach said. "Was you thinkin' of usin' him for a scarecrow in your raisin fields? If he was on my ranch, he'd scare the chickens to death."

"Well, he's yours — not mine!" Lates exclaimed, grinning.

"What's that?"

"I just drove him out for you, Roach. He don't belong to me. I thought I was doin' you a favor by bringin' out your new hired man. That's why I brought th' truck up th' drive."

"Yeh? Think that belongs to me? My broodin' houses are hawk-proof, an' I don't need him. Why, dang your —"

"Must be some mistake," said Lates. "He stopped me five miles down th' road and wanted to know if I'd ever heard tell of such a place as th' National Poultry Farm. He said he understood it was a small place somewhere in th' vicinity, and that th' hired man had left and he was goin' to get his job."

"Dang your hide! A ranch that sells chickens *and* eggs from th' Atlantic to th' Pacific, that's got thousands upon thousands o' feathered fowls peckin' grain, that ships eggs by th' trainload —"

"Don't make a speech, Bill. Think I'm a chamber-of-commerce banquet? He said it — I didn't! I reckon as how I'd heard tell of your place, and gave him th' proper directions; and he reckoned as how, if I was drivin' that way, he'd like to get in back and ride. So I let him, and he went to sleep. Thought I was doin' you a favor. He said he was goin' to work for you."

"He did, eh? You c'n drive him right on to your raisin patch —"

"Patch! A thousand acres —" Lates began.

"Oh! He's waking up!" Betty gurgled.

Lates ceased his oratory and turned to get a better view; Roach took a step nearer the hated "stink wagon," and Betty peered over the end gate.

The waking-up process of the somnolent one was intricate. The open mouth stretched wider in a yawn that disclosed more yellow and ragged teeth. Then it snapped shut, and the blunt nose wiggled from side to side. The elongated chin twitched, and a shiver seemed to run among the seams and wrinkles from the point of it, as ripples on the surface of a pool spread from where a stone strikes the water.

One eye blinked rapidly, then opened wide; the other conducted itself in a similar manner. The somnolent one gave a deep sigh and struggled to sit up, winning success at the second attempt. He drew his knees up under his chin, clasped his arms around them, and surveyed those around him.

"Is this here th' National Poultry Farm?" he asked, in a thin, quivering voice.

"It sure is!" Lates exclaimed. "We've arrived. Pullman passengers are at liberty to spend th' remainder of th' night in their berths after th' terminal is reached."

"I want to see the boss."

"You're lookin' at him!" Roach roared. "Have your look, and then be on your way! If my hens see you, they'll die of fright."

"Now ain't that too bad! I reckoned as how I might get a job on this ranch."

Roach snorted the improbability of such an event. The somnolent one unfolded his gaunt legs, let down the end gate with evident effort, and made his way to the ground. As soon as his feet touched the driveway, the truck sprang forward, wheeled, and started back down the drive, Lates roaring with laughter.

"You wait, Lates! Take this misfit along with you!" Roach screeched. But Lates merely honked his horn, waved a hand, and disappeared behind the palms around the curve. He had unloaded the joke on Roach, and for the time being his fun was at an end.

"So you thought you'd get a job here, did you?" Roach demanded, half angrily, as he whirled to face the new arrival. "Who the blazes are you, anyway?"

"My name's Dad Meek. I've been called Dam' Meek, which I ain't at times."

"Is right now one of th' times?" Roach wanted to know, stepping forward belligerently.

"Now don't you get yourself flustered. You can't scare me that-a-way. I've heard tell about this ranch an' some of th' funny things concernin' it. They call it th' Fuss an Feathers Farm down in Fresno."

"Yeh? And you'd like to have a job, eh? What did you ever do in th' line o' work to benefit th' human race?"

"I was a cow-puncher onct."

"Yeh? I s'pose some of them wise ones down to Fresno told you to say that, eh? They know I'm partial to old punchers, th' dudes! I used to have my thousands o' head runnin' th' old range an' had punchers by th' score. But when they turned Texas into town lots I trotted up here. I had to work an' I had to work with somethin' you c'd count in thousands, so I took up chickens. Chickens! Down in Texas we used to let th' women an' kids raise 'em for th' fun of it. But I've got th' biggest chicken ranch —"

"I heard tell 'bout that down to Fresno."

"An' every blamed cuss that comes along lookin' for work says he's an old cow-puncher so I'll take him on. I gave one a job last week, an' he didn't know a rope from a brandin' iron. Know what I did to him when I found it out?"

"I reckon I heard tell about that —"

"Down to Fresno — I know. Well, I kicked that imitation of a man clear across Lates' raisin patch to th' county road, an' threw him in an irrigatin' ditch. I roped him an' I branded both his eyes! If I'd had any sheep dip, I'd uv dipped him, that bein' th' greatest indignity known to man.

Comin' right down to th' truth, do you still reckon to be a cow-puncher?"

"I sure reckon I was onct. You can't scare me none. I've punched cows from th' Panhandle to th' Canadian line, includin' a term on th' old X Bar Z, in Montana, which shows I'm tough. My last job was in th' greaser belt."

"Sheriff run you out?"

"Not any," said Dad Meek. "It got so blamed settled up that a feller couldn't wheel a hoss 'thout tearin' up some woman's flower garden, so I quit."

"An' now you want a job here with th' chickens? Yeh?"

"Well," said Dad, "I never thought I'd ever ride herd on a passel o' chickens. I'm right glad my maw ain't alive to see it. But a man's got to earn his bed an' vittles. I thought maybe you'd have somethin' I could do in th' way o' work. I don't know much about chicken ranchin', but I'm willin' to learn. How do you brand th' critters?"

"We don't brand 'em; we keep 'em in pens."

"I used to be counted a pretty good hand at round-up," Dad said.

"Yeh? You don't have to sling a rope or knee a bronc to round up eggs and fries."

"Ever bothered with rustlers?"

"I am that! Lates keeps a mess of Japs to pick his grapes, an' I saw feathers behind their bunk house t'other day to fill ticks for a tourist hotel — an' they hadn't bought as much as a pullet."

"I used to be pretty good goin' after rustlers."

"Oh, give him a job, Father, and have it over with!" Betty exclaimed. "I can tell by the way you act that you're going to do it."

Roach glared at her, but she only giggled shamelessly.

"You sure don't want to make any mistakes," he said to Dad Meek. "You still reckon you used to be a real puncher?"

"I sure reckon I was onct."

"You're hired. You'll find th' bunk house an' cook's shack an' eatin' joint down th' driveway a hundred yards. Go right down an' get on th' job. You'll find a mess o' old punchers scattered around — I've got forty men workin' on this chicken ranch."

"Who's the foreman?" Dad asked.

"Bob Owen. You just pick out a bunk an' shake hands with th' cook, then come back here. Your job'll be to hang around th' office an' get in my way. I've got to have somebody to swear at once in a while, 'specially when Lates drives in here with the stink wagon. Wash your face, an' borrow a razor an' shave. I can't have my yearlin' hens scared. You'll get forty a month an' found."

"Much obliged," said Dad.

He yawned again, and started to shuffle down the driveway. Roach turned back into the office building. Betty, smiling and dimpling, hurried toward the house. Betty was glad that her father had ample funds, for only a man with ample funds could give an old puncher forty a month and found to sit around and tell yarns of the old days when the range was limitless and fences were unknown.

CHAPTER II

ENMITY

The "cook's shack," as Roach had designated it, was a model sanitary kitchen fitted with all the latest appliances and housed in a mission-style building connected by a narrow passageway to the "eatin' joint." This latter was a long, low building of concrete, scrupulously clean, with wide windows around which flowering vines had been trained. The National Poultry Farm was a model and modern ranch, save for the aversion of its owner to automobiles, yet Roach demanded that, for the sake of old days, the terms "cook's shack" and "eatin' joint" and "bunkhouse" be used by the men he employed.

Dad Meek was astonished when he reported at the bunkhouse and looked inside the door. There were rows of neat beds, lockers for each man, a private room for the foreman, and tub baths and showers in an apartment at one end.

"They've even got a he-chambermaid what makes th' beds an' tends to th' laundry," he said afterward. "There's a negro what shines your boots same as in a sleepin' car; and the he-maid mends your socks an' shirts. I reckon th' Old Man 'u'd get one of them valleys to help a feller put on his pants if someone u'd call his 'tension to it. That gang ain't no bunch o' delicate, hothouse plants, howsomever. You don't want to think that bunkhouse has a refinin' influence. Th' only was to refine some o' that crowd 'u'd be with an ax."

The "he-chambermaid" assigned Dan Meek to a bunk and instructed him how to shave in the bathroom before an adjustable mirror. Dad chuckled some as he shaved, for he remembered times when he had removed beard from face without the aid of any mirror whatever, simply feeling with a tough forefinger where patches of bristle remained and then scraping them off with a dull razor, and washing in ice-cold water afterward.

Properly washed and shaved, and his old clothes brushed, Dad wandered back to the office building and sat down on the steps. Roach was arguing over the telephone with the freight agent of some railroad concerning a delay in promised cars, and Dad grinned as he listened.

"Reckon that telefoam mouthpiece must be made of asbestos," he observed. "That's round-up language he's talkin'."

The telephone receiver was slammed on the hook, and Roach appeared in the doorway.

"Dang their hides!" he exclaimed. "Some day I'm goin' to buy a railroad an' show 'em how to run it! Here was me talkin' to th' freight agent 'bout delayed shipments, an' after I find out he don't know anything, as usual, I ups and asks him what time th' train that gets in her tomorrow afternoon leaves Los Angeles. I've got a new bookkeeper comin' on that train, an' I want to know. He says I've got to phone to another number, dang his hide! 'Ain't you workin' for the Santa Fe?' I asks him. 'I ain't in th' passenger department,' he says. 'I know it — you ain't swift enough,' I goes back at him, 'but can't you tell me somethin' about that train?' I asks. 'Of course, Mr. Roach, I know what you ask,' he says, 'but I dare not tell you, 'cause it wouldn't be official, comin' from the' freight department that-a-way. It's a matter o' red tape,' he says. I give him a bit o' my mind. I c'n talk when I'm mad!"

"Yes, I heard tell about that —"

"Down to Fresno, eh? I know. You're liable to hear anything down to Fresno. You sure stopped there long enough to get an earful. Now you get th' blazes outen here, Dad Meek, 'cause I've got some figurin' to do, an' if you're around I might get to talkin' 'bout hosses an' cows. Strut around th' place an' take a look, then get your supper. You c'n report here for work in th' mornin'."

"I guess I will take a look around," Dad said.

"Don't take any sass from th' men, old-timer. You got to stand up to th' bunch I've got on this range."

"I heard tell —"

"I bet you did! Get out!"

Dad Meek arose leisurely and walked down the driveway, past the bunkhouse, and out to where there were rows and rows of chicken houses side by side, each one numbered. He observed that all were marvels of ingenuity and constructed after the same pattern, and that the avenues between the rows were named after breeds of fowl.

"I wonder if that foreman, Bob Owen, is workin' on White Leghorn Street or Plymouth Rock Avenue," Dad mused. "I'm certainly anxious to have a look at that gent. Maybe he's restin' over in Black Minorca Park or at th' Bluff Cochin Club."

He asked the first man he met concerning the whereabouts of Bob Owen, and ascertained that the foreman probably was in one of the incubator buildings. It was some distance to these buildings, and Dad walked it slowly, chewing a twig he had pulled from a pepper tree, and ruminating.

"I c'n see right now," he told himself, "that merry blazes will be poppin' around this ranch before many days. Two particular gents are due for nervous shocks, and I ain't one of th' gents; but maybe I'll get a shock myself before this business ends. Well, I got a job, anyway, so I c'n stick around an' watch th' proceedin's. I sure want to get a squint at this here Bob Owen."

The door of the nearest incubator building stood open, and Dad, standing in it, squinted his eyes until they became accustomed to the semi-gloom inside. Two men were working in the middle of a big room, taking eggs gingerly from long, narrow baskets and placing them in the incubators. Dad stepped inside.

"I'm lookin' for Mr. Owen," he said.

The men stopped work and faced him; one, his fists on his hips, stalked forward until he stood within three feet of Dad Meek, and looked him up and down as a man might inspect a horse.

"I'm Owen," he said. "What's wanted?"

"I jus' wanted to take a squint at ye," replied Dad. "Th' boss said as how you was foreman of this ranch, and, bein' as how I'm goin' to work here, I thought I'd better size ye up and see whether we c'd get along."

"Is that so? Well, if you've got me sized up, what do you think?"

"I guess I c'n handle ye, all right. I reckon you won't be hard to get 'long with, if ye got some common sense. Foremen is funny critters sometimes. Onct I worked for one I had to smash in th' jaw regular every other night, but otherwise we was as contented as kittens at a bowl o' milk."

"Think you're funny, don't you?" exclaimed Owen. "I'll continue this little discussion with you tonight after supper. It's against th' rules to argue durin' workin' hours."

"I heard tell 'bout that down to Fresno. I heard a lot o' things 'bout this here ranch. I'm prepared."

"You are, eh? I'll take some of that prepared stuff out of you —"

"Don't get flustered, young man, or you'll spoil th' eggs."

"If you've got a job on this place, get out of here and go to work!" Owen exclaimed.

"Th' boss says as how I'm to go to work in th' mornin'. I'm to hang around th' office an' get in his way so's he c'n swear. I reckon I'll go round an' look at th' rest o' th' ranch now. See you later, Mr. Foreman."

"You can bet you will! Take your ugly face away from her now, before I make it look worse!"

"Why, cuss your carcass, I've chewed up an' spit out tougher men than you! I'm an old cow-puncher, I am, from

Texas. My name's Meek, but you don't want to gamble much on it. If you've got an idee that name fits *me*, I'll be settin' out in front of th' bunkhouse after supper ready to prove things. Why, cuss your carcass — I'm goin', I'm goin'. A man can't get any eddication in here. Don't you frown none at *me!* I'll bet every chick in them egg'll be birthmarked from them black looks o' yourn."

Bob Owen dropped his fists to his sides and breathed heavily. But Dad Meek gave him no chance for further conversation or combat. Dad turned around and went out into the bright sunshine and, chuckling low to himself, walked slowly down White Orpington Avenue toward the brooder houses.

When he was some distance from the incubator building, he allowed the chuckle to die away, and a look of deep concern came into his face.

"Just like his daddy, I reckon — as mean as you c'n find 'em," he mused. "Bob Owen, hey? Why, cuss his carcass! He's got th' same ornery look around th' eyes an th' same devilish way o' stickin' out his chin. Jus' like his daddy — a narrer-minded, crooked, wicked-eyed critter that couldn't scrap fair if there was a bet on it! Tough, hey? He'll need to be, cuss his carcass!"

At the brooder houses, Dad conversed at length with several of Roach's employees, taking care to state that he didn't begin work until morning, hence was to be looked upon at present time as a guest, and shown the sights. He remained at the brooder houses until the men left to go to the bunkhouse to prepare for the evening meal, and Dad went along with them.

As he waited beside his bed for the call to eat, it appeared that a fit of moroseness was upon him. He refused to recognize the banter of the men, declined to reply to remarks considering his facial appearance — merely sat silently, with head bowed, now and then sighing deeply and shaking his head slowly from side to side, meantime making with his thin lips sounds intended to indicate pity.

"Grub pi-ile!" roared a stentorian voice.

Dad almost chuckled again when he realized that the

ancient call to victuals of the range had been instituted here in Roach's model "eatin' joint." There was a sudden rush from the bunkhouse, and Dad brought up the rear, as became a newcomer. He took a seat at one end of a long table.

"I guess you'll think you're in clover here, old-timer, after eatin' cow-ranch grub for forty or fifty years," said one of the men seated near him. "This is a real hotel. I s'pose you're used to tin plates and iron knives and forks, eh? — burned beef and cold potatoes with th' skins on, and thin soup, eh? Yes, I reckon you'll feel like a pig in clover here."

"If he stays," put in Bob Owen from the head of the table.

"Oh, I reckon I'll stay," Dad said. "I heard tell down to Fresno that th' grub was good, but I've got me doubts. You generally got to beat a cook over his head with the butt of a quirt a few times before he gets good grub. I've had some experience with cooks."

"Your experiences ain't ended yet," Owen promised.

"No? Well, I'm ready to take her as she comes. I always aim to please. What's this stuff?"

"That's soup, old-timer," said the man nearest him. "That's mock-turtle soup. Th' Old Man insists we get th' best."

"I reckon it's a mockery, all right. It's as thin as some of th' brags I've heard about th' toughness of this gang. Down to Fresno —"

"Oh! Maybe you think we're a gang of kids!" Owen interrupted.

"I ain't thinkin' just now. It takes a *man* to make me think. What do you aim to call this here?"

"Braised beef, old-timer," said the man on his left.

"Braised be — What's that? Beef, you said, didn't you? I don't know where you was raised, but your paw and maw neglected your eddication. This beef? Not any! You c'n cut beef *an'* chew it! I see right now I'll have to tend to that cook. I recollect almost killin' a cook onct for servin' tough beef. It was down in Texas. Cuss his carcass, it makes me mad just to think of it! Worked for th' old X Bar Z Ranch, he did."

Bob Owen choked on a piece of meat, recovered, and looked down the length of the table at Dad Meek suspiciously.

"What ranch?" he asked.

"X Bar Z Ranch, down in Texas. You know it?"

"I — No, I don't know it!"

"I suspicioned you knew all 'bout it, th' way you spoke up like that. There's a town right where th' old ranch house used to be. That was some ranch. A puncher had to enlist for two years, like a soldier, 'cause th' place was so big that when he started out to ride line it took him a couple o' years to get back."

"It must have been some ranch," said the man on his right.

"*And* it had some history. Blood *and* gore was shed thereabouts. Man by th' name o' Taylor owned her when I worked there. Right next door was th' Crooked S, owned by a man name o' Sturm. There was strife continual."

"Feud?" asked the man on the left.

"Worse'n a feud. This Sturm was th' meanest, crookedest, narrer-minded excuse for a man what every polluted th' atmosphere o' Texas. He got his start rustlin' calves — that's how small th' critter was. He was th' cussedest —"

"That's about enough!" Owen exclaimed.

"What's th' matter, foreman? This Sturm wasn't a friend o' yourn, was he?"

"Never heard of him! But I don't like to hear a man run down."

"No? I never suspicioned you was that tender-hearted. As I was sayin', this was worse'n a feud. Th' punchers fought continual, an' th' bosses fought, too. This was some years ago, when they wasn't strong on law an' order down there. Th' war went on right merrily for some time. Dad fought dad, an' son fought son. One day Taylor was shot from behind a rock, but he got over it. Then th' boys caught Sturm raidin' an' strung him up. He had a son 'bout fifteen, an' Taylor had a son 'bout th' same age. This son o' Sturm's was like his dad — th' crookedest, meanest —"

"We're getting pretty tired of this story," Owen said.

"I'm about done, foreman. This son, aged fifteen, went an' hid behind a barn an' shot Taylor ag'in, perforated him twice. What do you think o' that? And right at that time Taylor was tryin' to help th' Sturm family, too, since th' old man was gone — sayin' as how Mrs. Sturm an' her brood warn't to blame for what th' old man did."

"What did they do to th' kid?" asked the man on the right.

"Taylor made 'em let th' kid go, an' he skipped th' country. Taylor died 'bout a week later. That was th' fightenest ranch ever. One day th' cook —"

Owen crashed his coffee cup down on its saucer. Clouds of anger had gathered on his face. He was not looking at Dad Meek, however, and those at the table supposed he had heard something spoken at the other table across the room and that it had angered him.

Dad Meek's sentence was left unfinished. He attacked the remainder of the meal like a hungry man, and the fit of moroseness seemed to have returned to him.

"You're lookin' blue about somethin', old-timer," said the man on his left, as the pie was passed around.

"I'm feelin' kinder sorry, that's all. I heard some bad news down to Fresno."

"Bad news?"

"Yes — 'bout this gang."

"What's that?" Owen demanded, glaring at him.

"I heard tell down to Fresno as how they called this ranch th' Fuss an' Feathers 'cause th' boss won't have any but he-men around it. They told me as how, whenever a new man showed up, he had to lick 'bout everyone before they'd let him alone. They said this here was th' *toughest* crowd within a thousand miles o' th' Tehachapi."

"Maybe it is at that," Owen said.

"I reckon you're foolin', foreman. This crowd tough? Why, I've been feelin' sorry for this crowd. 'Cordin' to what I heard tell down to Fresno, th' old man makes it hot for you if you don't trim every new man. They said as how Roach wouldn't have a man around 'less he'd fight at th' wink of an eye. Reminds him of old ranch days, they said."

"Well, what of it?" Owen demanded.

"I heard them tell down to Fresno that th' first evenin' a new man was here somebody picked a quarrel with him an' started th' ball rollin'. Seein' as how I'm a new man, I s'pose one o' this gang will try to pull my nose. An' I'm sure feelin' sorry for this gang."

"Why?" demanded the man on his left.

"'Cause if anyone starts to trifilin' with *me*, I'm goin' to run amuck. I'm a wolf when I get started. I'm liable to hurt somebody real bad; an' I hate to hurt folks, 'specially on short acquaintance. I'd issue warnin' so's you know better, but I reckon you have to start somethin', anyway, 'count of th' boss' orders. It's goin' to be mighty tough on this crowd, any way you squint at it."

There was silence for a moment, then a gale of laughter from forty throats. Someone at the other table sacrificed a piece of pie — it struck Dad Meek on the left ear. There was another gale of laughter, and then silence once more.

Dad Meek got slowly to his feet, wiping away the pie with the end of the tablecloth. He unfolded himself gradually until he stood at his limit of height. There was no flush of rage in his face, no flash in his eyes. Dad Meek was a picture of calm deliberation.

"What gent hurled that pie?" he demanded.

"Right here!"

"What's your handle?"

"My name's Paddon, old-timer. What about it?"

"I s'pose th' boss has got a list o' near relatives and friends o' yourn?"

"There wont' be any trouble about such little things as that."

"No?" said Dad. "As soon as these other gents are through eatin' what passes for food in this shack, s'pose we go out front an' have a little argument. I never did like my pie on th' left ear. I'm right sorry to do a thing like that, but I reckon there ain't any other way."

Paddon laughed. "Think I'm goin' to beat up an old feller like you?" he asked.

"Nope. I ain't thinkin' anything like that. I reckon I know who'll get th' beatin'."

"You don't aim to *fight* me?" Paddon cried.

"I aim to spank you some for throwin' that pie."

The laughing men were thronging to the door now, and Dad Meek followed leisurely. For an instant his eyes met those of Bob Owen, and the latter's were blazing. Dad noted that fact before Owen could turn his face away.

Outside, Paddon was waiting for him, and the men had formed a ring, going about it after the manner of men who did it often.

"It's a shame to do it," Paddon was saying. "How can a man fight with an old fossil like that? If he was a *man*, now —"

"From th' looks of him, he never *was* a man!" Owen snarled.

The words were struck from his lips. He reeled, and regained his balance to see Dad Meek standing before him, bent forward, eyes blazing, and fists clenched, Paddon for the moment forgotten.

"You talkin' to *me?*" Dad demanded. "Cuss your carcass, I'm more of a man right now that you an' your daddy put together. I don't mind havin' a little sparrin' match with this gent that hurled th' pie, but if I have to mix with *you*, it'll be one fight! I don't like your face."

The men were aghast. There was no mistaking the meaning in Dad Meek's tone. Here was not a man enraged suddenly by baiting; here was a fighter, cool and collected, deadly, acting as if the man before him was a being he hated more than any other in the world.

Bob Owen realized the state of affairs, and perhaps in a measure of understood them better than the others. His face went white, his lips shut tightly over his teeth, and he rushed.

He struck — and his wrist was caught in a grip of steel and his arm doubled behind his back. He struck with the other fist, to find that his antagonist dodged the blow. Against Owen's cheek the palm of a horny hand crashed with force enough to rock his head. Bob Owen realized the ignominy of it — it was the palm, not the fist, that had struck him.

"Cuss your carcass!" Dad cried, and he hurled Owen backward.

Curses rumbled in the foreman's throat as he rushed again. Dad did not grip his wrist this time, but he sidestepped the blow, and once more his palm cracked against Owen's face. The second slap turned the foreman into a maniac. He wheeled and rushed a third time, caught Dad Meek around the body, and tried to throw him. Back and forth across the driveway they struggled, neither gaining an apparent advantage. The men gave way for them — all except one. Paddon threw out a foot and tripped his foreman's antagonist.

Owen exulted as he felt Dad's body sink beneath him, but his exultation did not last long. With a snarl of rage at such unfairness, Dad Meek lurched to one side and twisted from Owen's grasp. This time it was his fist that struck the foreman, and the blow almost felled him. Then he whirled upon Paddon.

"Cuss your carcass, you crook!" he screeched.

In an instant two foes confronted him, each eager to get in a telling blow. Foot by foot they beat him backward, Dad warding off their blows, fighting to keep them from coming to close quarters. Foot by foot he retreated — until he found himself against the wall of the bunkhouse and unable to retreat more.

"Now, curse you!" Owen cried.

He charged in with Paddon; Dad Meek rocked both their heads with drives of his fists; they returned to the fray and finally got their hands on him and started to drag him down. It was dusk now, and once Dad Meek was helpless on the ground, a kick that could not be seen by the other men would serve to disable him.

Dad realized his peril, for he guessed the sort of men with whom he was fighting; and now he lashed out with both fists, trying to fight his way out into the open again. They hurled him back against the wall of the bunkhouse, and once more they started to drag him down, giving no attention to the mutterings of the men, who disliked this unequal combat.

"Stop that, dang your hides!"

It was the stentorian voice of Roach that rang in their ears. Panting and enraged, Owen and Paddon stepped back.

"That'll be all o' this!" Roach went on. "I heard th' whole argument. I like fightin' men, an' I like to see a man tried out when he's new on th' ranch, but I like to see fair fightin'. So it takes two of you youngsters to handle an old-timer, eh? Understand this, Owen — and you, too, Paddon — this ends right here. We'll call it a draw. You fellers let Dad Meek alone after this. I've a notion he won't start anything if you don't. Understood?"

They nodded their heads. Dad Meek wiped the perspiration from his forehead, returned his red handkerchief to his pocket, and picked up his battered hat.

"I reckon I must have lost my temper," he said. "I almost got started this time. I reckon I must have been misinformed some — this gang ain't so tough. Why, I heard tell —"

"Down to Fresno, I suppose!" Roach exclaimed. "Shake hands now!"

Dad extended his hand and grasped that of Paddon and shook it heartily. Then he stepped toward Owen and extended his hand again. Their hands approached, but by mutual consent they did not touch. The manner in which they were standing prevented Roach and the other men observing the fact. Each hand closed into a fists; and, though the eyes of Dad Meek glittered, his voice was soft when he spoke.

"I reckon that'll be all for th' present, foreman," he said.

CHAPTER III

THE NEW BOOKKEEPER

"Well, Dad," said Roach, the following morning, "I guess you'll have to tend to the office this afternoon. All you've got to do is set tight before th' desk an' smoke, an' throw out anybody what comes in. All except Betty — she's a privileged character, o' course. I've got to go to town."

"I reckon I c'n run th' office, all right, if there ain't anything to do 'cept smoke."

"I've got a new bookkeeper comin', an' I'm takin' a personal interest in him, you might say. I fired th' last one a month ago, dang his hide! He had an idee he was goin' to marry Betty an' inherit th' ranch, but I stepped on his corns. I never knew his folks, an' th' man that fusses round Betty has got to have *folks*, you c'n bet!"

"Maybe this new one'll try th' same thing," Dad suggested. "That daughter o' yourn is an eyeful for any male critter. If I was about thirty year younger, now —"

"Well, I know this man's folks," Roach interrupted. "His paw's dead now, but he was some man in his day. I ain't seen th' boy since he was ten year old, and he's twenty-five now, but if he's anything like his paw he's a sure-enough man."

"I've seen good men as had pretty poor sons," Dad said.

"Well, I'm takin' a chance, of course," said Roach, "but I ain't much afraid. Years an' years ago, when I had a cattle ranch down in Texas, I knowed this boy's father. Square as a man could be, he was. His name was Taylor, an' he run th' X Bar Z Ranch."

"Yeh?" said Dad.

"He had a thunderation feud on with a skunk on a ranch adjoinin'. Besides that, he didn't have good business luck. I was glad to help him out now an' then, but we sorter drifted apart, 'specially after I got to thinkin' 'bout leavin' Texas. After I moved up here, Taylor was killed."

"Yeh?" Dad said.

"A boy — th' son of th' neighbor I mentioned — shot him. He didn't leave th' family any too well fixed when he passed over th' range, but I didn't know it at th' time, or I'd have done somethin'. Th' widow sold th' place an' moved to San Antone an' educated th' boy. Young Taylor went through a business college."

"An' that's th' new bookkeeper?" Dad asked.

"Yeh. I understand he's some bookkeeper. I heard 'bout him accidental a short time ago. Supportin' his mother, he was, on forty a month, an' havin' to pay rent an' board. Great Jupiter! Know what I did? I wrote an' offered him th' job here, told him if he made good I'd see he got along all right, 'count o' his father an' me bein' old friends. Offered him sixty *an'* found to start. So he's comin'. Only one thing makes me mad. I meant he was to bring his mother, o' course, meanin' for them both to live up to th' house, which ain't any too full o' folks now that my own wife is gone. It'd save th' boy expense, too. But nope! Said he'd come first an' see if he made good. That looks promisin', eh?"

"I wouldn't be surprised but what th' boy's right," Dad

said. "A feller wants to be sure he's makin' a wise move."

"I'm drivin' in this afternoon to meet him, an' I'm bringin' him right out to th' ranch. If he's a man like his daddy was at his age, he c'n make sheep's eyes at Betty all he likes. An' if he ain't all he ought to be, I'll either make him over or send him back to Texas. There ain't goin' to be no halfway business about it."

"I s'pose he'll have to hate automobiles an' be ready to fight with his fists," said Dad.

"You c'n bet that! If he c'n handle Bob Owen like you did, I won't have no kick comin'."

Roach hurried out and toward the stables, and Dad Meek remained sitting before the mahogany desk, his feet upon it, puffing at his pipe and ruminating again. Once he chuckled, and then a thoughtful look came into his seamed and wrinkled face.

"Th' poor kid!" he sighed.

Half an hour later, Roach drove past the office building a team of thoroughbred colts hitched to a light road wagon. Dad Meek watched until he had disappeared around the curve in the driveway, then filled his pipe anew, lit it, took a preliminary puff, and put his feet on the desk again.

"Th' poor kid!" he repeated. "Cuss my carcass if it ain't a burnin' shame!"

An hour after Roach's departure, Dad was still sitting before the desk, smoking, and busy with his thoughts. He heard steps on the driveway, and a form darkened the door. Dad looked up to find Bob Owen standing before him.

"Boss gone?" the foreman asked.

"You know blamed well he is," Dad responded. "You waited until you was sure he was gone before comin' to th' office. An' I want to say right here that he left orders with *me* to throw outen this office anybody I didn't happen to take a fancy to."

"You're sure some bad man, ain't you?" Owen demanded. "I happen to be foreman o' this ranch, an' it ain't anything unusual for me to visit th' office buildin' for orders."

"Oh, you want orders, eh? Then I order you to get out. If you don't know what to do, go right down on Plymouth Rock

Avenue an' help th' boys clean th' pens."

Owen remained standing in the doorway, and began to fill his own pipe leisurely, glancing now and then at Dad Meek, who had turned half from him and was contemplating the driveway through the window.

"I don't know, Dad, as how we ought to be enemies," he said, after a time. "If you're goin' to work here, we'd ought to try an' get along. I'm th' foreman, an' you've got a job doin' odd things around th' office, I s'pose. We've got to see each other now an' then."

"Yeh?" said Dad.

"I didn't exactly like th' drift o' your conversation last night at supper."

"No?"

"No! Maybe I was too free with my talk afterward — an' I don't blame you for gettin' sore."

"That's real kind o' you."

"An' th' boss said that was to be th' end of it. I ain't a man to hold a grudge —"

"Th' hell you ain't."

"What makes you think I am?" Owen asked.

Dad hesitated a moment, looking at the man in the doorway; then —

"Oh, I just guessed it from your face," he said. "Cuss your carcass, what do you mean by all this loose talk? If you've got somethin' to say, relate your little piece an' then tend to your chickens!"

"I just thought we might have a little understanding," Owen said.

"I guess we understand each other, all right. I ain't a hand to make bargains with th' devil, but I don't mind, this once, havin' a little agreement. I suspicion you got an idee I know a few things."

"Er — maybe."

"That bein' the case, I'll say this: I'll just forget what I know, as far as relatin' it to th' boss is concerned, as long as you conduct yourself in a becomin' fashion. An' I reckon that'll be some hard job for you."

"Well — if I know what you mean —"

"I reckon you know what I mean, all right. You stay outen my way, an' I'll treat you fair. But don't come prowlin' round *me*, by gravy! Cuss your carcass, every time I get a squint at you I want to peel my coat — else reach for a six-gun. By time, I remember onct when a man got a vote o' thanks if he let daylight through a cuss like *you* — an' now I reckon they'd stretch a man's neck if he did. I'm glad I ain't got much longer to live — this world's gettin' too civilized. An' now I'll be obliged if you get outen that door an' let a little sunshine come in."

"Well, I'm glad we had this little understandin'," Owen said. "I guess I get you right."

"You'd better hope you do, cuss your carcass!"

Bob Owen wandered away toward Plymouth Rock Avenue. For the space of half an hour Dad forgot to refill his pipe; and then, having filled it, he forgot to light it for another half hour. At the end of that time he threw back his shoulders and sighed deeply, an alert look came into his eyes, and he showed plainly that his spell of meditation was at an end.

It was late in the afternoon when he saw Roach drive up to the house and get out of the road wagon with a young man who stood six feet tall and had a generous breadth of shoulder. An employee who happened to be working on the lawn was ordered to drive the rig to the stables, and then Roach and his new bookkeeper entered the house. Dad stood at the window, watching them, a wide grin distorting his face.

Later, when he observed that Roach and the new bookkeeper were walking down the driveway toward the office building, Dad turned his chair around so that his back would be toward the door, put his feet on the window sill, and puffed at his pipe until a cloud of tobacco smoke half obscured him.

"Dang your hide!" Roach cried, as he stepped inside. "You make as much smoke as Lates' stink wagon!"

"Yeh," said Dad, and he puffed again.

"Take your feet off that window sill, get up, an' meet my new bookkeeper!" Roach commanded.

Dad's feet crashed to the floor; he put his hands on the arms of the chair and lifted himself slowly from the seat. Suddenly he extended himself to his full height and turned, still grinning.

"Why — why —" the young bookkeeper gasped. "It's Dad Meek!"

"It sure is!"

"Old Dad Meek!"

The young man brushed Roach aside and sprang forward and gripped both Dad's hands. Roach stood against the wall, a picture of consternation.

"Dad — Dad! It's certainly good to see you!" the new bookkeeper cried. "This *is* luck — finding you here! This is the best yet!"

"You — you two fellers know each other?" Roach managed to gasp.

"Know each other!" the young man exclaimed. "I should think so! Why, I've known dad ever since I was twelve years old. He was one of my father's men. Know him? He taught me to ride a horse and throw a rope. He used to help father fight his battles. He was with us when — father died. And he was mighty good to mother and me afterward. Know him? I should think so!"

"Why, dang his hide!" Roach screeched. "You old fossil, you! You sat right here in this cussed room an' let me give you th' history of th' Taylor ranch an' family an' troubles. Why, dang your pesky skin! Let me tell it — an' you on th' spot when it happened! Why —"

"You never asked me no questions," Dad interposed. "I reckon I'm too polite to interrupt when a man's talkin' 'bout old days."

"You let me ramble on a-purpose, dang you!"

"I reckon it wouldn't be th' right thing to stop you, boss. I understood it makes you skittish when a man gets tangled up in your personal talk. I heard tell —"

"Down to Fresno, eh?" Roach roared. "I'll get that Fresno gang to write the history o' my life! Why, dang you —"

"But what are you doing here, Dad?" Richard Taylor demanded.

Dad managed to deliver a wink without Roach observing.

"I just dropped in yesterday an' got a job," he said. "Ain't that luck?"

"You — got a job —"

"Now don't you interrupt me when I'm talkin', Dick Taylor, or I'll take you over my knee. I heard tell —"

"Down to Fresno!" roared Roach.

"Yeh, I heard tell down to Fresno as how Mr. Roach generally had a job for an old cow-puncher, an', needin' a job that-a-way, I just come out an' got one. I reckon you an' me'll have to make good on this here ranch, Dickie, for th' honor of th' old X Bar Z."

Roach cleared his throat.

"While th' family reunion is in progress," he said, "I'll just take a run down to White Wyandotte Terrace an' see how th' pullets are gettin' on. Dang you, Dad Meek, I'll put one over on you yet for this!"

He left them still gripping hands and beaming upon each other, and hurried down the driveway. Then Dad Meek put an arm around Richard Taylor's shoulders and guided him to a chair.

"What the blazes does all this mean, Dad?" the younger man asked.

"What?"

"This about you getting a job. A job — you? You haven't gone and lost all your money?"

"I reckon I've got as much as ever."

"Then —"

"You see, Dickie, it's like this," Dad said. "I ain't seen you for about four years, now, only been gettin' letters from you sayin' what you was doin'. 'Spite the fact I promised your paw to kinder take care o' you, you wouldn't let me give you a cent —"

"I was getting along all right. I was making enough for myself and mother. So why should I take your money, Dad?"

"Your paw was mighty good to me, Dickie. Onct, when some misguided sons o' sin were stringin' me up, thinkin' as how I was a rustler, he saved my life. Then he gave me a job an' let me have a home. Wasn't that somethin'? Then he went broke, an' a skunk killed him, an' you was left in a pretty bad fix. I wandered away after you and your maw moved to San

Antone, an' turned desert rat. If I found a hole in th' ground as had ore in it, an' a fool gave me twenty thousand for it, why shouldn't I give you some o' that money? Eh? Cuss your carcass, what could *I* do with twenty thousand dollars?"

"I know. But I didn't need it."

"When I saw it hurt your feelin's, I stopped offerin' it, didn't I? But I'd promised your paw to look out for you, an' I knew a few things 'bout a certain deal, an' so I just spent a few dollars o' that money spite o' you — spent it findin' out things."

"But — being here —" persisted Richard Taylor.

"Well, Dickie, you see, you wrote as how Mr. Roach, an old friend o' your father's, had offered you this here job. So I just thought I'd run up here an' be on hand to see you got started right."

"But — getting a job — why did you do that?" You could have been a guest here, Dad."

"Yeh? I didn't want to be no guest. I had a reason, Dickie boy. I wanted a job so's I could live in th' newfangled bunkhouse they got an' mix with th' men — 'specailly one man. 'Cause, Dickie, some o' that money I been spendin' informed me you might have a little trouble here."

"Trouble — here? What do you mean, Dad?"

"That money I spent went to a wise detective feller in Los Angeles. He's been trailin' an trailin' for some time, an' he located a certain party for *me*. When I got that letter o' yourn, a feather could uv knocked me flatter'n a pancake. You was bound straight for trouble an' didn't know it."

"But — how can there be trouble for me here, Dad? Please explain what you mean."

"Let's see, Dickie. You're almost twenty-five now, ain't you?"

"In three months, Dad."

"An' there's a certain human bein' you don't want to meet before you're twenty-five, ain't they?"

Richard Taylor turned toward the window for an instant; and when he faced Dad again his lips were set tightly and rage was flaming in his face. His shoulders were thrown back, his hands clenched at his sides.

"Yes," he said, in a tense voice. "There's one man — I may kill — if I meet. And I don't want to do that — until after I'm twenty-five."

"O'course. I understand, Dickie. Well, you better get ready for some shock, boy. That — man's — right — here!"

"Here?"

"Just hold in your horses, now, Dickie. Yep, he's here. I had him trailed an' kept an eye on him. I was bound to see your paths didn't cross, but you took this job, and —"

"Why didn't you tell me, Dad — telegraph me? Why didn't you stop me?"

"An' let you get done outen a good job?"

"Why didn't you let me know, so I could stay in Texas? Oh, Dad! Why didn't you?"

"Boy!" Dad's voice was no longer thin and quavering; a bit of sternness had crept into it; the expression in his face was questioning. "Why did I let you come? Have I lived to see th' day when a Taylor runs away from a Sturm? Ain't you got th' courage your paw had?"

"Dad! I —"

"Would you stay away 'cause that man's here — let him keep you outen a good job? Ain't you a Taylor, boy?"

"I'm — a Taylor — all right!"

"Then you ain't afraid to face him!"

"He killed my father!"

"Yeh — I know."

"And — and my hands are tied, Dad — tied!"

"I know that, too, Dickie."

"I've got to be near him, on the same ranch, with my hands tied?"

"For three months, anyway."

"I — I can't do it! I'll kill him!"

"You're goin' to be a Taylor, boy — an' that means a lot more'n havin' nerve enough to kill. What you've got to do'll take more nerve than half a hundred killin's. I reckon it'll be a test o' your manhood, Dickie."

"Oh, Dad!"

Dick sank into the chair and covered his face with his hands. His body shook, but not with sobs.

"An' that's why I'm here — why I got a job," Dad went on. "I'm right here with you, Dickie, an' ready to take a hand in th' game. I'm goin' to help save you. I promised your paw I'd look after you, Dickie, an' your paw was mighty good to me — I'm keepin' my word. Just brace up, now. It could be a lot worse. You're goin' to live in th' house with Roach an' this other man lives down to th' bunkhouse where I'm keepin' an eye on him. Don't make any slips, Dickie. It wouldn't be playin' th' game to —"

"I'll tell Mr. Roach! He'll discharge him — drive him away!"

"Boy!" cried Dad angrily. "Don't you see that's th' thing you can't do? O'course Roach would send him away. Then everybody'd say you didn't have th' nerve to face him. It's be somethin' like a coward's trick, Dickie — an' a Taylor ain't a coward! You got to let him keep his secret, you got to face him, an' you got to keep your hands offen him —"

"He killed my father!"

"You got to, boy! You know why. Here's where you prove you're a man like your paw. Brace up, now! Roach'll be comin' back. An' remember, I'm right behind you all th' time. Cuss his carcass! You got to keep quiet 'bout me, too. Just let Roach think it's a happenstance, me bein' here this-a-way. I'm an old puncher what got a job — I ain't got a cent in th' world. Understand? You just knew me when I worked for your paw."

Richard Taylor stood up and walked to the window, and stood looking out at the driveway, yet seeing nothing. After a time he turned and grasped Dad's hand again.

"I'll play the game, Dad," he said.

"That's th' boy! That sounds just like your paw! Steady now, Dickie!"

"What is his name — here?"

"He calls himself Bob Owen, Dickie — an' he's th' foreman."

CHAPTER IV

THE MEETING

On the supper menu at the "eatin' joint" that night there was roast chicken and mashed potatoes, and for a wonder Dad Meek made no complaint regarding the food. Laughing and joking with the others, Dad gave evidence of the fact that he considered the unpleasantness of the night before a thing of the past, and regarded himself already as "one o' th' gang."

Bob Owen had done some ruminating himself that afternoon, and had reached the mistaken conclusion that Dad Meek, desperately in need of a job, was willing to keep his secret to gain the foreman's good will and made the possession of that job a surety. He realized, however, that Dad Meek held abundant animosity for him, yet cared not, so long as a truce was observed.

Desiring to convey to his men that he now considered Dad a welcome addition to the ranch, the foreman from time to time addressed a commonplace remark to the veteran puncher at the at the foot of the table, yet was careful to say nothing that would call for a caustic reply. It was while desert was being served — bread pudding this night — that Owen began talking of the new bookkeeper. He asked certain questions of Dad — and again he made a grave mistake. Owen considered that Dad, being of the bunkhouse and an old-timer, would have naught but contempt for a man who earned his living wielding a pen, hence would fall in with Owen's sarcastic remarks regarding the latest arrival. In a way he was eager to bind himself close to Dad Meek — and nothing will bind two men closer than having a mutual object of contempt.

"Well, I hear th' new pen pusher got here today," Owen said.

"Yeh," Dad replied, seeing that the remark was addressed to him.

"I didn't get a chance to see him. Young feller?"

"Oh, 'bout twenty-five," said Dad.

"I ain't set eyes on him, but I'll bet I c'n give you his photo right now."

"Yeh?"

"He's about five feet high and one foot thick; he's got yellow hair an' a little mustache; his hands is pretty an' pink, an' he talks like a girl an' dresses like a dude an' sticks out a little finger when he drinks his coffee. He's mighty glad he lives at th' big house, 'stead of down here with all these naughty, rough men. Ain't that his picture?"

"Meanin' th' last bookkeeper, or this new one?" asked Dad.

"That was th' picture o' th' last one, an' I'll bet it's a picture o' th' new one. All bookkeepers is ladylike."

"Yeh?"

"Well, ain't I right?" Owen demanded. "Tell us."

"Well, you ain't exactly right," Dad replied. "This new bookkeeper is six foot an' one inch, an' he's about two feet thick in th' place where he ought to be. He's got to turn sideways when he goes through th' office door, his shoulders are that broad. His hair's black, an' he ain't got any mustache at all. He don't stick out any little finger, an' he ain't a mite lady-like. He's a regular he-man."

"What's that?" Owen demanded, laughing. "A regular he-man an' a bookkeeper! I reckon you're foolin', old-timer."

"Not any! I'm tellin' th' truth. I've had some 'sperience, I have, an' I judge him to be a he-man. If you ask *me*, I'm sayin' he'd made any o' this crowd mighty hard to catch."

"Yes, he would!" Owen roared, laughing.

"Cuss your carcass! You asked me for my opinion, an' you got it!"

"If he's a he-man, why don't he live in th' bunkhouse?" Owen demanded. "There's a private room used to be inhabited by th' bookkeeper. Is he so blame much better'n this crowd that he's got to eat at th' boss' table?"

"That ain't th' reason," Dad explained. "Roach was th' friend o' th' new bookkeeper's father years ago. Th' new bookkeeper's sorter one o' th' family."

"Oh!" Owen exclaimed. "Then I s'pose we have to keep our hand s offen him, eh? Can't even try him out?"

"I don't know exactly," replied Dad, "but I got an idee

Roach lets a man fight his own battles. But I'd advise this gang to keep its hands strictly to itself."

"Yeh?" roared Owen. "Maybe this new bookkeeper could clean us up?"

"I said as how he was a he-man."

"What's th' name o' this he-man?" Owen asked.

The question had come; Dad had been expecting it throughout the meal. It was inevitable, of course, that Richard Taylor and the foreman should learn of each other's presence and should meet face to face sooner or later, since the foreman turned in daily reports at the office. Dad had considered the situation at length, and had decided upon a course of action. So now he answered Owen's question in a matter-of-fact way, as he wiped his lips with his napkin and started to get up from the table:

"His name? Oh! His name is Richard Taylor. His father used to own that X Bar Z Ranch I was tellin' you boys about last evenin'. Roach knew th' boy's paw down to Texas a long time ago."

Then, without a look at the foreman, Dad Meek turned his back and walked slowly toward the door, stopping an instant to exchange remarks with Paddon and one of the other men.

At one end of the bunkhouse was a row of benches. Dad Meek filled and lighted his pipe and sat on a bench at the end of the row, smoking in the gathering dusk. He heard some of the employees enter the bunkhouse, and knew that a card game had started. Others walked about, also smoking, before turning in. Two or three wandered up the driveway toward the gate, intending to go to an adjoining ranch on a visit.

The mist obscured the distant hills and crept down into the valley. The night deepened. Still Dad Meek sat on the bench at the end of the row, waiting.

And then Bob Owen came around the corner of the bunkhouse and walked slowly toward him. Dad had known he would come. Then bare statement made at the supper table would not suffice Owen.

The foreman sat down on the other end of the bench and regarded Dad for a moment without speaking. The foreman was too troubled to smoke.

"Was you tellin' th' truth?" he asked presently. "Or was you just havin' a little fun with me without th' boys knowin'?"

"What's that?" Dad replied.

"'Bout th' new bookkeeper."

"I was tellin' th' truth."

"It's Richard Taylor, eh?"

"Yep."

"You knew he was comin'?"

"You c'n bet I did."

"That's why you come here ahead o' him?"

"Maybe so, foreman."

Owen licked his dry lips and sat nearer, and when he spoke again his voice was low and trembled.

"What's th' game?" he demanded.

"Meanin'?"

"Don't play with me, cuss you!"

"Don't you cuss me!" said Dad. "You speak to me like a gentleman oughter be addressed, or I'll break your neck!"

"I ain't startin' any quarrel with you. I just want to know where I stand. It's Taylor's son, eh?"

"Yep, it's th' son of th' man you shot from behind th' barn."

"Easy with that voice o' yourn, Dad Meek! Well, what's goin' to happen?"

"Don't ask *me*, cuss your carcass! I ain't no fortune teller."

"I reckon you know somethin' goin' to happen, with him an' me on th' same ranch. Does he know I'm here?"

"He does," said Dad.

"You told him?"

"Yep."

"Then you're in on it, eh? You're playin' a game? Well, I'll just take a hand in it, Dad Meek. Th' both o' you can't get th' best o' me! You said you'd keep to yerself what you knowed —"

"I said as far as th' boss is concerned."

"Well? Do you s'pose this young Taylor won't run to th' boss with his story as soon as we meet? Maybe he's doin' it right now."

"Don't worry, foreman," said Dad, removing the pipe from his mouth. "I was hopin' you'd hunt me up tonight, 'cause I'm anxious to tell you some things. You both bein' on this ranch is a sorter accident. Roach don't know who you are; he don't know that I know who you are; and he won't know that Dick Taylor ever heard o' you before."

"Huh! I s'pose not!"

" 'Cause Dick Taylor won't tell him. He's fightin' out his own battles 'thout any help from Roach. An' I'm right here to see fair play."

"I s'pose you think I'll believe that!" Owen exclaimed. "Don't I know you're both playin' a game? You've follered me here — you've traced me —"

"I traced you, all right. But Dick Taylor didn't know you was here until today. An' now let me tell you somethin': There ain't goin' to be any row."

"With me an' a Taylor on th' same ranch?"

"I'm tellin' you straight. You got to meet, naturally, 'cause you got to go to th' office buildin' with reports an' to get orders. But you don't have to fly at each other's throats. You let him alone, an' I've a notion he won't say a word to you nor raise a hand —"

"Huh! That's th' game, is it? He daren't raise a hand!"

"Meanin'?" asked Dad.

"He's like th' rest o' th' Taylors — he ain't got any spunk. I reckon he'll be mighty glad if I don't start anything. Well, I can't live on th' same place with a Taylor 'thout takin' him down a peg. I ain't forgot what happened to my daddy."

"Th' Taylors didn't do it, you skunk! He was stretched up for rustlin' cows. An' you killed old man Taylor."

"Yeh, an' I c'n run his son outen th' country, too! I ain't afraid o' th' two o' you. I know why you come here — Dick Taylor was afraid to come alone — that's why. He's friendly with th' boss, livin' right up to th' big house an' all that, an' you're fightin' for him — but I c'n get him!"

"I'm tellin' you —" Dad began.

"An' I'm tellin' you, old-timer, that I'm gunnin' for any an' all Taylors. Ready to drop th' family scrap, is he? Sent you to give me th' hint, did he? I'll bet he's ready! Well, I don't drop it while there's a Taylor left walkin' th' earth. I s'pose you'll be tryin' to send me back to Texas for that shootin' — but if you try it I'll get Dick Taylor first."

"You ain't got a bit o' character!" Dad complained. "Old man Taylor forgived you for that, an' let you go, didn't he? Then that's settled, Mr. Owen, as you calls yourself. We ain't goin' to dig up any old history. If you get into trouble, it'll be for somethin' that ain't been done yet."

"It'll be done soon!"

"Then you'll make th' first move — the boy won't. An' I'm advisin' you to behave yourself."

"I just reckon I'll show him who's th' best man," Owen said. "We won't let th' matter go undecided. This ranch ain't goin' to be big enough for us both."

Dad put his cold pipe in his pocket and got up, and now he stood before the foreman and looked down at him. He spoke in a low tone, but his voice was tense for all that.

"Dick Taylor's goin' to do th' right thing for th' present," he said. "An' so are you! I'm right here on this chicken farm to see that you do! Understand that? Cuss your carcass, I'll massacre you if you make a move!"

"Why don't you let young Taylor do th' massacr'in? I reckon I know why — he ain't got th' nerve. He's a six-foot coward — like his dad!"

Dad Meek's arms trembled, and he raised both fists; his breath was expelled in a great gust that told of tempestuous anger checked for the moment. Yet he did not strike, though Bob Owen expected it. Dad knew a combat now with this man would lead to questioning by Roach, possibly to explanations that he did not care to have made.

"You listen to me!" he commanded. "I said I'd keep your little secret, as far as th' boss is concerned, if you behave. An' I don't want to hear you run down a good dead man in my presence — nor his livin' son. If you think them things, think 'em until you learn better — but don't speak 'em aloud, especially when I'm around."

Dad whirled around like an army officer on parade and walked briskly to the corner of the bunkhouse and around it to the door, leaving Bob Owen sitting on the bench in the darkness.

In the morning, when Roach was not in the office, Dad told Dick Taylor of the conversation with Owen, and warned him that a meeting must come soon, perhaps that very day. For an hour afterward, Dick worked at the books like a man in a dream, and finally threw down his pen and sprang to his feet, startling Dad out of his reverie.

"Where's Mr. Roach?" he asked.

"I reckon he went over to Lates' raisin patch, Dickie."

"And where would this foreman be liable to be at this hour?"

"Either at th' incubator buildin' else on Black Minorca Boulevard bossin' th' men."

"I'm going to find him right now, Dad. We've got to face each other sometime, and the sooner it is done the better. I'd rather have it happen when Mr. Roach is not around. I'd betray myself in an instant if we met under his eyes."

"I reckon you know best, Dickie," said Dad, "and I reckon I'll just got along, if you're goin' to hunt him up. But you want to remember —"

"I am remembering, Dad. You needn't be afraid. There's too much at stake —"

"Just what I reckoned, Dickie."

Dick led the way from the office building; and they walked down the driveway side by side slowly, as if on a tour of inspection. Dad gave a sigh of relief when they found that Owen was not in the incubator house. Being an outdoor man, Dad Meek had a horror of a scene within walls. He believed big emotion should be experienced in the open.

"That's him!" he whispered, as they turned into one of the little streets between the rows of chicken houses. "The one nearest, with his back turned toward us. Now you remember, Dickie —"

"I'll remember, Dad!"

Owen turned and saw them approaching, looked at them for a moment, then went on directing the men. Dad and Dick Taylor stopped with a dozen feet of him and inspected a pen of Indian Runner ducks. It was for Owen to make the first move, and he made it in characteristic fashion, with a sneer on his lips and a tone of sarcasm in his voice.

"This ain't visitin' day, Dad Meek," he said. "We can't be bothered to death by dudes trailin' around th' ranch. Visitors ain't allowed 'cept Sunday, when th' boys are down to th' bunkhouse an' don't have to look at a lot o' painful she-men."

"Yeh?" said Dad smoothly. "I reckon you're yellin' 'fore you're hurt, foreman. This ain't a visitor. He's th' new book-keeper, Mr. Taylor, takin' a look at th' ranch."

Now they stood face to face, with scarcely six feet separating them — the murderer and the son of the man he had killed — scions of two families that had lived in feudal animosity for three generations. Neither spoke at first. Owen was half bent forward, the sneer still on his lips, his eyes narrowed beneath their bushy brows, his fists clenched at his sides. Dick Taylor stood straight, his shoulders thrown back; his lips were in a straight line, his eyes piercing, his face deadly white.

"Your friend looks sickly, Dad Meek — as if he was scared 'bout somethin'," Owen said.

"I reckon there ain't anything round here to scare a man," Dad retorted. "Nothin' 'cept chickens an' ducks — an' geese!"

Dick Taylor took a deep breath. Owen turned and bellowed an order to one of his men. The new bookkeeper and Dad walked on slowly past the foreman toward the brooder buildings, not once looking back.

The first meeting was over. Neither Dick Taylor nor the man he hated had spoken a word directly to the other. But, considering the expression of their countenances, there had been no need for spoken words.

CHAPTER V

COMBAT REFUSED

Some masters of large affairs, if those affairs are prosperous, look only at the surface, and do not care to investigate beneath it. William Roach was such a man, hence he did not know of certain events that occurred on the National Poultry

Farm during the next few days until his attention was called to them by an outsider.

In those few days Roach became convinced of two things — that Richard Taylor was a good bookkeeper and business man, and that he was the sort of gentleman Roach had expected him to be, having known his father. In the office, at times when there was little work to do, Roach delighted in conversations in which Dick Taylor and Dad Meek had a part, and which related to old Texan days. In the big house, in the evenings, Roach was pleased at the manner in which Dick conducted himself, and soon grew accustomed to seeing Dick and Betty sitting in a corner of the big veranda getting interested in each other. At such times, Roach would grin knowingly and retire to his library, declaring on his oath that he hadn't looked at a newspaper for two days.

Twice each day Bob Owen journeyed to the office building with his reports and to get orders, were there any to receive. Dad Meek always made it a point to be present when these visits were made, and Owen was forced to content himself with throwing the reports down on the table in a disrespectful manner, speaking in a sneering tone, and showing that he had nothing but contempt for the new office man. At such times, Dick's face grew white and his voice was charged with emotion, but he conducted the business as speedily as possible and got Owen away.

On occasions when Roach was present, Owen was very businesslike in his manner, and so Roach suspected nothing, and no one sought to enlighten him. Dad Meek always managed to clothe the conversation in dry humor that attracted Roach's attention.

Owen got the feeling that these first days of Dick's presence at the ranch formed an armistice, that Dick was getting acquainted with his work before making a move. Knowing the Taylor stock, he did not anticipate that Dick was a coward, even if he did intimate as much in his conversation with Dad Meek and the other men. He was wise enough to do the most of his talking when Dad was not near, and refrained from discussions of the new bookkeeper at the table, fearing Dad Meek would retaliate in a way he would not relish. The clash was coming, Owen thought — it was only a matter of days and opportunity.

It came on a day when the men were building a row of new sheds near the fence that separated the ranch from the public highway. It was the middle of the morning, and Dad Meek had been sent down the road on an errand by Betty. Roach telephoned to the office from the house, and asked Dick to find Owen and tell him to have one of the men hitch up the road cart and prepare for a trip to town.

As he hurried down the narrow streets toward the point where he knew Owen was working, Dick realized that now he was to meet his foe face to face without the presence of Dad Meek to sustain him. He, too, had heard how men were tried and tested at the National Poultry Farm, and anticipated that he would be no exception.

Owen was directing a gang of men near the iron fence; and in the road outside sat Lates in his "stink wagon," passing the time of day and asking about the improvements. Dick walked briskly toward the foreman, who saw him coming and straightened up to stand with his fists resting on his hips. It was the opportunity for which Owen had been waiting.

"Mr. Roach wants you to have one of the men hitch the road cart and drive to the house for orders," Dick said, in a matter-of-face voice.

"Yeh?" asked Owen. "It's a burin' shame a nice feller like you had to walk clear down here on an errand like that. An' all these naughty, rough men around, too."

"The man is to make a trip to town," Dick went on, ignoring the other's manner, though it made his blood boil.

"I s'pose he was afraid to send you, eh?" Owen said. "The horsy might run away an' throw you out."

Raucous laughter came from a dozen throats at that, and the foreman looked around at his men and grinned.

"I never did care much for bookkeepers," Owen went on. "They're a pretty worthless lot, seems to me. Look at this one, fellers. He looks like a regular he-man, but I reckon his looks is deceivin'." He took a step forward, as if to inspect Dick closer, and under his breath he hissed: "You damned Taylor!"

Dick's face went white and his hands clenched. Owen, an

evil smile on his face, waited.

"Well, do you care for a little argument?" the foreman taunted. "Generally it's agin' the rules to have arguments durin' workin' hours, but I reckon th' boss'll overlook it once, seein' as how we'd never argue 'less we did do it in th' daytime. I ain't seen you foolin' round th' bunkhouse much as if you was lookin' for anything."

Dick's eyes narrowed until they were two tiny slits, and his breast rose and fell because of the angry breaths he was taking, but he restrained an impulse to lash out with a fist toward the foreman's grinning face.

"Well, I've got my orders," Owen continued. "You'd better clear out o' here now, 'less you care to argue. We're doin' men's work here, an' don't care to have th' scenery cluttered up with a lot o' worthless human bein's."

The men had stopped work and were waiting for the battle. Half enjoyed this baiting of the bookkeeper, and the other half expected to see Dick charge into the foreman and give him a thrashing, nor would have wept had he done so.

"On your way, dude!" Owen exclaimed, bending forward slightly. His chin made a tantalizing target that Dick ignored. "You don't seem to have much backbone. Your paw must have been a weak-kneed sort o' feller."

Owen half raised his fists as he spoke the last sentence. That, he expected would precipitate the clash. The men would not understand, of course, why that remark was fraught with peril, but Dick Taylor would understand.

Dick bent forward suddenly, and his fists were half raised also. His face was ashen; his body trembled with rage. Then he remembered that he must stay his hand — and the fit of rage passed. He turned without a word and started to walk away.

"Well, th' damned coward!" Owen exploded. "What do you think o' this, fellers? If Roach lets that she-man stay on this ranch, it'll be an old maid's home in no time."

Jeers, catcalls were hurled at Dick's retreating back. These men had no use for a man who would not fight at the drop of a hat, especially a man of broad shoulders and weight. In that instant each one of them promised himself to make the further existence of Richard Taylor on the National Poultry Farm a nightmare, to torment him, treat him like a baby, throw him aside, belittle him, taunt him, drive him away.

Not once did Dick look back. When he was a safe distance away, a single sob shook his body. He had won for the time being, but he told himself that the next clash with the foreman would bring disaster. Such scenes were not to be endured by a proper man.

He was glad, when he reached the office, that Dad Meek was not there. Slowly he regained his composure and went to work at his books. A short visit from Betty also served to put him in a better humor. And when Dad Meek finally did return to the office building, Dick Taylor had decided to refrain from telling him of the encounter. There had been no bad consequences, hence it was not worth the telling, he thought.

But there were consequences. Late that afternoon, when Roach and Dad Meek were swapping yarns in a corner of the office, and Dick was making out the monthly payroll, there came the sound of an auto horn, and Lates drove his light truck rapidly down the drive toward the office. Roach was standing in the doorway when the machine stopped.

"Lates —" he began.

"Now take it easy, Bill," said the raisin king, jumping from the seat and walking toward the door. "I didn't suppose you'd have any objections to me drivin' in this afternoon."

"Why not?" Roach demanded. "Have you seen any indications that I'm gettin' foolish?"

"I've seen an indication that you've given up some o' th' bloodthirsty ideas of yours," said Lates. "Great Jupiter! I'm glad to see it, Bill — glad you're gettin' to be a human man 'stead of an old bear with a sore toe."

"What in time you talkin' about?" Roach demanded.

Lates had entered the office now, and when he caught sight of Dick he began chuckling.

"So that's your new clerk?" he asked.

"That's my new bookkeeper, Lates. His name is Richard Taylor. Dick, this is Lates, who's got a little raisin patch across th' road. He runs a stink wagon."

"You'll be runnin' 'em next, Bill, now that you're chang-in' your mind about things."

"This mind-changin' stunt is news to me," Roach said.

"Well, you ain't as crazy as you were to have this farm populated with pugilists, I take it. I saw this new clerk o' yours back water in a hurry today when that foreman you've got pretended to be a bad man."

"What's that?" Roach demanded.

"Backed him down, th' foreman did. Made a monkey outen this young gent, an' th' said young gent turned ground an' walked away as if nothin' had been said. Great Jupiter! I expected to see a fight."

Roach turned and looked at Dick, whose back was toward him. He looked at Lates again, and knew that Lates had spoken the truth.

"Richard," he said, "there's on thing I demand of every man that works for me. I didn't make any mention of it in your case, 'cause I knew your paw an' th' stock you come from. I don't have any man on this ranch that ain't a man. Every man here's got to know just where every other man stands. What's this about you an' th' foreman?"

"Oh, he was a little insulting — it wasn't anything," Dick said, with an effort.

"Not much!" roared Lates. "If it had been me, by time, I'd have peeled my coat and slammed him one. He called you a dude, didn't he? He made fun o' you to your face. Great Jupiter —"

"Richard," said Roach, "I want you to understand that you don't have to take any sass from any man on this ranch. You're new here, an' I suppose you didn't want trouble, thinkin' I'd believe you was a nuisance. Any time one of th' men gets gay with you, Richard, you give him th' best thrash-in' you can. Slam right into him an' make him eat dirt! I won't kick if you get your face spoiled an' have to lay off work a week — I'd rather have that happen than have a man as works for me back down in front of any male critter. You under-stand that, Richard?"

"I understand, sir."

"If that foreman makes another remark you don't like,

black a couple o' his eyes. Remember that, boy. Don't hesitate on my account. I knew your paw, an' I reckon you c'n fight — you don't look like a weaklin'. Every man's got to stand on his own feet on this here ranch, whether he's foreman or roustabout. So you take your own part — I'm expectin' it o' you."

"Very well, sir."

"Remember — I'm expectin' it o' you!"

Roach gave his bookkeeper a speculative look, as if the first doubt of Richard Taylor's fitness had entered his mind.

CHAPTER VI

THE ROUND ROBIN

Given an object of scorn, rough men can change to persecuting beasts — a fact Richard Taylor had driven home to him during the week that followed.

That evening, after Roach's ultimatum and Lates' departure, he told Dad Meek the entire story — told it in a tense voice, as he stood at the window looking down the drive toward the bunkhouse, his body trembling with rage.

"If it keeps up, I won't be able to stand it, Dad," he said. "It's more than flesh and blood and stand. If he faces me again — talks that way again —"

"You *got* to stand it, boy!" Dad interrupted. "You know what it means to fail, don't you? I suppose you think you're playin' into th' enemy's hands by lettin' him pretend he thinks you ain't got any sand, an' puttin' the other men agin' you — but you'd be playin' into his hands a lot more if you let him coax you into a fight, wouldn't you, boy? Think what it'd mean for you to let yourself go an' take satisfaction outen his hide! An' there's a time comin' —"

"Yes — there's a time coming! I'll make him pay, Dad — I'll make him pay!"

"Then you just swaller his insults now, an' store 'em up agin' him. When th' day o' settlement comes, take your pay, boy, every cent o' it, outen his carcass! It's a hard row to hoe, boy, but I'm here to help."

Curling lips, disrespectful tones thought the words were

respectful enough, actions that expressed contempt — these Richard Taylor received from Bob Owen day after day, when the foreman went to the office building to make his report.

There were times when Richard Taylor saw red, when he shut his eyes quickly to keep from seeing the face he wanted to strike with a fist. There were hot words choked back, palms torn by fingernails because of hands tightly clenched in restraint. Ignominy, insult, scorn — such things as made a man give battle — were heaped upon him. Not only did he endure these things from Bob Owen in person, but he felt them whenever he neared one of the men.

He remained near the office building and the big house. He kept away from the other employees. He spent his days with Dad Meek and Roach and at his books. He spent his evenings with Betty on the veranda, or driving on the broad highway. And he spent the greater part of many a night in tears of rage and sobs of despair.

"I can't stand it another day!" he told Dad Meek often. "I'm going to let myself go! I want to fight — to *fight!*"

Then Dad would speak at length and in a low tone, and Richard Taylor would endure it for another day.

It was his fortune that love should come to him at this time, when he felt that he was not playing a man's part, as the majority of the world looked at it. From that first day there had been something like a bond between Betty Roach and himself. Betty, who had looked upon possible suitors as nuisances before, looked upon Dick Taylor with more favor than she ever had shown to another man. And at the end of the first fortnight, Dick knew he had found the one woman.

There was no question of speaking, of course. He was a bookkeeper with nothing but a small salary, and he had a mother to keep — and a sacred trust left him by his father. Looking into the future, he could not see success, peace, contented existence. So his love remained unspoken, yet it grew. And the evening in Betty's company helped mitigate the miseries of the day.

Three weeks passed without another direct clash with Bob Owen. It was evident to all that Dick avoided the foreman. There could be no open clash in the office or near the big house, and Dick did not walk the driveway at night, nor visit the bunkhouse, nor did he go about the ranch during the day except when Dad Meek accompanied him. Without Dad's services, this sort of thing could not have endured for long without Roach understanding that something was wrong. Dad made things looks natural to Roach.

"How much longer is the big boss goin' to let that she-clerk stay around th' office?" one of the men demanded of Dad at supper one night.

"I reckon he's got a steady job," Dad said.

"What's this ranch comin' to? Is th' old man gettin' old? It's th' first time we ever let a coward stick around here longer than two days."

"I reckon he ain't a coward."

"You're sure wrong in your reckon," Owen put in.

"Yeh?" Dad asked. "How you come to call him a coward?"

"Great roosters! Didn't he back water when I bluffed him?"

"He ain't a coward because he refused to smash into you just 'cause you showed bad trainin'," said Dad.

"Well, he ain't showed much bravery since," said one of the other men. "He's afraid to meet one o' us alone. He's a six-foot coward, and that's all. And if th' boss lets him stay here much longer —"

"You listen to *me*, cuss your carcass!" Dad cried. "That boy ain't a coward, an' don't you think it for a minute. An' it's my private opinion he c'n lick any two o' you 'thout gettin' warmed up. I'm givin' you a piece o' good advice when I say it's be better for you all to lay offen that bookkeeper. He comes from fightin' stock, an' he's in th' pink o' condition."

Roars of raucous laughter greeted Dad's announcement. The supposed cowardice of the bookkeeper became a standing joke. Bob Owen was but one of the mob now — every man on the ranch except Dad Meek and William Roach beheld in Richard Taylor an object of scorn.

Things like that seem to travel in the air. Roach got the feeling, and, though he could not analyze it, he began looking askance at the son of his old friends. There seemed to be something wrong between Dick and the men. Roach wondered if it was because Dick had not taken the foreman to task that first time they clashed.

"You ain't had any more trouble with Bob Owen, have you, boy?" he asked one afternoon.

"No, sir."

"Um! You remember what I said — if he gets gay, smash both his eyes. You don't have to take a thinks from him. He's smashed other men on this ranch. You go after him if he don't show respect. Whether you lick him or not, at least put up a fight."

Roach was in the office later that day when Owen came in with the reports. There was no words passed that lacked respect, because of the boss' presence, yet Roach felt hostility in the air.

"That foreman an' Dick's goin' th' mat one o' these days," he told Dad Meek. "There's bad blood betwixt 'em. You c'n smell bad blood a mile. Don't tell *me!*"

More puzzled than Roach, however, was Bob Owen. The foreman knew that the Taylors were fighters. He had expected a combat royal with Richard Taylor long before this — a show-down — either victory or defeat. In Dick he saw the remaining ancient enemy of his family, and to the foreman it was incomprehensible that they should be on the same ranch without discovering which was the better man.

He tried to decide whether it would be the greater victory to attack Dick openly in the office, running the chance of his identity becoming known and himself losing a good position, or to have him ridiculed as craven and driven from the ranch. The latter appealed to him after mature thought. He could cast upon the name of Richard Taylor the shame of cowardice — and the man himself would remain to be beaten another day.

Owen swayed his men, because he had beaten all of them and because they found it paid to be in the good graces of the foreman. He talked with them now, when Dad Meek was not around, concerning the open disgrace of the ranch in having such a man as Richard Taylor working there — a tall, broadshouldered man who would not fight. He spoke a word to a friend in Fresno, and the expected happened. Two of the ranch employees, in town, with loads of chickens, found themselves taunted.

"That Fuss and Feathers place of yours is getting mighty tame, I understand," one of them was told. "You fellows used to have a reputation for being scrappers, but you're losing it. That new bookkeeper is about the weakest specimen of man you ever had on the place. It's a wonder Bill Roach stands for him."

The men drove back to the National Poultry Farm charged with anger. They spread the news — it was being whispered around town that one of them was a weakling. Their reputation was being ruined.

Their hostility to Richard Taylor grew. Men on adjoining ranches heard of it. Dad Meek's declarations that Dick was all right fell upon deaf ears. They assumed Dad had taken a fancy to the bookkeeper, and so left him out of their conversations.

There came a night, then, when one of the men appeared at the big house and asked for the boss, and when Roach came out to the veranda and stood before him, the employee said respectfully that the men would be obliged if Mr. Roach would step down to the bunkhouse alone for a few minutes.

"I'll be right down," Roach said, and turned in to the house for his hat. It was not the first time he had received such a summons. Generally it meant that the men wanted his permission to form a baseball club, or his subscription for a Sunday picnic, or a day off in which to attend some affair in Fresno.

Dick and Betty were sitting in the corner of the veranda as Roach left and started down the driveway, whistling. He walked briskly to the bunkhouse, threw open the door, and entered. The men were not singing, playing pranks, or laughing and shouting, as they were generally. They sat on the benches and the sides of the beds, somber in manner, serious of face.

"Well, boys," Roach asked. "This looks like a funeral. Want me to chip in for a phonograph or somethin' like that? Dang your hides, you're as solemn as owls. Loosen up, somebody — I ain't got all night."

Paddon got up from his place near a corner and cleared his throat.

"I been 'pointed spokesman, Mr. Roach," he said. "We didn't want our foreman to do th' talkin', 'cause we didn't want you to think he started this — which he didn't."

"Let it come," Roach encouraged.

"We been proud o' this place," Paddon went on. "We been proud because there ain't ever been nobody but he-men workin' here — until now."

"What's this?" Roach demanded.

"We've been known as huskies, ain't we? We never caused trouble any wrong way, but it's been understood nobody could get gay with the National crowd an' get away with it. You've let us try out men as come her to work, and we've got a pretty good bunch. I reckon you're as proud of it as us."

"You can bet I am!" Roach said. "Come to the point, Chauncey Depew."

"An' when it gets so everybody's laughin' at us an' callin' us a lot o' old maids, it's time we done somethin', we reckon. They're talkin' 'bout it on th' other ranches, an' even in Fresno. We can't stand it, boss. We got a little paper, here, everybody's signed —"

"You're a liar, cuss your carcass! I didn't sign it!" cried Dad Meek from a corner.

"All signed 'cept Dad Meek," Paddon corrected. "I guess it explains things, Mr. Roach. We don't want no hard feelin's, an' hope you'll look at this right."

Paddon held out the paper, and Roach took a quick step forward and grasped it. Standing beneath one of the lights, he read:

> We, the employees of the National Poultry Farm, respectfully ask our boss, Mr. William Roach, to fire his new bookkeeper, Richard Taylor, because said bookkeeper is a coward and not a he-man, and if he stays here it will make the ranch and men a laughing-stock.

Roach, dumbfounded, looked from the paper in his hand to the men around him. There was no mirth in this. The men were in earnest. Roach could read men, and the attitude of these before him said they had weighed Richard Taylor and found him wanting, that they did not desire his presence among them on the ranch.

An ordinary employer would have resented such a thing, have told the men that it was his business who he engaged for a certain position. But Roach was not an ordinary employer. He believed in *esprit de corps*. He wanted his men to be one large family, content with their lot and with one another. He always let them fight their own battles as long as they remained loyal to him, and settle their own differences, and he never stepped between them. If a new man won their regard, he remained and became one of the family; if he did not, then he left.

And this was the first time his men had banded together and appealed to Roach against any person on the ranch. It was something he could not overlook under the circumstances.

"What does this mean?" he demanded.

"It's all on th' paper, Mr. Roach," Paddon replied.

"I see all of you have signed it except Dad Meek. Why didn't you sign, Dad?"

"Why, cuss your carcass, it's a dirty trick!" Dad exclaimed. "It's a damn' lie! That boy a coward?"

"The men seem to think so. They seem to have decided agin' him for some reason. I reckon I'll have to look into this."

"We've made up our minds, sir," Paddon said. "O' course you been too busy to notice things. I reckon he's chicken-hearted. An' they're talkin' 'bout it is Fresno and on th' other ranches — makin' fun o' us, sir, and of th' ranch."

"You've made up your minds, have you?" Roach asked. He looked around him slowly, searched the face of every man there, and every man gave him a straight look without dropping his eyes. Yes, they had made up their minds — it was serious.

Roach's lips set in a straight line, his eyes narrowed, and he whirled without a word, the paper still in his hand, and strode through the door and toward the house. This thing had struck him deeply. He didn't understand it, but he intended to put it up to Richard Taylor immediately. That his old friend's son should be termed a coward by the men of the ranch, and in such a manner, was beyond his comprehension. It was a thing that demanded explanation. It demanded more than that — it demanded that Richard Taylor remove the stain put upon his name, else leave for other parts. Roach had welcomed him to his home, had fondly anticipated that his daughter and his old friend's son might marry and inherit his worldly goods, and now his castle was crashing about his ears.

The heels of his boots ground into the hard surface of the driveway angrily as he paced toward the house. He wanted a "show-down," and he wanted it at once. This was a thing that could not be evaded on the National Poultry Farm, a charge that had to be answered in a deliberate way. He didn't try to excuse the men or the boy. It wasn't his business, he told himself. He was merely the judge — the boy had to fight his own case.

Twenty feet from the corner of the veranda, he heard Dick's low voice and Betty's answering. Even the knowledge that Betty was beginning to look upon Richard Taylor with some favor did not stop Roach now. He mounted the steps and saw them sitting in the corner of the veranda beneath a porch light. Their faces were solemn, too, but Roach did not notice it as he strode toward them.

"Here's a paper you'd better read, Dick!" he said. "It's signed by th' men. They're sayin' you're a coward!"

CHAPTER VII

IN THE BUNKHOUSE

Betty and Dick had gone to the veranda immediately after the evening meal, while Roach remained in his library reading the newspaper, and their conversation had become more intimate than before. They had passed the point of wit and mirth, song and joke, and had begun to talk of more human and serious things, which shows how they were drifting.

"I wish your mother was with us," Betty had said. "I'm sure it would do her a great deal of good."

"Perhaps I'll have her here later," Dick said.

"You like the place, don't you?"

"You know I do, Betty."

"And you like father?"

"Yes — and you."

"I'm so anxious for you to — to get along," she said. "I mean — father's so anxious, because he knew your father —"

"I understand, Betty."

"I'm quite sure he wants you to make good in every way, because — well, I guess you'll not always be just his book-keeper if you do. He may see that you have an interest in the business."

Dick visioned other things between her words, of course. He moved nearer, and presently took her by the hand.

"Dad didn't leave me anything but a good name, Betty," he said. "I've got to fight the world to win a place. There are things — that I must do. But I want to make good. I'm thinking about my mother — and my own future, too. And some day I want to be more than your father's bookkeeper — closer to him than that. I can't even speak my hopes now — it wouldn't be right. Perhaps some day I may."

"Father is very anxious for you to make a good impression on everyone in the neighborhood," she went on, "and I'm sure you can. There is always help here, always friends here, for a man of the right sort. That's what has made the State."

"I know, Betty."

"You're getting along all right — aren't you?"

"I think so," he said.

"Please be careful, Dick. I'm beginning to like you, and so I want everyone to look up to you — respect you. People are different in different places — a person has to study them and learn how to get along."

"Why the sermon?" he asked, trying to laugh.

"You'll not be angry if I tell you?"

"Why certainly not."

"It's the — the men. They are — peculiar, you know. They are quick to judge, and once they have made up their minds it is difficult to change them."

"Well?"

"I've heard whispers, Dick. Most of the men have known

me for years, and I am a sort of pet of theirs, I suppose, and they talk freely before me. Dick, they — they are intimating that you're a — a coward."

He seemed to flinch as she spoke the word. He turned toward her quickly to find her regarding him gravely.

"It appears," she went on, "they think that because you didn't thrash Bob Owen that day when he was impudent to you."

"I had a good reason, Betty."

"I do not doubt it, Dick. I just thought I'd speak of it. Now that you know, perhaps you can do something to make them change their opinion of you."

"I'll try," he said.

Then there was a silence for a time, while Dick's thoughts were bitter. To face scorn and discourtesy had been bad enough; to have the woman he had begun to love mention that other men called him craven was all he could endure. He had a vision of himself facing Bob Owen and having it out — and then he remembered.

Betty's words had aroused his fighting spirit as it never had been aroused before. He trembled as he sat beside her, and would not trust himself to speak, save to answer in monosyllables to her questions. He was wondering how he could get away to his room, to be alone with his thoughts.

Then Roach returned from the bunkhouse and threw a paper into his lap.

"Here's a paper you'd better read, Dick. It's signed by th' men. *They're sayin' you're a coward!*"

Roach's words were goads. Dick read the paper in an instant, saw the signatures, felt rage welling up within him. So they had determined to run him out!

Bob Owen was one thing — he had a reason for keeping his hands off the foreman, as difficult as it was — but this was quite another matter. There was no reason why he should refrain from putting hands on another man.

Roach was standing before him, waiting, his attitude noncommittal. Betty was regarding him in astonishment. He handed her the paper, and she read and gave a little cry. Dick laughed mirthlessly, then got slowly to his feet.

"Mr. Roach, I'd like to have you accompany me to the bunkhouse," he said. And then, without looking at the girl beside him, he walked swiftly to the steps and down them to the driveway. Roach's heavy boots pounded behind him.

"Coward, eh?" he cried, as he strode. "I'm a Taylor, and a coward, am I?" And Roach exulted in his heart, for his castle had ceased tumbling about his ears. At least the foundations of it were left. And behind, Betty Roach gasped and hurried into the house and to her room, wondering how long she would have to wait before her father told her what had happened.

Roach spoke no word as he followed his bookkeeper down the wide drive through the shadows cast by the palms. Richard Taylor did not present the appearance of a man who desired to hold conversation. He walked swiftly, but Roach kept at his heels. As they neared the bunkhouse, they could hear sounds of a heated debate.

Dick threw open the door. Silence reigned. Every man there looked up and into his face, and saw Roach standing behind him. They had not expected this. The wondered what would come of it. Even Dan Meek, in his corner, gasped his astonishment, and felt sudden fear. He started to get up.

"I understand you think I am a coward. I suppose it is because I didn't thrash your discourteous foreman the first time he insulted me. I believe all of you signed that document?"

"I didn't, Dickie!" Dad Meek cried.

"Thank you, at least, Dad. Anybody else who didn't sign it? No? Then every man in this room has as much as called me coward to my face. One is not better and no worse than another in that regard, eh? I'm a coward and should be driven off the ranch — is that what you mean? Do you?"

He shot the question at Paddon, who happened to be standing nearest.

"I reckon if you look at that paper close, you'll find my name on it," Paddon exclaimed.

"You'll do as well as the next man, then! I'm a coward, am I?"

His hand shot out; the palm of it crashed against Paddon's cheek.

"Fight, you cur!" Richard Taylor cried.

Bob Owen sprang forward.

"Here! Let me handle this! I started it!" he cried.

But Dad Meek had been expecting something like that, and he sprang before Owen and grasped him by the arms.

"One at a time, foreman — one at a time!" he screeched. "Do you an' Paddon always fight in pairs? Cuss your carcass!"

The interruption served. Paddon was engaged in battle now, and there was Roach standing by to see that everything was fair. Though he did not show it in his face, the heart of Roach was exulting again. The boy was like his paw, after all!

There was nothing scientific about that combat. Richard Taylor, who had some knowledge of boxing, was too angry to use it. His fist clashed first between Paddon's eyes. He took a return blow on the cheek. They clinched, stood foot to foot, and tried to beat through each other's guards. Paddon was no weakling, but he could not stand against his equal in strength when that equal was enraged. He fought his best, giving blow for blow, knowing it was a losing fight.

"Coward, am I?" Richard Taylor cried. "You want me to fight, do you? Sign a paper, eh? You sniveling curs!"

Paddon closed and attempted to trip him. This was not according to the rules of combat as Dick understood them. It angered him the more. He backed away, then rushed forward, his arms working methodically, his blows distributed where they would be most effective.

"That's th' boy!" Dad Meek was crying. "I told 'em you was fightin' stock an' in th' pink o' condition, an' th' fools wouldn't believe it! Go it, Dickie! Put it on his chin!"

Dick stepped forward again and did as requested. Paddon shot through the air to fall among his fellows, his face covered with blood, unconscious.

But there was no end of it there. Dick whirled, and his fist crashed into the face of the man nearest.

"You signed it, too!" he cried. "Fight, you cur! Coward, am I?"

He struck the man again; struck another man. Despite the shrieks of Dad Meek and Roach, they rushed him now, half a dozen of them. He taunted them as he fought, retreating toward the wall foot by foot, and when he reached it he stood there, fighting them off...

"Come on — half a dozen of you!" he cried. "We'll see who's the coward!"

Determined, angry, and frenzied, they closed upon him. Roach was unable to stop them, unable to get near the center of the fight. Dad Meek was busy keeping between Bob Owen and the crowd. Dad didn't want the foreman to get where one of Dick's blows could land on him. The bunkhouse was a bedlam of shrieking, cursing, fighting men. Some stumbled away, their faces streaming blood. Above the din rose the voice of Richard Taylor.

"Coward, am I? Come on!"

Roach fought to get to the front, but the men hurled him back. Things were beyond his control now. Dick's taunts were enraging the men. They fought now to get at him, get their hands on him, drag him down; they had no thought of fairness. Dick saw the flash of a knife and dodged the blow.

"You would use a knife, would you?" he shrieked. "Come on, curs! Come on, cowards!"

The knife flashed again, the point of it bit into his arm. He could not see who wielded it. He sprang to one side, hurling half a dozen men out of his way. In an instant he had grasped the end of a bench and lifted it. He swung it before him; it crashed against those nearest and then to the floor. A leg was torn away from it. Dick picked it up and used it as a bludgeon, swingin it before him, driving them back — actually driving them back.

"Stop it, dang your hides!" Roach shrieked.

"At 'em, boy!" Dad Meek was screeching.

And then, as the throng parted, both Roach and Dad found themselves in the front. Dad grasped Richard Taylor about the arms, tried to calm him. Roach faced his men.

"Back!" he cried. "Great Jupiter! Haven't you had enough? Worryin' what they say in Fresno an' on th' other ranches, eh? What'll they say now? What'll they say when they find this crowd ganged a single man? Hey? An' what'll they say when they know he licked you? You're a nice gang to call *him* a coward, ain't you? I reckon you're satisfied now. Is he a coward? Want him run offen th' ranch? Hey? If I ever find out what fool forgot himself an' flashed that knife —"

Now that their fit of passion was passing, the men began to feel ashamed. Some there were with broken heads who grinned and looked at Richard Taylor admiringly as he stood with his back against the wall, the bench leg still clutched in his hand, his face streaked with blood, his eyes flashing, chest heaving. Surely this man was not a coward! Hadn't he stood up to them? Hadn't he proved himself?

"I reckon we must have made a little mistake," one of the men said sheepishly.

"I reckon you did, cuss your carcass!" Dad Meek shouted. "That's Dickie Taylor — that boy! He's from Texas! Him a coward! Hell, I knew his paw!"

Following his custom not to "take sides," Roach did not express in face or manner his delight at the outcome of the battle. He spoke merely as a man who was glad an issue had been decided and possible turmoil among his employees ended.

"Everybody satisfied?" he demanded, in a matter-of-fact tone. "Still got th' opinion he's ladylike an' not fit to 'sociate with you? Anybody got any remarks?"

"He ain't fought me yet!" said Bob Owen surlily.

Dick, gasping from weakness, took two paces forward and faced the foreman.

"And I don't intend to fight you — now," he said.

"I should think not! Not after you've just licked th' rest o' th' gang!" Roach exclaimed. "Take time to get your breath!"

Only Dad Meek knew Richard Taylor's true meaning.

CHAPTER VIII

THE UNPARDONABLE PHRASE

Richard Taylor no longer avoided the men — but he avoided the foreman. Before the purple-and-orange spots had disappeared from his bruised face, the employees of the ranch noted that. They no longer termed him a coward, since he had proved himself to be otherwise, yet he puzzled them.

They treated him with respect when they met him — while Bob Owen sneered at him and about him openly, and went unrebuked.

"You're goin' to get an awful lammin' one o' these days," Paddon told his superior one night at the bunkhouse. "That bookkeeper's just storin' it agai' you."

"He's afraid to lay hands on me!" Owen boasted. "Laugh, you fool! I say he is! Come up to th' office with me tomorrow when I make my report, an' I'll show you somethin'."

So, the following morning, Paddon accompanied the foreman to the office, pretending that he was going to the other side of the ranch as soon as Owen gave him orders.

"Here's your stuff!" Owen exclaimed, throwing his papers down on the desk in such a manner that they scattered among Dick's books. The acme of disrespect was in his voice.

Dick collected the papers carefully, checked them over, and put them in a file.

"I want some more blanks," Owen went on. "Well, get a move on you! I ain't got all day to wait while a dude book-keeper trims his fingernails!"

Dick turned and faced him, white with anger. Dad Meek got up quickly from his chair in the corner and stepped between the two men.

"Cuss your carcass, foreman!" he exploded. "You make more noise'n a threshing machine. You never come in this office when I'm thinking; 'thout disturbin' my thoughts. I'm a-sayin' you want to stop your fussin' around *me*."

"Get out of th' way, so this she-clerk c'n give me my blank reports!" Owen exclaimed. He sneered at Dick as he spoke.

Dick took a pad of blanks from the desk and threw them on a table before Owen. The foreman picked them up, grinned again in derision, and stalked from the office.

"See?" he said to Paddon. "He may smash into th' men, but I've got th' Indian sign on him!"

"It looks mighty funny to me," Paddon said. "You ain't so much worse than th' rest o' us."

Behind them they left a Richard Taylor who stamped from one end of the office to the other, sweeping his fists from side to side, expelling his rage in great breaths.

"I can't stand it — can't stand it!" he said.

"You've *got* to, boy! It's only a little longer," Dad replied. "When th' day o' reckonin' comes —"

"Ah! When it comes —"

Meanwhile, Paddon talked, and word went among the men that Richard Taylor, who had attacked the crowd in their bunkhouse, took words from the foreman that no self-respecting pygmy would take from a giant without resentment. Owen began to boast:

"He's afraid o' me! But I'll get him! I'll make him fight. I'll torment th' life outen him until he hauls off an' takes a smash at me, then I'll beat him half to death — th' dude!"

Yet Owen asked himself continually why Richard Taylor did not offer him combat. The man could fight, and Owen had slain his father. They were ancient enemies; their families had lived in a feud. They were about evenly matched physically, though Owen fondly believed he would be victorious in a combat. That he and Richard Taylor could exist on the same ranch without coming to blows was beyond his comprehension. It began worrying him a great deal. As an ignorant man will, he began to fear that which he could not understand. And one day he wrote a letter.

Scarcely a man is so low as to be without a single friend, be he fugitive, murderer, swindler, or thief. Owen remembered he had a friend in Texas, though he had not communicated with him, nor anyone else there, since his flight at the age of fifteen. He spent an entire evening over the letter, and mailed it himself the following day when he went to town with a load of eggs.

During the week that followed, he continued his systematic persecution of Richard Taylor. In vain he sought to meet the bookkeeper in the open, away from the office and the house, when Dad Meek was not near. He did not want to strike the first blow; he had a superstitious idea that victory would perch on his banner if the first blow came from his enemy. His plan was to taunt Richard Taylor to the point where endurance became impossible; Taylor would make the attack — and the big question soon would be decided.

Then came the reply to the letter he had written. Half

a dozen times during the day Owen read it. His manner changed. He laughed boisterously. He had found the solution — it was only a part of the answer, but he did not know that. During the evening meal he scarcely spoke, but repeatedly looked down the length of the table to catch Dad Meek's eyes and grin.

"I want to see you a minute, Dad," he said, as the men left the table; and they went to the bench at the end of the bunkhouse, where there were no others near to hear.

"So this Taylor won't fight me, eh?" he said. "He'll take anything I say without as much as answerin' back? Mighty funny, ain't it, Dad Meek? Well, I've got th' answer."

"Oh, you have, eh?" said Dad. "I s'pose you worked it all out by yourself, in your head."

"Not much I didn't! I wrote a letter, an' today I got a letter back. Won't fight me, eh? I know why, Dad Meek. An' do you think I'd let a Taylor get away with a thing like that? Do you think I won't spoil his little plans? Huh! I'll make him fight — an' I'll make him hit th' first lick, too. If I hit th' first lick, they might say as how he acted in self defense o' his life, or somethin' like that. Oh, I'm smooth enough to see that, all right."

"Oh, yes! You're sure smooth!" said Dad. "I heard tell down to Fresno —"

"Cut the talk, Dad! It won't do you any good now to try and act funny. I'm wise, I say. I'm goin' to spoil his little game. No wonder you kept stickin' in your nose an' preventin' us comin' together. Lookin' for a slice, was you?"

"Cuss your carcass —"

"That's right — get mad. I'm on to you, that's what! I'll make him fight, an' I'll spoil his plans! An' I'll make him hit th' first blow, like I said. I'll treat him like dirt — th' damned Taylor! I'll do everythin' I c'n do, an' say everythin' I c'n say to make him fight. Th' damned coward!"

"Cuss your carcass, don't call that boy a coward! Didn't he clean out th' gang?"

"Yeh! An' you was mighty careful to see he didn't come to clashes with me! Oh, I'll make him come to clashes, all right!"

Owen laughed loudly and whirled around to go into the bunkhouse. Dad Meet spent the next hour in ruminating more earnestly than he ever hand in his life before.

And the next day Owen began his campaign.

"Good morning, she-dude!" he called to Dick, as he entered the office. "I see your bodyguard's settin' in th' corner as usual, afraid I might take a smash at you. Did he tell you I'm wise to th' little game? How much'll you stand before you're man enough to try to take a smash at m' face?"

"I don't know how much he'll stand, but I ain't goin' to stand much if you come pesterin' round *me!*" Dad cried, hurrying forward.

"Back up, old man! I know your game. I'm talkin' to this half specimen o' human bein' that plays with th' books — this six-foot calf. He must have had a sheep for a daddy!"

"A-ah!" Dick Taylor whirled upon him with a snarl of rage, like a lion at bay, nostrils distended, eyes flashing, body poised as if to spring forward.

"Boy!" Dad cried.

"Why don't you hit me?" Owen taunted. "Why don't you take a smash at me — you white-livered pup!"

"Boy! Remember!" Dad shrieked, rushing forward again. He grasped Owen by the arm and hurled him toward a corner of the room. "Get out, you scum!" he roared. "Out o' this office!"

"That's right — protect th' baby!"

From the end of the desk came a cry of enraged despair:

"Dad! I can't stand it! I don't care! I'll —"

"Get out, you scum!" Dad shrieked again. He knew this was a crisis. Dick was at the point where he could endure no more. One blow — and everything would be lost.

"Let me at him, Dad!"

"Back, boy!"

"Let th' baby at me!" Owen cried. "Let th' son of a sheep —"

"A-ah!"

Dad Meek felt Dick rush against him from behind. It was a moment for quick action. He thrust one shoulder backward and struck Dick in the breast, sending him reeling, checking him for a moment. Then he did something he hoped to avoid — his hand dived beneath his shabby coat, and an old, loved "six-gun" came into view, its muzzle menacing the foreman. He charged forward.

"Get out, scum!" he shrieked.

His body struck against that of Bob Owen, and to save himself from falling the foreman was forced to spring out of the door. There he regained his balance, put his fingers to his nose, turned, and swaggered away.

"Dad! Why didn't you let —"

Dad Meek faced the bookkeeper from the opposite side of the table. He had returned the gun to its hiding place as quickly as he had taken it out.

"Boy, boy, you've got to do better than this," he said. "He almost won over you then. You know he's tryin' to do it. Why, think what you almost lost, boy! Your sacred promise — your chance —"

"I know, Dad — I know!"

"This man is wise — don't forget that. He'll try everythin'. He's tryin' to drive you to th' breakin' point, an' then he'll laugh an' say a Sturm conquered a Taylor. For if you give way, that's what it'll mean. He'll make you lose out, an' then he'll laugh. Let a Sturm wreck th' Taylor honor — eh, boy?"

"I can't — stand it."

"Keep a-thinkin' what it all means, Dickie. Just store it up agin' him. Your day's comin'. Cool down, now. I see Roach prancin' down th' drive. Get a smile on your face! Cuss your carcass, you made me break a rule o' th' old days — I drew a six-gun an' never shot."

Roach strode in at the door.

"What th' blazes has been goin' on here?" he demanded. "Up to th' house it sounded like a free-for-all scrap."

"Nothin' much, boss," Dad replied. "Bob Owen made a crack at *me*, an' I threw him outen th' office, by gravy!"

"Um!" Roach said. He glanced toward Dick, but Dick was busy thumbing the pages of a ledger.

Owen's campaign continued. He didn't care who knew it. He was challenging Richard Taylor to fight. He was taunting him to combat, searching for fresh slurs to sling at him, new epithets to hurl at him, insulting him every chance he got — and the bookkeeper of the National Poultry Farm did not double up a fist to resent it.

At first the employees were dumfounded. They had witnessed an example of Dick's fighting ability. They had thought him no coward. Had they been mistaken? Was he craven, after all? Had he fought that night because he had been goaded to it by Roach, because the eyes of his employer were upon him? Even cowards, forced by circumstances, will give battle on occasion, then relapse into cowardice again. Was Richard Taylor that sort of man?

They began believing it, for Bob Owen was no more formidable than some of them. Now and then a man observed indications of Dick's apparent fear of the foreman. They began to think they had been tricked into thinking the bookkeeper a proper man — and they began turning against him again.

Dad Meek was doubly alert during those days, for he knew the danger. Dick would stand just so much, and no more, Repeatedly Dad's warning cry stopped him as he was about to launch himself upon his tormentor; repeatedly Owen left his presence with a scornful laugh.

"I can't stand it any longer!" Dick cried; but the days went by.

"A little longer, boy — just a little longer," Dad implored.

Roach, eager to find whether Dick was respected by the men after the bunkhouse battle, began hearing whispers. He was looking below the surface of things now. One night he called Dick to the library.

"My boy, we've got to have a serious talk," he said. "I reckon you don't know what about?"

"No, sir."

"You've got to lick that foreman! You can't dodge it any longer! I don't know why you've let him go this long, Dick. From what I hear, he's makin' life miserable for you. Maybe you don't like th' idee of getting' a reputation for bein' a man beater, but I reckon it won't hurt you to beat up one more, 'specially when he give you good reason."

"I understand, sir."

"What in th' name o' Heaven's th' matter with you, Dick? You're a Taylor — you got spunk an' brawn. Don't you know I want you to make th' men respect you? Don't you know I got idees about you, boy? No use beatin' 'bout th' bush with me. How you an' Betty gettin' along?"

"Sir?"

"You know what I mean. I ain't blind — an' I'm pleased at th' way things are goin'. If you get to love my little girl —"

"I do now, sir — but I can't speak of it yet."

"Speakin' won't hurt, Dick, boy. O' course she'll have to wait, if you're th' man I think, an' want to stand on your own feet 'fore you take a wife — but she'll wait if she loves you. She'll wait for th' weddin' ring, boy, but you needn't make her wait to hear th' words she wants to hear. That's why I want you to make good. You're a business man. I knew your folks. I want you to get goin' right, then get your mother here, an' later other things'll come as a matter o' course. 'Cause I ain't got a he-heir, boy, an' I'd rather see you — Understand?"

"I think I do, sir — thank you."

"Sometimes it's necessary for a man to turn brute an' teach another he-human manners. Betty won't think any th' less o' you — an' you c'n be sure I won't. Don't take another word o' sass from Bob Owen. Beat him up — let him know you're a man as can't be taunted. I reckon you got to go down to his level to make him see you're above him."

"I understand, sir."

"Take th' very next chance you git, an' go to th' mat with him. That'll end it, I reckon. Th' men'll shut up, then, an' you'll have clear sailin'." Roach reached out and patted him on the back. "Remember, Dickie, I knew your paw!"

"I am thinking of my father now, sir."

"That's th' boy! You'll never go wrong thinkin' o' him!"

"And I want to ask you, sir, to let me handle this in my own way. I'm not a coward, sir."

"I know it, boy."

"I'll attend to the foreman in time. I've remembered every look, word that has been disrespectful. I'll make him pay."

"Why not now?" Roach demanded.

"I can't tell you, sir. Just trust me — if you will."

"I never did like talk 'cept it was straight from th' shoulder, but I'll gamble once on th' Taylor blood. I'll leave it to you."

"Thank you, sir."

When Dick went up to his room — and he did not go to the veranda to talk to Betty this night — he looked at the calendar.

"Seventeen days!" he said. "Only seventeen days! Maybe I can hold out. But it's going to be a hard job."

Two of the seventeen days passed without disaster, for it happened that Roach was in the office whenever Owen called, going over the books with Dick and planning some improvements in marketing methods. The day following, Owen was in town, and Paddon brought the reports. And the next day was Sunday, and Dick did not see Owen at all.

"Thirteen days more," he told Dad.

"We'll make it, Dickie!" Cuss your carcass, we got to make it! An' then —"

"And then —" said Dick; and the look in his face was not good to see.

Then the torment began again. Dick was forced to go about the ranch a great deal, but Dad managed to keep at his heels, always ready with a warning and prepared to prevent a clash. Owen was trying everything he knew.

"You pup of a coward!" he shrieked at Dick, down by the incubator building, where half a dozen men heard. And then, stepping close behind him, his fists held ready, he hissed: "You damned Taylor! You know what I did to your dad, an' I c'n do th' same for you!"

Dad Meek threw himself between then just in time; and Dick, whirling about on one heel, walked away swiftly, afraid he could not control himself, tears of rage streaming down his cheeks.

Owen searched his brain for new methods of insult. He insulted brutally and with finesse. He sought in vain for the weak spot in Richard Taylor's armor. Then he gathered courage to go the limit, to speak the fighting words of the white race.

Dad Meek and Dick had been to the Lates ranch to get fresh fruit. Returning, they entered by a private gate and made their way up one of the streets between the rows of chicken houses. They turned a corner to come upon the foreman and a dozen men crating hens.

Owen pretended not to notice their approach. But as they passed close to him he lurched to one side and crashed against them.

"Get out of the way, you —"

He spoke the unpardonable phrase.

He looked straight at Richard Taylor as he spoke. No man that could be called a man would let that pass unpunished. It was the limit of insult. About them was a sudden silence. Not a man moved. Just a flash of silence, then —"

Dad Meek's mind acted like lightning. Dick would never allow that to pass, he knew, no matter what hung on the outcome — no man would. Disaster, failure loomed big. And Dad acted.

"Me?" he shrieked. "I'll kill you for that!"

He sprang at the foreman.

"I didn't mean you —"

"Don't crawfish, you pup! I'll learn you to call *me* that!"

Like a whirlwind of rage he was upon the foreman, striking, kicking, deadly in his intent. He beat Owen down before the foreman could begin to defend himself. Dad Meek, who had known Dick's father, who knew his sweet mother, took that insult to himself and fought to avenge it, as well as to save the boy he adored.

In his frenzy he was more of a maniac than Richard Taylor had been that night in the bunkhouse. The foreman was a beaten man before he could begin to fight. He crashed to the ground; fists and boots struck him, even the heavy butt of the "six-gun" Dad Meek whipped from beneath his left arm. A minute — and the foreman was a senseless, bleeding thing stretched on the ground at the feet of his men.

"There — cuss your carcass!" Dad cried. "Maybe you'll keep your dirty mouth shut now!"

Then he staggered away, clung to Dick's arm, and went toward the office building. Behind him was a squad of men undecided whether it had been a trick or whether Dad Meek in reality had believed those words addressed to himself.

CHAPTER IX

FORBEARANCE

Roach paced back and forth across the veranda, pulling at his chin, a look of perplexity in his face. Betty was sitting in the hammock that hung in the corner. It was mid-afternoon.

"I can't make th' boy out!" Roach was complaining. "There's somethin' about this that I can't understand. He showed grit enough when he tackled th' gang down in th' bunkhouse that night, but he sure acts as if he was afraid o' th' foreman."

"But that fight in the bunkhouse —" Betty persisted.

"Betty, there's men as are cowards nine-tenths o' th' time an' brave only in spots," said Roach. "Sometimes a man like that'll get so mad, suddenlike, that he'll tackle th' greatest scrapper on th' earth. An' th' next minute he'll take back talk from a skinny little runt that couldn't knock down a mockin' bird. Them kind is the worst excuses o' men in th' world, 'cause they *can* take care o' themselves but ain't got th' nerve to do it. If I thought Dick Taylor was that kind of man —"

"Father! I'm sure he's not!"

"You're beginnin' to think a lot o' him, ain't you, Betty? Well, I hope things turn out all right. I'd hate to have my little girl's heart broke."

"If he ever showed me he was the sort of man you mentioned, father, my heart wouldn't break. It would be so full of scorn for him that I couldn't even feel sorry."

"I reckon I understand, Betty — that's th' kind o' girl you are. I'm givin' the boy every chance. Maybe he'll lick that foreman yet. There's sure somethin' funny 'bout it. I've talked to some o' th' men, an' they saw Owen insulted Dick, not Dad, an' that Dad took up th' words 'cause he knew Dick didn't have th' nerve to fight, an' such a thing couldn't be let pass 'thout somethin' bein' done. I'm sure hopin' he proves himself. Bein' a Taylor —"

Roach did not finish his sentence. He stalked down the steps and toward the office, digging his boot heels into the hard driveway at every stride.

It was three days after Dad's beating of the foreman, and Bob Owen had done little in that time to arouse Dick's fighting spirit, for the foreman was in no condition for combat. Dad's kicks and blows had bruised his chest and arms so that moving them was painful. He contented himself with sneering at the bookkeeper at such times as he was obliged to visit the office, and waited for his wounds to heal. There was animosity in his heart against Dad Meek, too, now. The men knew it, and in "eatin' joint" and bunkhouse they kept at a distance from Dad, afraid to be over-friendly with the man who did not stand in the good graces of the foreman.

"I'll get th' dude yet!" Owen told his men. "He knew I was talkin' to him that day, all right, an' Dad Meek knew it! He took up th' scrap 'cause he knew th' she-clerk didn't have th' nerve to fight even after that. I'll get him! I'll be in shape, now, in a couple o' days more — I'm gettin' the soreness outen my arms. An' if I can't do it any other way, I'll walk up to th' coward an' smash him between th' eyes. Maybe he'll have to fight then."

He was outspoken to Dad Meek, too.

"You saved th' damned Taylor a good beatin' t'other day, but I'll get him!" he boasted. "I'll spoil your little game! This ranch ain't big enough to hold th' both o' us, an' I reckon he'll be th' one to go, 'less th' old man protects him. An' if I'm th' one as has to go, I'll spoil this Taylor's little game first, all right!"

"Cuss your carcass! Don't come blattin' like that round *me!*" Dad replied. "I'm gettin' awful tired listenin' to you."

"Think you're a bad man 'cause you smashed me down when you knew I was lookin' for a different man to start th' scrap, don't you?"

"Oh, I ain't sayin' I could trim you in a regular stand-up an' prize-ring fight," said Dad. "But I reckon I got years an' 'sperience. I generally c'n get in one good smash before I'm counted out. 'Cordin' to m' age, I got th' right to go after a man with fists, gun, or club; an' if you start anythin' more with *me* I'll use th' first thing I c'n put my hands to, by gravy! I'm tellin' you ag'in you'd better lay offen that boy, or some o' these days th' ground goin' to raise up an' smash you side th' head!"

Every night Dick Taylor looked at the calendar on the wall of his room. Every time he marked off a day he gave a sigh of relief. These were days of conflicting emotions for Dick, for he had hours of despair when he thought of the forbearance he must practice, and hours of rapture when he sat beside Betty Roach on the veranda.

"Four days more, Dad!" he said one morning.

"We're goin' to make it, boy! Ain't it been worth it?"

"I don't know," Dick replied. "And when my time is up —"

"You're goin' after him?"

"I am, Dad, I've remembered every word, every action, every sneering look. I'm remembering who he is and what he did years ago. And I'll make him pay!"

"I been waitin' to talk to you 'bout that, Dickie. Just what do you figure you'll do?"

"I'm not sure."

"I reckon you won't kill him?"

"I — I may."

"Then you'll find a Sturm conquerin' a Taylor in th' end, boy. You know what killin' will mean?"

"I don't care, Dad."

"You don't? Killin's too good for that skunk. His troubles'll be over if he's kilt. An' yours'll just begin. There'll be th' disgrace o' bein' hung or goin' to th' pen —"

"I wouldn't consider it a disgrace — he killed my father!"

"Just th' same, people'll be able to say a Taylor swung by th' neck. Think o' your mother, Dickie, an' what it'll mean to her. An' you'll lose th' girl, Dickie. You'll lose th' chance to have a wife an' a home an' kids, an' to make somethin' outen yourself, an' you'll die on th' scaffold. You'll suffer, an' a Sturm will look up from Hell an' grin to think you're sufferin' 'count o' him."

"But what can I do, Dad?"

"Break him, Dickie! Break him forever! Beat him down an' cripple his spirit, then tell why you done it. Make him walk th' earth a twisted, whipped thing men'll laugh at! That'll hurt him more'n killin'. An' when th' story's known, nobody'll blame you for it. They'll say you're a man 'cause of how you did it. Punish him, boy — make his punishment good an' lastin'!"

Two more days passed. Bob Owen felt that he was in condition again now to give a good account of himself in case the bookkeeper gathered enough courage to fight. He never met Dick except in the office, however, and Dad Meek always was there. Dad did not sit in the corner these days when the foreman called, but got up and stood beside the desk, ready for anything that might occur; and his humor had give way to a facial expression that was menacing.

"I'll get him!" Owen boasted to his men as they worked. "I'll get him at th' raisin dance — if he's got the nerve enough to go."

"Oh, I reckon he'll go, an' with Roach's daughter," Paddon said.

"Well, Dad Meek can't hang around him all th' time at th' dance. There'll be a chance to face him, if a feller watches for it. I'll get him, an' I'll make him hit th' first blow, else take talk no other man ever took."

"If you're so blamed anxious to git him, why don't you slam into him an' make him fight back?" one of the men asked.

"I got a reason for wantin' him to hit th' first lick. He ain't goin' to have th' chance to say he acted in defense o' his life. I'll git him, all right. I've tried 'bout everythin', but there's a few moves I ain't made yet. I'll git him afore a crowd an' give him talk that he'll have to answer, less have every decent human critter turn back on him."

*

The raisin dance, so called, was held annually at the Lates place. Men from adjoining ranches were guests; so were other ranch owners and their sons and daughters. A few young men and women journeyed out from the city to take in the affair. There were no stiff formality about the raisin dance. Everyone went for the sole purpose of having a good time. Bars that separated social classes at other times were dropped the night of the raisin dance. Ranch hands and owner's wives and daughters met on a common footing.

Once inside the big gate at Lates', everyone was equal to everyone else.

"You want to watch out, Dad, at th' dance," Dick warned. "That pesky foreman might get a chance there."

"Why, cuss your carcass, o' course I am! Think I'd miss a shindig like that? But I reckon I ain't as young as I used to be when I worked for your paw, an' it's likely I won't be on th' dance floor much. I'll hang round an' keep both my eyes open, but you want to be careful, just th' same. If you don't have to go —"

"Remaining away is out of the question, Dad. I'm to escort Betty."

"I sorter reckoned that, boy. Course you couldn't refuse 'thout explainin', an' you can't do that. You go to th' dance an' keep your eyes peeled. Enjoy yourself, Dickie, but don't let that pesky foreman catch you alone in some corner when I ain't around. He'll be watchin' to do that. An' if you lose that temper o' yourn —"

"I've stood it this far, Dad. I've got to stand it two more days — I've got to win out!"

"That's th' talk, Dickie!"

The dance was Thursday evening, and Dick Taylor arose that morning, exulting. It was the last day!

"Less than twenty-four hours now, Dad!" he said, when he reached the office.

"Just when is th' time up, Dickie?"

"Friday morning at five o'clock. Think of that, Dad — tomorrow morning at five o'clock! And then — Oh, it'll feel good to be free! It'll feel good to know that I can be a man again!"

"I reckon you've been pretty much o' a man right along, boy, an' other folks'll think so when they know. Be careful, Dickie, today an' tonight. There's been many a hoss race lost in th' last hundred yards, an' that goes for other things, 'sides hoss-racin', I reckon."

Bob Owen reported at the office that day at the usual time for orders. Though Dad Meek stood beside the desk, ready to take a hand, the foreman did not spare Dick Taylor. Every word, every glance, and every gesture was an insult. But Richard Taylor was strong in determination this day, and the foreman could not get beneath the armor of the bookkeeper's resolve.

"By thunder, I guess you ain't got a speck o' manhood in you," Owen exclaimed finally, standing in the doorway. "But I'll make you toe th' mark, you damned quitter! Your time's a-comin', you cussed Taylor, an' comin' soon!"

Roach and Betty and Dick drove over to the Lates place in a surrey that night, to find the house of the raisin king ablaze with lights and strings of Japanese lanterns running from tree to tree along the driveway. Groups of men and women were scattered over the great lawn, filling the night with merry laughter. At one side of the house, a large, raised dancing platform had been constructed and illuminated with flaring oil lamps, and at one end of the platform an orchestra, imported from Los Angeles for the occasion, made sundry noises as the musicians tuned their instruments.

Lates and his wife met them at the door after one of the men had taken the surrey toward the stables, and the greetings were joyous! Dick, used to the cordial hospitality of his native Texas, found it almost overdone here. By the time Betty descended the wide staircase and signified she was ready for the first dance, the music having started, Dick Taylor was feeling that it was good to be alive and working at the National Poultry Farm as Bookkeeper.

It appeared that Betty Roach was not afraid to show her colors. She danced the first three numbers with Dick, refusing other men and making it impossible for Dick to choose another girl. Such a state of affairs cannot endure for long at a raisin dance without comment being made. Men and women — and especially women — began whispering that it looked as though Betty Roach had lost her heart at last. Dick was appraised and analyzed, and received many tributes unknown to him. He began to feel a glowing sense of proprietary interest in the radiant girl his arms encircled.

Once during the third number a couple bumped against them, and Dick, turning to apologize, found himself looking into the sneering face of Bob Owen. He had almost forgotten the foreman's existence, and the incident served to recall it forcibly. The smile left his face, and a troubled expression came in its stead. He was glad Betty had not noticed.

But his fit of moroseness did not last long, for it could not in that atmosphere. He danced a couple of times with other girls, yet for the greater part he answered his partners in monosyllables and kept his eyes on Betty when possible.

He saw the grinning features of Dad Meek now and then. Dad had taken a seat at one end of the platform, and was holding convention with half a dozen other old-timers from other ranches. Once, between dances, Dick walked over to him.

"I've been keepin' my weather eye on a certain party," Dad whispered. "He acts like he's too busy havin' a good time to bother you tonight, but you never c'n tell. If he does happen to run afoul o' you, for Heaven's sake don't let go your temper, boy. Remember, th' time's almost up."

As Dick walked around the edge of the platform to claim Betty again, he kept promising himself to be careful. Since he had taken so much from Bob Owen, he felt that anything the foreman could do or say tonight could be allowed to pass unnoticed, since the time for reckoning was so near.

He whirled Betty through a waltz. Once they passed close to Bob Owen and his partner, and Dick noticed that the foreman scarcely glanced at him. Perhaps, he decided, Owen had no intention of forcing things at the dance. And there would be no opportunity on the way home, unless the foreman was willing to affront Roach, too. Dick felt safe now — felt nothing could occur until the next day — and then he wanted it to occur. He hadn't decided yet just how he would handle Bob Owen, but handle him he would!

The waltz came to an end. A radiant, blushing Betty clung to his arm.

"Let's talk a walk, Dick," she said softly. "I'm tired dancing for the present."

They left the platform and went down the steps, along the driveway, past other couples, and past groups. Betty directed his steps down a narrow path that led to a pergola. There were but few Japanese lanterns here, but the moonlight filtered through the trees. From the distance came the music of the orchestra. Low laughter sounded from a happy couple on the bench beneath a palm tree nearby. Dick could not resist the impulse that came to him then.

"Betty — Betty!" he said.

She was in his arms — neither of them knowing exactly how it happened — before the words had died away. For an instant their lips met. Then Dick put her away.

"I — I shouldn't have done that, Betty," he said. "It isn't fair to you. I should have waited —"

"Why?" she asked. "I wanted you to do it — I've been wanting you to for days and days."

"But I —"

"I know what you are going to say, Dick," she said. "So, you see, there is no need for you to say it. You want to wait until you've made a place for yourself. Well, can't I wait, too? And the waiting will be easier because you've shown me —"

Again she was in his arms, and his lips on hers, and thus they stood for a time, and then, without speaking, they turned to retrace their steps toward the driveway.

Half a hundred couples were scattered along the walks now. Stern-faced and broad-shouldered ranchers, who did not dance, walked up and down and smoked and talked of business. Waiters who had come out from Fresno were busy preparing the long table under the palms for the supper Lates always served.

"Let's dance one more before we eat," Betty said.

Dick started with her toward the dancing platform. A group before them parted to let them through. And in the middle of the path, the sneer upon his lips, stood Bob Owen.

"Well, look at th' dude bookkeeper!" he exclaimed.

Dick knew his face had gone white. He knew forty persons, at least, had heard the foreman's words. He knew it couldn't be passed off with a retort and laugh. He took Betty by the arm and started on, stepping past the man he hated.

"Th' finest milk-fed coward in captivity!" Owen taunted.

Betty felt Dick's arm grow rigid, and he quickened his

step. Owen turned and started to follow.

"Ain't he th' pretty little thing to be out so late? Him'll catch cold in th' night air!"

"Dick!" Betty whispered. "That brute is making you ridiculous! People have heard — they are laughing."

It was past the limit of endurance for Betty that anyone should ridicule a person she admired.

"I — I know," Dick gasped.

"Don't mind me, Dick. I know you're trying to get me away and then go back after him, as a gentleman should. But I'd rather you left me right here and went back now. I've seen fights before. I can go on to the platform alone."

"Six feet one inch o' nothin'!" Owen called after him.

Betty glanced up at his face — she had felt his arm tremble again. A little doubt of him entered her mind. Had her father been right? Was Richard Taylor one of those men who can fight, but will not?

Dick was in agony that moment. The words of the foreman were as nothing compared to those he had used often before, but that they were spoken in public, and before Betty Roach, made matters worse. He kept imploring himself not to give way to his desire to turn and clash with Owen. Only a few more hours, he kept telling himself — only a few more hours!

"Th' dude seems to be in an awful hurry to dance!" Owen taunted. "'Tain't possible he's a coward, is it?"

"Go back, Dick — go!" Betty whispered angrily. "A man like that should be half killed."

"He's just a fool, Betty — or drunk."

"But —" she began.

Owen's words interrupted her:

"A woman shows mighty poor judgement to hang to th' arm of a feller like that."

"Oh!" Betty gasped angrily. She let go Dick's arm and half turned.

She had expected Dick Taylor to whirl like a madman and smash his fist into the leering face of the man who taunted. Owen had played his game with consummate skill. He had done as he wished — caught Dick and Betty together and slurred the girl. Richard Taylor would ignore insults hurled at himself. Would he allow to pass a slur hurled at the girl he escorted? Dick half hesitated, looked at Betty, stepped toward her, and started to walk slowly onward.

But Betty Roach stood firm in the middle of the path.

"Dick! Did you understand what he said?"

"Yes, Betty, I —"

"Go back there and thrash the brute!"

"I —"

"Pick up with a critter like him when there's real men around!" Owen said.

"Dick!" Betty's word was a command.

Dick half turned to face his tormentor. He was aware that a crowd was gathering. He saw Dad Meek in the distance, hurrying toward him — Dad Meek, who had missed him and search the wrong part of the grounds.

"Well, come on, baby! Want to fight?" the foreman sneered.

"Dick!" Again that tone of command from Betty.

Richard Taylor was fighting himself now more than any man guessed, even Dad Meek.

"Only a few hours more — a few hours more!" rang in his brain.

"Dick! That brute has as good as insulted me! Go back and thrash him," Betty cried. She began to feel some shame herself now. To think her escort failed in such a crisis — and when other girls were there to watch!

"Betty, I — I can't!!" Dick whispered.

"Why?" she demanded.

"I — Oh, Betty, let me explain later! Come, let's go to the platform. I can't now — I can't! I —"

"Are you afraid? Are you a coward? You let a brute insult me and make no move to resent it? Are you the man who whipped the gang in the bunkhouse?"

"Why, th' weak-kneed critter!" Owen cried, laughing boisterously.

"Betty —" Dick implored.

But Betty stood firm. Her eyes were flashing now. The situation was hurting Betty more than any guessed, for she had given her love to this man before her, given him her lips —

"You coward," she hissed finally. "This — after what happened a few minutes ago! I'll never hold up my head again! You — a Taylor!"

She laughed scornfully and turned from him, held her head high, and swept up the driveway toward the house. Owen's laugh rang out. A few jeers greeted Dick's ears. Rage welled up within him, and he took a step forward. In that instant there flashed through his mind what this foe of his had done. Publicly he had been dubbed coward — publicly he had been scorned by the woman he loved because of what he had refused to do. Another step forward —

"Dickie!" came the thin, quavering call of warning from a breathless Dad Meek.

It saved him. His arms fell to his sides. A few more hours —

"Well, he don't want to fight, after all!" Owen jeered. "Some man, he is!"

Dick whirled around and started toward the platform. He felt sick, miserable. He wanted to be alone with Dad — he wanted to see Betty and beg her forgiveness — he wanted —

"Taylor," the ranch owner said, "I reckon you've worked your last day for me. In th' mornin' you get out, get offen my ranch! You a Taylor? Like hell you are! Let a man insult you — insult my girl — and you walk away from him like a weaklin'! You six-foot rag! Pack your grip an' git! First thing in th' mornin' — and remember if, or I'll manhandle you myself! No coward works for Bill Roach!"

Roach turned aside, mumbling to himself. Dick made no attempt to answer.

CHAPTER X

FACE TO FACE

Back and forth, back and forth between the rows of chicken shed, Dick Taylor paced, shoulders thrown back, head held high, arms swinging by his side at times, and at other times his fists beating his breast. Hatless, coatless, the sleeves of his shirt rolled above his elbows, he strode a score of paces to the north and retraced his steps back and forth, like a tiger pacing the length of its cage.

The noises of the dance across the broad highway had died away. The last carriage, last automobile had gone; the lights were extinguished. Palm fronds waved in the gentle breeze that swept down from the distant hills, and their soft rubbing was the only sound save for the steady thread of Richard Taylor's boots as he continued his ceaseless pacing.

"What time is it, Dad?"

"Three o'clock, boy. You'd better sit down an' rest."

"Two more hours! Two more hours! I don't want to rest. Dad, I — I don't know whether I can wait two more hours!"

"You've got to make it three hours, boys, so there won't be any mistake. We don't want any mistake."

"Three hours! I can't wait —"

"You got to wait, Dickie!"

Back and forth, back and forth again, up and down the gravel street! Dad Meek sat with his back against the bole of a pepper tree and offered no word. Richard Taylor did not want words — he had thought that kept him busy. A tumult of emotions seethed through his brain — rage, despair, pain, love!

"What time is it now, Dad?"

"A quarter to five, Dickie. You'd better set down a bit!"

"Come!"

Dad arose and followed. Dick led the way to the drive, and along it to the office building, and there he stood looking through the breaking day at the big house. Betty was there — a Betty who had given him her love and who now was ashamed of him, hated him! Only Betty did not hate him, but he did not know that. Could he have seen through the side of the big house, he would have seen Betty tossing on her bed, her pillow tear-drenched, her tiny hands doubled until her fingernails cut into the palms — a Betty who prayed that it could not be true, and at the same time told herself she had seen it, heard it.

"Come!" Dick ordered again.

He went back down the driveway. Halfway to the bunkhouse, he stopped.

"As soon as it is over, Dad, I'm going into town," he said. "That is, if I'm able. And I want to go alone."

"Now, Dickie, I reckon I'll just go along."

"No, Dad. Do as I say. Come in later, if you wish. I hope you do. You'll find me at one of the hotels. I'm going into town and send a message. I want you to send one, too, when you get the chance."

"I understand, Dickie."

"I'm going to end this business as quickly as I can, and then I'm going back to Texas. I'll get my old job back, Dad."

"Aw, Dickie —"

"I'm done here!"

"Aw, boy, when they know —"

"I'm done! One thing could make me stay — and that thing cannot happen now. What time is it?"

"It's half past five, Dickie."

"Ah!"

Dad Meek faced him and extended a hand. Richard Taylor grasped it, clutched it, then let go. He stood for a moment in the middle of the driveway, looking down toward the bunkhouse. Smoke was issuing from the chimney of the "cook's shack." One of the cook's assistants had opened the door of the "eatin' joint" to let in fresh air. In a few minutes all the men would be up. They would have been up before this, except that they had been to the dance the night before.

"Dad, give me that old six-gun of yours."

"Now, Dickie, you don't' want to do murder. What did I tell you t'other day? He'll th' same as conquer in th' end if you kill him. He'll look up from hell an' —"

"Give me your old six-gun, Dad. I won't disgrace it by using it to kill such a skunk. Just let me have it — and leave the rest to me."

Dad took the six-gun from beneath his arm and handed it over.

"Remember, Dickie!" he advised. "His life ain't worth yourn. We don't want 'em to say as how a Taylor was swung by th' neck."

"Come!" Dick commanded again.

With his shoulders thrown back, he swung off down the

driveway. Dad hurried along at his heels. Straight toward the bunkhouse went Richard Taylor, with much of determination and nothing of fear in his stride.

In front of the building he hesitated a moment, then stepped forward swiftly, clutched the knob, and hurled open the door. For the second time in his life he confront all of Roach's men in their living quarters.

Some were just crawling out of their beds, some were half dressed, some were splashing in the bathroom, some smoking a before-breakfast pipe and some discussing the events of the night before. Conversation ceased as they looked up and saw who confronted them. Silent, motionless, they waited for him to speak.

"Where is that man who calls himself Bob Owen?" he demanded. "Where is the bully who has heaped insults upon me for three months? Where is the cur who calls a Taylor a coward?"

"Are you referring to me, you pup?" Owen demanded, stalking in from the bathroom.

"I'm referring to you!" Dick said. "We've got some things to settle that can't wait a moment longer."

"Oh! Goin' to fight, are you?" Owen sneered. "Why didn't you put up a scrap last night?"

"I had a reason for keeping my hands off you until today, that is why. That reason does not exist now. We'll see now who's the better man, unless you're afraid —"

"Afraid of a Taylor?" Owen cried. "Why, curse you —"

He started forward. Richard Taylor's arm swung from behind his back, and Bob Owen found himself looking into the black muzzle of Dad Meek's six-gun. He stopped in his tracks, flinched.

"Afraid I'll shoot you down like a dog, are you?" Dick cried. "Perhaps that is what I should do — you deserve it. But we won't have any gun play this morning. We're going to fight as men fought before there were such things as six-guns. We're going to fight like *men*, with our hands. We're going to see who is the better *man* all around — a Taylor, or a cur like you!"

He stopped and looked around at the others.

"Get out!" he commanded, raising the weapon again threateningly. "Every man get out! Leave me alone with this thing that calls himself Bob Owen. Leave us along in here, with our bare hands. Get out!"

"Boy —" Dad began.

"I'm handling this, Dad. You wait a moment, though. Just run your hands over him and see whether he has a weapon. Then you get out, too."

Threatened by the revolver, the men obeyed. Calmly Dick stood at the doorway and checked them off. Bob Owen remained standing in the center of the room, a sneer upon his lips, his rage gathering.

"Look in the lavatory, Dad," Dick ordered. "Anybody there? We're all alone, eh? Now pull down the shades at all the windows. The men don't need to see what happens — nothing but results will could in this affair. Thanks, Dad — to the door, now!"

Dad stood beside him. Dick reached over and took out the key and put it on the outside.

"I'm going to hand you back your gun, Dad, and then you're to go out with the others," he said. "Lock the door and stand guard at it. Don't let anyone in until this is over. And don't you come in! In time, one of us will come to the door and knock. Then you can open it, and not before."

He looked at Bob Owen again, an when he spoke the men outside could hear his words:

"Now it'll be a fair battle. I suppose you men do not know all that is between us, but we know it. It's going to be a fight to the finish. For I'm going to break you — I'm going to make you a twisted, crippled thing that men will laugh at. I was going to kill you, but a good friend showed me the better way. You haven't got a chance against a Taylor. You're going to be punished now for all you've done!"

"I'll be right here when th' punishin' is bein' done, you damned Taylor."

Dick handed his weapon to Dad Meek. Dad went out and closed the door. The key was turned in the lock. In the semi-gloom of the darkened room they stood face to face again, and this time alone — the murderer and the son of the man he had killed.

CHAPTER XI

THE OUTCOME

For a full minute they stood silently glaring at each other, calling up visions of the past to give them rage. Then they started to circle, crouching forward, each watching for the other to rush in, each with arms extended and fists held ready, two deadly fighting men with lips set tightly over teeth, eyes narrowed to slits, breaths flowing audibly through distended nostrils.

Inch by inch that circle narrowed. Now they were less than three feet apart. Now their fists almost touched. Now their eyes blazed into each other, and still each man waited for the other to make the first offensive move.

"You damned pup of a Taylor!"

"You whelp of a Sturm!"

They clashed.

Back and forth across the floor they struggled, each locked in a grip he could not break, neither able to strike a blow. One of Dick's arms slipped. In a flash the grips were changed, yet each as secure as before. A sudden twist — and Owen got an arm free. He swung it. His fist went over Dick's shoulder.

They broke away; they rushed. Now arms flung like flails and blows thudded against flesh. Shirts were torn to strips, breasts and backs became smeared with blood. Now one gave ground, and now the other. Back and forth across the room they fought, without a word, without even a curse.

They broke again, and for a moment stood two paces apart, panting, glaring at each other. Again they rushed and were locked in each other's arms. There was more frenzy in their wrestling now. They crashed against one of the beds and sprawled over it, fought their way off, fell to the floor. They rolled against a table and crushed it against a wall. On their feet again, they stood face to face and exchanged blows, giving and taking brutal punishment.

They choked, they kicked, the scratched. In this battle it

was permissible to use any of nature's weapons. Here there were no ring rules to be observed. Here the man who lost perhaps would be crippled for life, a repulsive thing at which to look.

Now rage got the better of caution. Guards were dropped. Like beasts they fought now on their feet, and now on the floor. Other tables were overturned and crushed. Lockers were knocked over. Beds were jammed against the walls. They were covered with blood now. One of the foreman's eyes was closed. Dick's cheek was ripped open. They breathed with effort, but still they fought.

And now they found their voices again, for they needed new insult to refresh their jaded anger.

"You damned Taylor!"

"Dog of a Sturm! I'll make you pay! I'd kill you — but my father — forgave! But I'll mark you! You'll carry — a Taylor's mark — to the grave!"

They had reached the crisis now, the point where a telling blow might mean victory or defeat. Their strength was going speedily. Their arms began to feel as heavy as lead. Their breathing pained their lungs.

Owen began to give ground again; and Dick, exulting, beat him back. Again they grappled, and now they shrieked in rage as they fought. They crashed to the floor, fought their way to their feet again. The foreman's arm was bent backward, snapped! With a shriek of pain he broke away and ran. He picked up a heavy vase from the floor, where it had fallen when a table went over, and hurled it at Dick's head, to have it miss its mark and crash against the wall beyond. He wrenched a leg from one of the tables and swung it around his head as he advanced. Dick rushed in, and the table leg struck with all the foreman's strength against his left shoulder. Another bone snapped.

Again they were clutched, screeching in pain, clawing at each other's eyes, growing weaker and weaker. Again the foreman slipped and went down, with Dick on top. But he called upon his remaining strength and managed to get to his feet.

The fight was nearing an end now. One of Owen's arms

hung at his side, one of his eyes was closed, his face was cut to ribbons, he limped. Dick's face was no better, and his left shoulder had been shattered. There was little fight left in them, still they tried to get in a conquering blow. There would be no mercy for the man who was stretched unconscious on the floor. Three generations of Taylors and Sturms had fought like this, and the feud was to have an ending here.

Dick charged forward again, determined to make an end of it if he could, for he realized he could not hold out much longer. Slowly but surely he beat the foreman back. And suddenly, with a cry that sounded like one of hysterical fright, Owen turned and ran.

He ran the length of the room to the door of the little apartment that was his privately. With a cry of victory, Dick ran after him. He had no intentions of letting his crippled enemy get inside the smaller room and lock the door.

Owen hurled the door open and dashed inside. He made no attempt to slam the door shut behind him. Dick charged after him. Owen was fumbling at the head of his bed. He whirled, gave a last great cry of rage, and threw up a revolver he had taken from beneath his pillow. There came a flash of flame, a puff of smoke, an ominous crack!

Outside the door of the bunkhouse, forty men huddled together and listened. Before the door stood Dad Meek like a soldier on guard, his beloved "six-gun" held in his hand. Dad Meek said nothing as he listened to the sounds of combat, but if ever an old sinner prayed, Dad Meek prayed on.

"There goes a table!" Paddon cried tensely.

"That sounds like a bed!"

"Great guns! Listen to them blows!"

"They'll kill each other!"

"Owen'll beat th' livin' blazes outen th' coward!" Paddon exclaimed.

Dad thought it his place to put in a word.

"I wouldn't call him a coward that-a-way, Paddon," he said, "seein' as how he gave you a unmerciful trimmin' onct on a time. 'Tain't a compliment to yourself."

Paddon sneered at him and turned away.

"Also," said Dad, "I reckon you're in line for th' foreman's job, an' I've got an idee there'll be an openin' for a foreman on this ranch in a few minutes."

"You needn't think he'll clean Bob Owen. Bob's got an extra card up his sleeve, I reckon."

"He'll need a pinochle deck," said Dad.

"If it comes to a show-down, I reckon Bob can git to his room. An' there's a little six-shooter under his pillow —"

"If th' skunk tries anything like that —" Dad began.

Another crash from inside the bunkhouse interrupted him. They heard the two combatants shrieking at each other, heard them crash to the floor. Quick footsteps, another cry of rage, and then —

The snappy bark of a revolver shot!

"Cuss his carcass!" Dad cried. "If th' skunk ain't played fair, I'll shoot him to bits!"

He whirled toward the door.

"Wait a minute, old-timer!" Paddon called. "Play the game th' way your man told you! You'd better wait —"

Dad stopped. Crouched near the door, he listened. Not a man spoke.

They heard faltering steps inside. One of the two lived, then. One was able to walk about without fear of attack by the other. But which?

They could tell that the survivor went into the lavatory. They heard water splashing. Then the steps again. A know at the door — a weak knock.

Dad turned the key and threw the door open.

In it, his face raw and bleeding, his eyes half closed, his head and shoulders drenched with water, his shirt torn from his back — staggering from weakness, breathing with difficulty — stood Richard Taylor.

"You'd better — attend to your foreman," he gasped. "His foul shot — didn't strike home!"

"Dickie! Dickie!" Dad cried joyously.

"Help me, Dad! Where's my coat? My shoulder —"

He lurched forward, and Dad Meek caught him to keep him from falling as the men charged past them into the wrecked bunkhouse.

"Hurry, Dad! I want to get away! Get my coat!"

"You're hurt, boy! You've got to have 'tention!"

"I've arranged that. That's why I phoned from the office when we got home from the dance. I've got an auto waiting just below the gate. There'll be a doctor — I want to go alone, Dad. You come in later — to the hotel."

He closed his eyes a moment, then started up the driveway, Dad supporting him with an arm. At the office they stopped for Dick's coat and hat, and Dad threw the former over his shoulders and buttoned it under the chin. Then on up the driveway they went.

Roach was on the veranda for his early-morning breath of air. He looked down in astonishment as Dad and Dick stopped at the foot of the steps.

"You'll probably need — a new foreman — Mr. Roach," Dick said. "But maybe you'll understand — now — that a Taylor can't be a coward."

"What th' de—"

"I'm leaving your ranch. You can send my things — and pay — by Dad."

Roach looked down the drive and saw the excited throng at the door of the bunkhouse. He ran down the steps and toward his yelling, gesticulating employees.

Richard Taylor staggered toward the gate, his back to the big house where Betty Roach had cried herself to sleep on her tear-drenched pillow.

CHAPTER XII

PAYMENT

It was a morning five days later, and Roach sat on the veranda beside a sober-faced Betty. The honk of an auto horn sounded in the distance, then nearer, nearer still.

"Cuss that Lates!" Roach exclaimed.

He got up and walked to the top of the steps. Expelling clouds of smoke, the Lates truck sped around the curve of the driveway and stopped with a clatter. Dad Meek was on the seat beside the raisin king.

"Not a word, Bill!" Lates cried. "I brought this specimen o' humanity here th' first time, an' I reckon I'll bring him this time, which may or may not be th' last."

"Why, dang your hide, Lates —"

"I found him in Fresno an' offered him a lift. Knowed you wanted to see him. Knowed you'd been lookin' for him several days an' couldn't find him. Thought I was doin' you a favor."

"I reckon you have this time, Lates. You might as well get outen that stink wagon an' hear what's to be said."

The raisin king followed Dad Meek up the steps. It was a different Dad Meek — a Dad Meek dressed like a man of means, and who bore himself with that conscious superiority that comes from having a roll of bills in a pocket.

"I reckon you didn't find me 'cause I was outen town a few days," Dad said. "I had business to tend to."

"Where's th' boy?" demanded Roach.

"He's been taken care of in Fresno at a private house. He's all right now, 'cept he's got some funny-lookin' spots on his face, an' one eye's kinder puffed, an' there's a shoulder in splints. He'll be all right in a couple o' weeks."

"I couldn't find him —"

"I reckon he didn't want to be found," Dad said. "He seems to have an idee you cussed him out for bein' chicken-hearted, which is a funny thing for a man as runs a hen ranch. Told him to git offen your ranch an' stay, didn't you?"

"Dad, don't try to be funny! There's somethin' 'bout this I don't understand, an' I want to be told."

"I sorter thought that, so I came out in Lates' buzz buggy to tell you. I know you always like to know th' facts in a case. Heard tell 'bout that down to Fresno."

"Dad!" Roach thundered.

"You might give *me* th' news first," Dad suggested.

"You talk!"

"All right. In th' first place, that foreman's name wasn't Owen, but Sturm. He's th' boy that kilt Dickie's father."

"What! He's —"

"Exactly. Hold your hosses, now, an' I'll get 'long faster. You see, I got hold o' some money after I left th' Taylors, an' Dickie wouldn't let me give him any of it, so I just helped him from a distance, you might say. When I heard he was comin' here to take a job, I come on ahead an' got one, 'cause I knowed he was headin' for trouble, an' I wanted to be near an' help. I knew this Sturm was here."

"Why didn't you tell —"

"Hold your *hosses!* There was a reason. So Dickie comes here, an' this Sturm, knowin' who he was, an' bein' a Sturm, naturally wanted to start th' old family feud. Dickie's hands was tied, 'cause no matter what that Sturm did or said, he couldn't start a fuss until a certain time."

"What damned nonsense —"

"Now you *wait!* Under th' circumstances, if he'd told you th' foreman was a Sturm, it'd been takin' advantage, 'cause you, knowin' Dickie's father that-a-way, would of threw this Sturm offen th' ranch. Then it might'a' been said Dickie didn't have th' nerve to face him an' fight it out."

"I see that, all right," Roach said. "But why in blue blazed didn't he go after him th' first crack Sturm made, an' fight it out?"

"Ha! That's th' story! You recollect, maybe, that Dickie's father had a brother as was a preacher, a sorter religious cuss that didn't believe in fightin' o' any kind, an' deplored th' feud? Well, this uncle o' Dickie ups and dies, leavin' five thousand dollars for Dickie, not havin' any other heirs an' not approvin' o' Dickie's maw 'cause she believed in th' feud —"

"Come to th' point, dang your hide!"

"There's a string to this five thousand — see? To get it, Dickie mustn't fight this Sturm. He mustn't lay a hand on this Sturm until after he's twenty-five years old, 'cept in defense o' his life. Dickie's uncle, bein' a preacher, reckoned, so he said in th' will, that if Dickie didn't go a-feudin' till he was twenty-five, he wouldn't go a-feudin' at all, bein' by that time a gent o' balanced mind. Do Dickie just naturally had to take this Sturm's bad talk until he was twenty-five. Well, he got to be th' age o' twenty-five at five o'clock in th' mornin' followin' the shindig over to Lates place. Soon as his time was up, he went an' showed a few little things to that Sturm an' a few other people hereabouts."

"Oh!" The cry came from Betty as she sprang to her feet

and confronted Dad Meek. "So he did it for money — for *money!* He let the man who shot down his father taunt him and belittle him and shame him — for money! For a measly five thousand dollars! He's lower even than I thought! That's worse than being a coward! He took slurs and jeers and hisses for money! He sold his manhood for *money.*"

"For a Taylor to do that! For th' son o' my old friend to do that!" Roach exclaimed. "Why, I'll kick him offen my ranch like a dog if he ever comes on it ag'in!"

"Waal, he's comin'!" Dad said. "Here he comes up th' driveway now. He got out at th' gate to walk up!"

"Ha!" Roach cried.

"If I was you, I'd just hold my *hosses* a minute! Let th' boy have his say!"

"I'll do that! And I'll have mine! I'll tell him how low th' Taylors have fallen through him!"

Dick approached slowly, his head bent forward, limping a little, his left arm in a sling. He hesitated a moment at the bottom of the steps and looked up at the group — at Dad, grinning reassuringly, Lates uncommittal, Betty white of face, Roach with a half sneer on his lips. He took off his hat and slowly he went up the steps. There was no word of greeting.

"Mr. Roach, has Dad told you?" he asked.

"He's told me you sold your honor for money!"

"Possibly," said Dick, and his voice sounded distant. "Just as my father was dying, he told me of a debt he owed. My father died poor, as you know, because of business reverses, but he owed only this one debt. He made me give my word of honor as a Taylor that I'd pay that debt as soon as I could. It was a matter that touched him deeply, a matter upon which his honor rested. The amount was large, and I despaired of ever paying it. Then came my uncle's will."

He hesitated, but no one spoke in encouragement. He sighed and went on:

"I saw my chance then to do as I had promised my father. You'll never know what it cost me. I fought myself hour after hour. One blow in answer to a sneering word — and my chance to pay the debt would be lost. But I won. And then I punished the man who had taunted me, and I went into town and arranged to get my legacy. I've got it, Mr. Roach."

"At the price of your honor!"

"I'm sorry you look at it that way, sir." Dick tossed his hat on a chair and took a long envelope from his pocket. He handed it to the ranch owner. "There it is, Mr. Roach — the five thousand dollars you lent my father years ago, without security, and which he never was able to repay. I have repaid it as a great price, it seems, but I've kept my promise."

"Why — why —" Roach gasped. "Cuss it all, I marked that note paid and returned it to your father twenty years ago!"

"But that didn't cancel the debt, sir. A Taylor doesn't pay a debt of honor that way. And now I'll go!"

He picked up his hat and turned down the steps, Dad Meek rising and starting to follow.

"Wait!" Roach cried. "Boy — boy —! You must forgive me! I never knew — I never guessed!"

"It was something I didn't care to talk about, sir. And I asked you, you'll remember, to let me settle with the man in my own way. Oh, yes! If there is interest, I'll have to pay that later."

"Ah! You shame me, Dick! Wait! Don't go like this! I don't want this money — I'll not have it — I don't need it! I'd rather have you, boy — here! I'll chase that crippled Sturm outen th' country! I'll bring your mother here! I want you to stay! Forgive me for th' things I've said —"

"I do that, sir, freely."

He walked on down the steps. Roach started after him.

"Dick — Dick! Don't leave like this!" he implored. "I want you here, Dick! You're a real Taylor! No other man in the world would have done it — could have stood it! Stay here, Dick! He one of us!"

"I think — I'd better go, sir."

He started to turn away again. But there was a flash of a white dress at the top of the steps, and Betty stood there holding out her arms, the tears streaming down her cheeks.

"Dick — Dick!" she sobbed. "Forgive *me* — too! And please stay, Dick! I — I want you so!"

Richard Taylor hesitated a moment, searching her eyes

for what he might find there to decide him. And then he smiled.

"I told Dad — that there was only one thing in all the world that could make me stay," he said. "And you're that one thing — Betty! I guess I'll stay!"

She ran down the steps toward him.

Dad Meek, who always disliked emotional scenes, whirled around and faced Roach and Lates.

"Cuss your carcass if I don't buy a place round here an' raise chickens!" he cried. "I got to stay round Dickie. An' I'll get a stink wagon. There's one I c'n get for five hundred dollars. I heard tell 'bout it down to Fresno."

DEMONS OF DISASTER

SQUATTING on his heels beside the fire in front of the small log cabin, old Lee Chung ate gobs of rice and chunks of boiled pork with his chopsticks. His cousin, Wong Chin, a younger Oriental, sat on the opposite side of the fire and ate also.

The brilliant sunset had died in the western sky, and dusk was descending into the rocky canyon through which the tumbling whitewater creek rushed to empty into the Yuba River. The firelight played over the faces of the two men as they devoured their evening meal.

Wong Chin was watching old Lee Chung's countenance carefully, hoping to read therein some inkling of what Lee Chung was thinking, what he intended doing about the situation that confronted them, and hoping it would not be something he would dislike.

For there was an important problem to be solved. The demons of disaster had been visiting this modest gold-seekers' camp on the bank of the creek again. So it followed that the gods were displeased about something, and Lee and Wong should do whatever would appease them and gain their favor.

What did it profit them to work from daylight until dusk each day and wash out gold-dust and nuggets if evil men came and robbed their sluice boxes and took the rewards of their toil? And once the masked visitors had even located the poke which Lee Chung believed he had hidden so cunningly, and had taken that.

Wong Chin wished half a hundred times a day that he had remained in the thriving city of San Francisco instead of coming out here to this lonesome rocky canyon on the Yuba river to help his elderly kinsman on the claim.

A Chinese could make good money in San Francisco

washing shirts for miners and gamblers, and many of their own kind lived there. They could play fantan and dominoes together; and with the frantic gold-rushers coming to the diggings on every ship, there was always amusing activity.

Lee Chung again silently filled his bowl with rice and boiled pork from the big pot over the cooking fire, grasped his chopsticks, and looked across at Wong Chin.

"There must be a swift end to it!" he declared. "We have suffered more than our proper share at the hands of the thieves. The gods must be appeased so they will grant us a season of good fortune."

Wong Chin began jabbering in his native tongue, but his elderly cousin halted him with a gesture.

"You will spleak Melican," Lee ordered. "Must learn language well." Then he dropped into his native tongue himself. "I have considered our problem. The demons of disaster are preying upon us. They must be driven away, so we may profit in peace from our hard toil."

Wong Chin nodded his head vigorously in agreement.

"A low thief stole our poke," Lee continued.

"Three times our sluice boxes have been robbed of gold. One time a masked man held a flaming stick to my naked toes to make me tell where our dust and nuggets were hidden. It is too much!"

Wong nodded in agreement again, so vigorously this time that his queue, which had been wrapped around his head, became undone and slapped him in his face.

"A certain amount of trouble and adversity is good for a man, but we have had too much," Lee announced. "So, I have made a decision. At dawn tomorrow you will start for Saclamento."

Wong Chin's slant eyes opened a bit wider than usual at that and he sat erect, but otherwise did not reveal he had been startled. So he was to journey to Sacramento! Next to San Francisco, he liked Sacramento best. He had several cousins there, younger than Lee Chung.

"You will go to the joss house and see the priest," Lee instructed. "You will burn many punk sticks in front of the joss. You will get plenty of sacred firecrackers which have been blessed by priest, and you will return here swiftly. We will shoot off sacred firecrackers and frighten away the demons of disaster."

Wong Chin thought that would be an excellent idea, especially since it would give him a trip to Sacramento. It was the proper thing to do under the circumstances.

He would go to Sacramento and see the head priest at the joss house, burn punk sticks before the sacred joss, make a suitable donation, get the blessed firecrackers and return at top speed. Then he and his elderly cousin would shoot the loud firecrackers a string at a time and make a terrific din. The demons of disaster would be frightened and driven out of the canyon, out of the Yuba River district, and bother them no more.

Now that everything was planned, Wong Chin gave his attention to the meal. He filled his bowl from the pot again and ate ravenously, his mind on the forthcoming journey.

A loud "hee-haw" made him jerk and almost drop chopsticks and bowl.

"It is the devil animal belonging to the men up the gulch," Lee said. "You encourage him, my cousin. His evil master, known to men as Chuck Gardon, is the chief of the sluice robbers, I believe."

A burro ambled into the circle of firelight and stood waiting with his head extended. He was a shaggy beast, generally docile, but known to have a fit of energy at times, especially when frightened. He made a habit of coming down the canyon and stopping at the cabin, for Wong had made the mistake once of giving him sugar. "It is good to be kind to animals," Wong said.

He got up and hurried into the cabin, and returned with a handful of sugar. The burro licked the sugar from his hand, voiced his thanks, and walked around the fire to return up the canyon.

"It is a waste," Lee complained. "Feeding good sugar to a donkey. You must learn thrift, my cousin. Go now, and stretch on your pallet, for you must rest and be up before dawn to start your journey. I'll have a package of cold food ready for you."

It was just at dawn when Wong Chin bobbed his head in farewell to Lee Chung and left the cabin to hurry down the canyon beside the tumbling stream. Hidden on his person was a tiny poke containing a couple of pinches of gold dust for his traveling expenses.

He carried the package of cold food Lee had prepared. And he wore his oldest and most comfortable sandals, which gave with every movement of his feet and helped him cling safely to the surfaces of slippery rocks.

Where the tumbling creek emerged from the canyon and emptied into the Yuba River, Wong came upon a comfortable cabin. A man was working at the edge of the stream, and a girl stood in the cabin doorway.

Eli Madison, a kind middle-aged man, was the owner of this claim. The Chinese in the district liked him because he was honest and fair in his dealings. His wife had died of a fever in Sacramento the year before, and he had brought his daughter Elsie, only twenty, to the claim with him.

Wong Chin bobbed his head in greeting, and Madison stopped shoveling gravel to talk.

"Making a trip to Marysville?" Madison asked.

"Me glo all way to Saclamento," Wong explained, proudly. "Glet back soon as can."

"I'll walk up the creek and visit Lee while yuh've gone," Madison promised. "I want to tell him that I've sent word to Marysville to the Vigilantes. We've had more'n enough of sluice box robbers around here. I shot at a couple the other night, but missed 'em."

Wong bobbed his head to show that he understood, and drew in his breath sharply to indicate that he was sorry Madison had missed. "The Vigilantes have a pretty good idea about who's doin' the sluice box thievin' around here," Madison continued. "Chuck Gardon and the two men who live with him up the gulch above yore claim. They don't do much work on their property, but they always seem to have plenty of dust to spend."

Wong bobbed his head in agreement. He and Lee Chung had suspected Gardon and his friends.

Elsie Madison called to Wong from the doorway, and he

bowed to her and looked at Madison questioningly.

"She's made some cookies," Madison told him, laughing. "Wants to try 'em out on yuh. Go get some."

Wong hurried to the cabin. Elsie Madison handed him a small paper bag filled with cookies, and he muttered his thanks and bowed again and hurried away. All this ceremony was delaying him, he thought. But the cookies were welcome.

He hurried on down the creek and turned into the trail which ran along the bank of the Yuba to Marysville. He dog-trotted at times where the trail was smooth, and covered the miles easily and without much fatigue. At times, he slowed down and munched cookies.

It was dusk when he reached Marysville, and lights were burning in the shacks and business establishments. Wong sought out one of his own kind he knew, had a meal, and arranged for a pallet upon which to sleep. Then he went down to the principal street.

Nobody gave him special attention, for pigtailed Chinese were not strangers in the district. He shuffled along, keeping his eyes and ears open. He heard bearded miners talking about the sluice box robberies, and of the dreaded Vigilantes, and once he came to where men were reading a freshly painted sign which had been nailed to the side of a store building.

Wong listened as a man read it aloud:

NOTICE!
We have good idea regarding the identities of the sluice box robbers in this district. One more theft, and the guilty men will receive what they deserve. If they are wise, they will leave these diggings immediately.

The Committee.

"Well, it's about time the Vigilantes got after 'em!" a miner standing near Wong said. "If them thieves ain't stopped now, no sluice box along the Yuba will be safe. String 'em up, I say!"

Wong thought that was a good idea. He remembered how Lee Chung's feet had been blistered by a flaming stick. And he knew that all men feared the Vigilantes. Perhaps this warning would stop the thieves, he thought.

He slept at his friend's house and at dawn hastened on, making his way as rapidly as possible toward Sacramento. When he reached his destination, he located some of his cousins and told them of his errand. He rested for a time, ate, then went to the joss house.

Following Lee Chung's orders carefully, Wong burned many punk sticks as he kowtowed humbly before the joss. He gave the head priest a pinch of gold dust and told him of his desire.

"Evil men should be undone," the priest declared, after Wong had finished his recital. "It is a terrible crime to steal. I shall bless many strings of firecrackers, and you shall carry them back and explode them and frighten away the demons of disaster. Then peace will come to your mining claim, and you can enjoy the fruits of your toil."

Fatigued from his journey, Wong spent two days and nights with his cousins in Sacramento, marveling at the manner in which the town was growing, and eating much rice and pork. He was a guest, and did not have to pay for it.

Then he began his homeward trip, the firecrackers safe in a bundle wrapped carefully in waterproof silk, which he hung around his neck and carried on his back. He was eager to get home.

Fired in the narrow rocky canyon, he knew, the firecrackers would make a loud noise and frighten the demons of disaster so they would never bother around the canyon again.

In time, he came once more to Marysville, and decided to rest there during the afternoon and night. He visited his friends again, and found them excited.

"Great news came to us yesterday," they told Wong. "There has been a great strike of gold on the Yuba River, just above where your creek empties into the larger stream. The man Madison has found many rich pockets and will be a person of wealth. And the report said also that your cousin and ours, Lee Chung, washed gravel in a new place on your own claim and is now a man of much wealth also."

"Lee Chung and I share alike," Wong told them, trying to

keep an expression of happiness out of his face. It was not proper to flaunt his good fortune in the faces of those less fortunate.

"We are your cousins," one of them reminded him. "You must come to Marysville again soon, and perhaps bring us gifts to show that you are truly thankful for the good fortune the gods have given you."

Wong finally managed to get away from them, and hurried down to the crowded street to watch and listen. Men were outfitting feverishly to go to the scene of the new strike. Claims were being staked far up the Yuba, they were saying.

"There's a bunch of Chinese in the little canyon," Wong heard one man say. "We can stake claims above 'em. We won't bother 'em any. It's bad luck to bother a Chinese."

WONG shuffled on, watching and listening, and trying to gather information. So he came, presently, to the rear of a large building which held the town's biggest saloon and gambling hall. The windows were open, and the roar of the rollicking crowd rolled out.

Wong stepped up close to one of the windows to peer in at the scene. He heard two men talking only a few feet away, as they sat across a table from each other, a bottle and glasses before them.

Wong knew one of them by sight. He was "Chuck" Gardon, who had a claim above Lee's and was suspected of being the leader of the sluice box robbers. The second man was thick in body and heavily bearded, and Wong decided he had mean eyes.

"You don't own the country, Gardon," this man was saying.

"I ain't claimin' I do," Chuck Gardon replied.

"I'm sayin' that I was playin' the Yuba River diggin's first. Why can't yuh stay over on the American River and work there?"

"Because the pickin's are gettin' better over on the Yuba," the other man replied. "And it got too hot for us over on the American."

"It's goin' to get hot here, too, Knowles," Chuck Gardon —

there ought to be some fat pokes to pick up if a man acts quick."

"I've got the same idea, Gardon."

"Yeah? Well, I'm warnin' yuh, Knowles, to keep away from the Yuba district, 'specially where I've been workin' with my two men. That man Madison belongs to me. I happen to know that he's the feller who sent for the Vigilantes. I want his gold and his hide, both. And that pair of Chinese in the canyon — they're my meat, too."

"Not unless yuh can get to 'em before I do," the other man told him.

Wong heard somebody approaching, so had to move on swiftly and silently to avoid being caught listening at the window, and possibly getting a stiff cuff on the side of his head.

He understood that Chuck Gardon was preparing to steal again, and that the other man was of the same sort. Lee Chung and Madison would be at the mercy of them both, unless Wong hurried with the sacred firecrackers and drove the demons of disaster away.

He entered a shop and bought a few cheap presents with a tiny pinch of gold dust and took them to his friends. Later, he stretched himself on a pallet to rest, but did not sleep.

When all his friends were asleep, Wong slipped out of the shack, put on his sandals, fixed his pack, and was ready to start for home. As he neared the street, he heard a tumult. Men were shouting and running toward the big saloon and gambling hall.

"Chuck Gardon and Bart Knowles are fightin'!" he heard somebody yell.

Wong got in the fringe of the crowd to watch.

Gardon and Knowles were in the street, slugging it out. The crowd was cheering them on. They seemed about evenly matched, until Gardon picked up a bottle somebody had thrown out of the saloon, and crashed it down on Knowles' head.

Knowles collapsed, and men rushed in to end the battle. Gardon and his two men got through the crowd and started up the street. Unobserved, Wong followed them and saw them enter a shack.

He felt he had an interest in this and that it would not be wrong to play eavesdropper, especially since these men were evil. He got on the dark side of the shack and listened beneath a window.

One of the men was bathing Gardon's cut and bruised face, and the other was opening a box of salve. Gardon was raging.

"I'll get Knowles if we ever meet again!" he threatened. "This country ain't big enough to hold us both! But first we'll make our haul. We'll slip out of town before daylight. You boys get everything ready. We'll beat Knowles to it. We'll travel fast and hit hard, then go over the hills and make for Frisco. The game's played out here."

"If Knowles is able to travel in the mornin', he'll be startin' up there with his men," one of Gardon's companions said. "He's got three men, I happen to know."

"We'll beat him to it, I said. Neither of us can make a haul till tomorrer night. We'll make our plans while we're gettin' to the canyon."

Wong understood all that. And he was eager to learn the plans so he could warn Lee Chung and Eli Madison. He decided he would wait and trail the trio when they left the town.

He went ahead and waited outside the town, hiding behind some brush. Before daylight, Gardon and his two men appeared, walking at a steady pace. They passed Wong, who trailed at a distance, keeping to the shadows. His sandals made no sound when he walked, and besides the wind was blowing toward him.

At a spot where the trail was almost obscured by shadows, Wong got closer, for the wind was carrying their talk to him. Gardon led the way off the trail and up a ravine.

"We'll cut across so's nobody'll see us," Wong heard him say. "We'll rest in the cabin a few hours, and get everything ready. The dust and nuggets we've taken and got hid — we'd better not carry it on us. We'll pack the burro with our stuff, and put the dust and nuggets inside a flour sack. It'll look like we're just quittin' the diggin's."

"What about this last haul?" one of the men asked.

"Accordin' to what we heard, them Chinese and Madison have struck it rich. Ought to have fat pokes ready for us. We'll go down the canyon and hit the Chinese first, then go on and clean up Madison. I want to handle him! If he's got gold hid, we'll shore make him show us where it is. We'll grab that girl of his and threaten to hurt her if he don't. That'll make him talk."

Wong shivered at that. He didn't want these men to hurt Elsie Madison, who was always kind to him and old Lee, and who baked cookies. He didn't want them even to affront her. He decided he would listen and hear all he could of their plans.

"If Knowles tries to get ahead of us, we must beat him to it," Gardon said. "It'd be rich if we got the dust and nuggets and Knowles got blamed for it and him and his men got strung up. Serve 'em right!"

"How about the Vigilantes?" one of the men asked.

"That's troublin' me some," Chuck Gardon admitted. "We've got to be mighty careful. If they catch us at it, they'll either fill us full of lead or make us stretch rope. I ain't hankerin' for either."

"Yuh reckon the Vigilantes are there already, Chuck?" the other man asked.

"Mebbe. I'll bet they've been slippin' up the Yuba a few at a time since they posted that sign in Marysville. It's my idea they'll gather there and be in ambush. We've got to smell 'em out."

They were not traveling so fast, off the trail; and since they had left Marysville a little before daylight, Wong knew it would be dusk when they reached the canyon. Now that daylight had come, he was compelled to be careful. If the men ahead saw and recognized him, and thought he was spying on them, they might resort to any kind of violence.

And Wong was compelled now to follow them, for he was utterly lost. Since leaving the regular trail, they had been going through ravines and up slopes. Chuck Gardon evidently was following a path he knew, one he had used before. But Wong did not know it. To return to the regular trail and follow that would mean loss of too much time. If he dropped back and followed their tracks, he would come to the canyon finally and could go home. Cautiously he watched ahead, to be sure that while ascending some hill they would not look back and see him. Their boot tracks in the soft earth were easy to follow.

Wong realized they were not traveling as fast as he had been, going to Marysville from the canyon, and this route was longer. And it had taken him from dawn until dusk to make the trip. So he knew it would be night before the canyon was reached. The men ahead stopped in the middle of the day to rest, and Wong was almost discovered as he approached them, scanning the ground for tracks. He hid behind some brush until they started on again. He saw them eating cold food, and knew the gnawing of hunger, for he had brought none himself.

When daylight faded, Wong went faster and got behind them as close as he could and be safe. The wind was still blowing from them to him, and his sandals made no noise. He could hear their boots crunching gravel and striking against rocks, and followed them by sound.

There came a time when Wong could hear, from the distance, a sound he knew came from the rushing of the creek over rocks in the canyon. A glance at the stars told him it was almost midnight. Just before dawn was the most auspicious hour, he knew, for shooting off the sacred firecrackers.

He was eager to get home, awaken Lee Chung and go through the ceremony. After what he had heard, he knew there was no time to lose if the demons of disaster were to be driven away before Chuck Gardon and his men made their raid.

Wong shuffled on in the wake of Gardon and the others. They went through another long ravine, then began climbing among the rocks. The noise of the rushing water came nearer.

The moon was up now, and Wong had to be careful that he was not seen. The men ahead were talking again, and the wind carried their words to his ears. "We'll take a little rest, then get ready," Gardon was saying. "Make up the burro's packs and put the dust and nuggets among the stuff, like I said. Have a little snack to eat."

NOW they were working down among the rocks, and Wong had to follow them because there was no other way to go. They were descending to the floor of the canyon. Wong could see the whitewater below tumbling over the rocks in the moonlight.

And he realized that he was in a trap. Gardon and his two men were ahead of him, between him and Lee's cabin. The canyon was narrow along here, and there was only one path, and the walls could not be scaled. To get out of the canyon and work his way around to the mouth of the creek would take hours, Wong knew.

Finally they came down to the path and went along it, the men ahead hurrying now. Wong dropped behind, shuffling cautiously over the rocky path. When the men ahead reached Gardon's cabin, Wong went into hiding behind some rocks, to watch for an opportunity to pass the cabin and go on home.

They entered the cabin and lit candles, and one man emerged before Wong could make a move. The man built a fire, put on a coffeepot, and sliced bacon into a skillet. Through the open door of the cabin, Wong could see Chuck Gardon and the other man making up packs.

The burro smelled the smoke of the fire and came wandering up the path from below, heehawing a welcome. The odors of boiling coffee and broiling bacon almost upset Wong's stomach because he was so hungry. He wished they would eat and all enter the cabin and close the door, so he could slip past.

The man at the fire called, and Gardon and the second man emerged and began eating.

"If Knowles and his men are intendin' to raid, they'll try it just before dawn," Wong heard Gardon say. "We want to get down the canyon and hit them Chinese while they're dopey with sleep, finish it there quick as we can, and go on down to Madison's place."

"How about the Vigilantes?" one of the men asked again.

"There's a chance we'll have to take. Mebbe they're not out here yet. But, on account of this new strike, they may be.

Mebbe they're in ambush. If they are, I hope Knowles runs into 'em first."

"Suppose we run into 'em, Chuck?"

"If so, there's only one thing to do, and you both want to remember it. Drop everything and run. We're the same as swingin' at the end of ropes if we don't."

"If the dust and nuggets are in a pack on the burro —"

"We'll take time to grab that stuff, then make a getaway. There's a trail up the side of the canyon a quarter of a mile this side of the cabin them Chinese live in. We'll use that, get over the hills, and back to Marysville. Mebbe folks'll think we never left there. And we'll get on to Frisco as fast as we can."

They finished eating, but did not go into the cabin. Outside, by the fire, they were making the burro's packs ready. Wong could not get past them unseen. There was no sort of cover between the cabin and the wall of the canyon. And the firelight, added to the light of the moon and reflecting from the rock walls, made it so light that even a shadow could have been seen drifting past.

Crouching behind the rocks, Wong tried to think of a way out of the trap. Instead, when he looked toward the cabin again, he found instead a new peril. The burro was wandering up the path directly toward Wong's hiding place.

Wong crouched lower. He regretted now that he had made a friend of the burro by giving him sugar. "Get that burro and bring the jackass back here!" Wong heard Chuck Gardon howl to one of the men.

The burro was coming on, and the man after him. Wong hugged the ground in the shadows. If they found him, he was done for, he thought. He had no weapon on him except a sharp knife.

But the man after the burro did not suspect anything, evidently. He yelled at the burro, who trotted on toward Wong. Then the man ran, caught the burro and turned him back just in time. Wong began breathing normally again.

Beside the fire, the three men put on the burro's pack frame and began packing it.

"Don't forget that this flour sack holds the stuff," Gardon told the others. "If we run into trouble, we'll tell a yarn about our claim bein' no good, and that we're goin' over to the American River and try our luck. Nobody'll think of investigatin' a flour sack. They'd expect us to be packin' any gold we had ourselves."

Wong prepared to make a wild dash if they all went into the cabin. They would be starting down the canyon soon, he knew, and he must get ahead of them and warn Lee and explode the sacred firecrackers to drive the demons of disaster away.

Finally, Gardon led the others into the cabin and closed the door. That gave Wong his chance. He left the protection of the rocks and began running, bending almost double, his worn sandals making but little noise, and the sound of the rushing water drowning that.

He came even with the fire, and the burro saw him and hee-hawed with evident delight.

Wong sped past him and went on. The burro began following, no doubt thinking of sugar. Wong got to some rocks and dropped behind them just as Gardon opened the door.

"Catch that fool burro and fetch him back!" he called to one of his men. "He's carryin' the stuff! Somethin' must have made him loco."

Wong crouched in a state of terror until the man had caught the burro and led him back. Then he went on, keeping in the shadows. When he got around a curve in the canyon and was hidden from the sight of those at the cabin, he put on speed.

He reached home and shook Lee Chung awake.

Gasping and panting, he poured out the story.

"We must shoot the sacred firecrackers," Wong said. "They will drive away the demons."

"I will hurry down to the Madison cabin," Lee Chung told him, "and let him know about this, while you shoot the firecrackers. Some of the Vigilantes are here. They caught a man named Knowles early last night, and three men with him. They were sluice box robbers. Madison and the Vigilantes will come to help."

"I thlink sacred firecracker maybe dlive demons away," Wong declared, remembering to speak "American."

Lee Chung hurried down the canyon trail. Wong washed his hands to purify them, unpacked the firecrackers, and got them ready. He muttered certain incantations. He strung out one string of the firecrackers, ignited a sulphur match, and lit the end of the string.

The firecrackers were good and loud, and the explosions echoed among the rocks. Wong began shouting his incantation in a shrill voice, determined to frighten the demons away. He ran into the cabin and got a huge pistol Lee kept there, but which he had never used on the thieves because they had always caught him asleep. Running outside again, Wong fired the pistol. It made a deafening roar among the rocks.

Wong would have been startled then if he could have seen what was happening and heard what was being said a short distance up the canyon.

Gardon and his men, the burro following, had neared the cabin on Lee's claim. They had pulled up neck handkerchiefs for masks. Suddenly, the night erupted. Explosion blasted and roared along the rocky canyon walls. Flashes of flame were reflected on the rocks.

"Gunfire!" one of the men said.

"Knowles got there ahead of us, and the Vigilantes are after him and his gang!" the second added.

They heard shrill yelling, and the thunderous explosion as Wong fired the old pistol. Gardon did not hesitate.

"Back!" he ordered. "Travel fast. They may come this way. Get up the trail to the top — it's only a hundred yards back. Hit for Marysville. We don't want any of this. Let Knowles have it!"

"The stuff on the burro — ?" one questioned.

"Grab the flour sack and come on. Let the burro go. No time to lose!"

But the burro was gone already. The explosions and the flashes of fire were too much. He stampeded, running down the trail toward Lee's cabin, bucking and kicking to get off the packs.

A rope broke as the burro neared the cabin. The flour sack holding the pokes of dust and nuggets flew off to one side. Some of the cooking utensils dropped off also.

Wong had just lit the second string of firecrackers. They began exploding. The burro turned and rushed back up the trail, went past Gardon and the men like a streak, and continued. The three let him go. They were scrambling up the trail frantically, to get out of the canyon and away.

Lee Chung came back with Madison and several grim-looking men who were heavily armed.

Wong was dancing around excitedly.

"Velly loud sacred firecracker," he told them. "I think they drive demons of disaster away."

"You stay here with Wong, Lee," Madison instructed. He turned to the men with him. "We'll go on up the canyon and see if Gardon and his two men are in their cabin. If they are, we'll drive 'em out of the district."

They started on their futile errand, for Gardon and his men at that moment had reached the top of the canyon wall and were on their way to Marysville.

Wong was tired and hungry, but happy. Lee Chung started to build a fire to cook food. Wong wandered a short distance up the trail, listening to the sounds in the canyon.

But soon he came rushing back, holding a flour sack and shouting for Lee Chung.

"Look!" he cried. "Find this beside trail. Here is the poke they stole from you. Here is the little package of nuggets. Here is more gold in little sacks. Not only did the sacred firecrackers drive away the demons of disaster, but the gods make the burro drop this sack at our feet, and we have the stolen gold and some extra. Perhaps that is because I gave the burro sugar. The gods like men who are kind to animals."

"The gods at times have what seem to us to be strange ways," Lee Chung told him, "but they are always profitable. Come and eat your rice and pork, and drink your tea."

www.ingramcontent.com/pod-product-compliance
Lightning Source LLC
Chambersburg PA
CBHW050730250626
47155CB00005B/1741